Totally Bound Publishing books by January Bain

Brass Ring Sorority
Winning Casey
Chasing Lacey
Romancing Rebecca

TETRAD Group
Racing Peril
Racing the Tide
Racing the Whirlwind

I0658900

Manitoba Tea & Tarot Mysteries
Magic, Mayhem & Murder
Movies, Moonlight & Magic
Moonshine, Magic & Murder

Sin City Wolf
Howl
Hunt

Collections
A Little Bit Cupid: Lovestruck

Sin City Wolf

HONOR

JANUARY BAIN

Honor
ISBN # 978-1-83943-772-4
©Copyright January Bain 2022
Cover Art by Claire Siemaszkiewicz ©Copyright February 2022
Interior text design by Claire Siemaszkiewicz
Totally Bound Publishing

HONOR

Dedication

Thank you, dear reader, for picking my story. I
am truly blessed.
Thank you, Rebecca, mistress of words and
stories, for making my stories shine.
My ever thanks to my husband for telling me to,
"Go for it!" when I first mentioned I wanted to
write. The journey with you has been beyond
amazing and I am humbled by it.

Chapter One

Lucius

"Look! There's a halo around the moon tonight, Lucius. You know what that means?" Veronica purred. Her mouth was coated in far too much red lipstick for my liking, though I more than appreciated her luscious body and adventurous spirit.

"What do you think it means?" I asked, not particularly interested in her take on it. I couldn't imagine the notorious party girl having done much digging into mythology or history.

If I wanted facts, my twin brothers, Maximus and Alexandro, would be the ones I'd call on. One of the things I did like about Veronica's type though — easy to forget. I didn't need any complications as enforcer for the House of Luceres beyond those necessary to protect my pack.

"It means something momentous is on its way. Could be good. Or evil. It depends on the intentions of the spirit." Veronica shivered for effect in a dress that barely covered essentials. She looked up at me, her eyes huge, reflecting not only the light of the roaring bonfire kept alight for the entirety of the Lupercalia festival, but I swear I caught a glimpse of myself.

Easy to look at, I've been told. Like all my pack brothers, I kept my *GQ* looks highlighted with exercise and good grooming. And all the Luceres were blessed with good genetics and lots of money.

The howling of a lone wolf in the distance cut short the woman's unexpected announcement and I went on high alert. In the desert, on a clear night such as this, sound was deceptive. The interloper could be miles away…or nearby.

I glanced around the firepit, checking out the pack members milling about. Emily, one of the cousins, was dancing with wild abandon. I frowned. Wasn't she a bit young for this? The festival was notorious for events that would curl a human's hair. Rumors abounded and things that probably should not happen…happened.

Case in point, headed right toward me was a former one-night stand, her finger pointed at me like she had something to say. Something I was certain I would prefer not to hear. What was her name again? *Serena, Simona, Sawyer…*

Before it came to me, she was right up in my face. "Lucius Luceres, I got some…thing to say to you you're not go…ing to like." She poked at me with a sharp red fingernail, her words slurring and her body language suggesting something vastly different.

"Step back, if you know what's good for you, cur!" Veronica yelled at her.

"What you go…ing to do about it?"

Right, *Simone*, one of the more jealous ones. Why was one night never enough for them? *Not like I ever promised anything more.* I stepped back. Let them have at it. A gorgeous female standing farther from the fire winked at me, her eyes taking in the foolish provocation with obvious interest. I gave her my patented cool-billionaire smile.

She replied with an air kiss, pulling me forward with all the magnetic pull of true north. Just the way I liked it. *And man, those curves, highlighted in a tight dress that leaves nothing to the imagination.*

"Hey, where are you going?" Veronica quickly noticed my mental desertion…soon to be followed by a physical one.

I turned back and sighed. The two women had each other by the hair. Soon they'd shift, by the look of things. I didn't want the hassle, but after all, I had caused it, even though they'd both been warned that I never dated.

"Come on, ladies, the festival is almost over. Wouldn't you rather be having fun than fighting?"

"This is fun! I'm going to beat her ass!" And with that Veronica shed her clothes and shifted, one second vanishing through the otherworldly portal in a shimmer of light, and in the next back again as a blue-eyed gray wolf. It had been explained to me by my scholarly brothers that the dimension was only one of the eleven that create the multiverse. *Whatever.* I was just satisfied it worked.

I mean, who doesn't want to be wolf?

One second later, Simone followed Veronica, her leaner and meaner wolf appearing in a flash of light. Of course, she was the more perturbed of the two, giving her the edge. The pair squared off. Simone growled as she lowered her head to bully her opponent, the thick ruff on her spine fully erect.

Instantly, others picked up on the change of energy. Bodies began streaming in from everywhere, surrounding the two females in mere seconds. This was what the pack wanted. *Craved.* The music shifted, became a louder drumbeat that stirred the blood.

I gave a nonchalant shrug to the gorgeous female on the sidelines watching the antics as if to say, *What can I do? Females will be females.* She rolled her eyes.

Turning back to the action, I decided not to intervene in the fight, not unless they began to inflict real damage. These kinds of fights could be more about posturing than anything else, useful for ratcheting down minor disagreements and aggressions. Which was why this festival was held in the first place. It allowed pack members time to listen to their wolf, step away from the imposing limits of civilization. *Freedom, baby.*

But I had apparently misjudged the level of anger and animosity between the pair. Claws and fur flying, they lunged at each other, rolling in the desert sand and sending a blanket of dust into the air.

The crowd roared their approval. Someone had appointed themselves the holder of the bets and numbers were being tossed around the ring like confetti. Eager faces, alight with the excitement I'd imagine rather common to the Colosseum of ancient days, began to holler loudly for their favorite. Seemed that Simone was holding sway, her anger the most apparent to the catcalling crew. Hell, half of them were half undressed now, probably looking to take a turn.

Great, a bloom of blood had appeared on Veronica's fur. Now I had to shift. Not really a bad thing, as I loved to be wolf. The power, the freedom, the pure sense of being removed from this world—it didn't get any better.

I shucked my clothing, knowing I was being checked out by the new female. *Have at it. I'm choice.* I jumped into the fray and in seconds, had Veronica by the scruff of the neck, subjecting her to dominance, forcing her to give over to her alpha. She whined, then lay down. Simone stood on four stiffened paws, her tongue lolling, still defying me.

I flew at her, catching her by the throat, taking her down to the ground. Not hard enough to break the skin, but enough to inflict some pain. She needed to learn her place.

When she gave me proper respect, I let her slink away, then dusted myself off and redressed. The interested female was still watching, and I nodded at her. She sauntered over, her spectacular hips swaying to the rhythmic beat of the snare drum one of the pack members was pounding on, her smile coy.

The crowd clapped and stamped their feet loudly, naked breasts bouncing to the delight of the males who watched with approval, obviously having enjoyed the show. Money was paid out to the victors and backs were slapped. Just another night at the Lupercalia. And mild compared to some events I won't get into.

"Nice moves," she said, getting closer enough to pick an imaginary piece of lint from my jacket.

"I aim to please."

"I take it you're not worried that a rare witch moon is causing chaos this night?" The new female pointed at the night sky. A dark cloud was now creeping across the luminous surface, lending an even more eerie appearance to proceedings.

"*Witch moon?* Where did you hear that?" A cold finger traced my spine. I shook the odd sensation off. *An old wives' tale.*

"Big strong wolf like you—you have nothing to fear."

Never trust a witch.

The warning from an elderly Italian relative came to mind. Well, not like I had any in my pack or knew of any in my round of acquaintances. And I certainly wouldn't bed one. Now, the wolf throwing herself at me at the moment, sure.

I'm partial to blondes and easy tail...

* * * *

Isadora

I placed an arm around Elena's thin shoulders, my heart breaking for my younger sister who was the mirror image of me with her smooth fall of Titian hair, legs that didn't quit and a bod that drew more than her fair share of attention. But she didn't look like a goddess at the moment. She was sobbing as if her life were over. I'd never seen her this upset, not even when her first boyfriend had dropped her just before prom...though it had been fun enacting a spell to cause him to grow horns and a tail for the event.

Of course, I wouldn't do anything like that again. If I'd learned anything, it was the cost of being rash in such endeavors. *Everything one does has a karma attached to it, like it or not. Good deeds attract good energy.* It was the way of the witch – or a good witch, which was what I considered myself. Okay, I had to work on it at times. *Nobody's perfect, right?* But hell yeah, I tried to stay in the good-witch zone.

Elena turned her tear-stained face toward me. Her beautiful hair was tangled, oily from needing a washing, her eyes were red-rimmed and I swore she had lost weight in the past few days. Was she even eating? My sister, who prided herself on being well-groomed and whom I loved for her big generous heart, was beyond devastated, her eyes hopeless pools of pain.

"I know I was stupid to care so much. But he was so kind to me, so handsome and romantic. I thought we'd made a real connection. I wouldn't have gone with him otherwise. You know that, right? I'm not easy. I've only been with a few guys."

I rubbed her back. "He's a damn fool. And no, you're definitely not easy. You're the best he could ever imagine being with. It's his loss."

"I should have known better. He's too good for me, being a Luceres and all."

My ire heated. "You're as good as any Luceres. In fact, this proves you're better. Why, your little finger is more special than all of him put together."

"Then why didn't he think so?"

My stomach squeezed into a fist. "Which Luceres was it? I've got an idea. We're not going to let him get away with this."

Elena sat up straighter, a bit of hope in her beautiful teary eyes. "It was Lucius Luceres from the Glitter Palace. What are you going to do? Make him come back to me?"

"Sorry, sweetheart, that I can't do, not without doing something we'd both be sorry for. That kind of action comes with a steep cost. But damn it, I can make him pay!"

"Okay. That's something at least." She looked disappointed, then gave me an odd look, like she was trying to decide something. Maybe her tender heart was saying not to do the guy harm that she had once admired? No way would my sister try to deceive me, she didn't have it in her.

"But I should tell you, we didn't *actually* go all the way. Lots of kissing and hugging though. But the connection, I swear it was there. You believe me, right?"

I nodded, though I had thought differently on the matter. I'd assumed they'd made love all night long. "Of course, sweetheart. Promises can be made without actual sex."

"What do you want me to do?" Elena pressed onward.

At least Elena's tears had dried up. I gave my options a quick perusal. "I think he needs a taste of his own medicine. And I think we'll do this by calling on the power of the coven. Lots of them were done wrong by men. Why not let them be the catalyst for inflicting a fair revenge?" I relished the quick look of interest that instantly appeared on my sister's lovely face at this idea.

"*Ooh*, that could work! You'd do that for me?"

"Of course, sweetheart." There was nothing I wouldn't do for my family. I'd even picked up the heaviest debt of all, one that I would take on again, if need be, though the cost was beyond belief. I'd be enslaved to the end of my days. But that didn't bear thinking about now. I had something I could do to help my sister — though spells weren't really my thing — but it wouldn't cost too much if I chose wisely and avoided the evil one. *Shouldn't. Hopefully…*

"Now, you take a quick shower and I'll assemble the pieces."

Elena gave a grimace, suddenly aware of how far she had let herself go. "Yeah, you're right, I stink. I'll be right back."

"No, it's best you don't get involved. Let me bear the fallout." *And it's not like I haven't had lots of practice.*

She looked disappointed, then gracefully gave in. "Okay, as long as he pays."

My sister scurried off and I set to work, first lining up photos of my coven in a nice precise row. Twelve in all, me being the thirteenth. I didn't want to bother them for this undertaking that I could easily handle myself. Most of my sisters of another mother had such busy lives…and they wouldn't be very happy with what I was doing. But photos captured the spirit at a moment in time, giving images energy that could be used for future events, so they'd do.

I turned next to my array of gleaming crystals, green glass containers of hard-to-find ingredients as they all had to be handpicked and ground by mortar and pestle and vials of shimmering liquids that moved of their own accord, catching the light as they bubbled and swirled.

Hmm, how far do I want to carry this? For Elena—hell, for all those harmed by the notorious womanizer—nothing was more important than stopping the wolf dead in his tracks. A devious plan suddenly formed in my mind.

Well, well, wolf, by the hair on my chinny chin-chin, you'd better look out, for here I come…and guess what? You won't!

Chapter Two

Lucius

"I'm on my way." I snapped my phone off and strode toward the bank of elevators on the main floor of the casino.

Idiots. One more damn thing that needed my attention. Some of our human employees acted more like children during a full moon, even though our wolves had a far more ancient right to howl. *Fighting over a female. Again. Damn it.*

The final night of the Lupercalia festival and my wolf was craving some no-holds-barred sex. Or I'd be a candidate for moon sickness, like my pussy-whipped twin had had the audacity to suggest earlier tonight. *He finds his Forever Mate and suddenly he's the expert.* A twinge of jealousy I couldn't quite ignore made me even more pissed off.

Cristaldo marking his one-year anniversary of his marriage to Everly was making him far too smug. *Yeah, right, like I couldn't control my urges. I'm the enforcer for our pack. No need for a mate.* Love 'em and leave 'em had worked so far and allowed me all the time necessary to do my job to the very best of my ability.

Pack safety was my number one priority, no matter that I secretly envied my brother his gorgeous mate. Something I'd not be sharing with anyone was that my nights had become lonelier since I'd watched that pair walk around like lovesick puppies, forever fawning over the other. When was their damn honeymoon going to end anyway? Surely a year of sweet nothings was sufficient to bond them forever?

Stepping onto the first available elevator, I caught an amazing scent in the small space. My nose wrinkled with keen interest. Neither entirely human nor wolf, but totally intoxicating with a powerful range of uplifting notes combined with an earthy lust that held my full attention. *What is this?* I narrowed my eyes at the lone occupant. A female stunning even by Vegas standards leaned against the gold railing opposite me, watching me intently. A goddess standing near six feet tall, just a few inches shorter than myself and impossible to ignore, with her siren-red dress barely covering the essentials.

And what essentials. Long bare legs that went on for miles, curvy hips that nipped into a tiny waist, and full breasts that led up to a Madonna-like face surrounded by loose waves of shiny light auburn hair, a shade richer than strawberry blond. My wolf fired to full alert, mirroring my rapidly hardening cock. *She's mine.* I had never heard him so certain.

"Good evening," she said, running the tip of her pink tongue over shiny red lips. Her voice matched the exterior. The kind that called to unwary sailors who smashed their ships to smithereens on distant rocky shorelines. All low timber and sexy overtones. Chocolate and liqueur.

"It is now." I pressed the button for the twenty-first floor without taking my eyes off her. Her lips quirked up in a small smile, her amber-colored irises smoldering with hidden intent. I swore I could see bright flames flaring in their depths. I shook my head to dispel the odd image.

"Got a light?" she asked.

I glanced at her hands. Neither held a cigarette. Instead both held on to the rail behind her as if her life depended on it. "Sure, what would you like lit?"

The elevator began to ascend. Depending on her reply, I could let it arrive on its scheduled floor or hit the emergency button and shut it down between floors. This encounter had the definite potential to make up for missing the Lupercalia orgy.

"I'm game for anything, sailor. No holds barred. Except for kissing and hanging around afterward."

A wet dream sprung to life.

In a single bound I crossed the short distance that separated us. She leaned into me with her legs splayed open, her hands still holding on to the rail, and I jerked her dress down to expose her incredible breasts with tightly budded deep pink nipples. This woman wanted me. *Now.* Her arousal filled my nostrils with the scent of musk and honey, and that faint underlying herbal fragrance I couldn't quite identify.

I clamped my lips down on a perky nipple while I swept my hands around her tiny waist to pull her in tighter to my fully aroused cock, grinding myself against her.

"Oh, yeah, baby, you want it bad. I got just the cure."

I yanked her dress up her thighs uncaring if it tore — I'd buy her another — exposing a fully waxed pussy gleaming with moisture. I thrust my hand between her legs and rubbed her, finding her lips swollen and drenched with lust. Slipping two fingers up inside her channel, I circled her clit with my thumb.

"No panties. I like that."

"We aim to please, sailor."

I'd had quick encounters in Vegas, but never one that came even close to this fantasy. A tryst without dinner and a show, or even an introduction. What else could a hunting man want?

I dropped to my knees and spread her lips wide with my fingers, seeking her core with my mouth.

"So wet, baby," I murmured. I nipped at her clit, enjoying how her body jerked in response. "You like that."

A low moan slipped from her lips, jacking up the excitement. I applied myself further, her taste dancing across my tongue.

"Ow, bit rough," I half-protested, an odd sensation stinging my scalp. Had she pulled out some hair?

Suddenly, the elevator jerked to an abrupt halt, making our bodies slam hard against the railing. *What the hell! Guess the fates are on my side for this one.* Now I could take my time to finish her, find out what her deal was.

At that exact second in time, the clatter of something dropping to the floor caused me to glance down. The gleam of a blade attached to an ornate handle of carved bone lying on the marble tile stilled my breath. *What is this?*

In a flash I came up from my knees and fisted her hair, yanking her head straight back, making her look me straight in the eyes.

"What the hell are you doing? Why did you have that weapon?"

She shot daggers at me with her expression. I kicked the knife farther away from me. She didn't look like a killer. And she sure in the hell didn't feel or react like one.

"No more than you deserve after what you did. But no, I wasn't trying to kill you. You're not worth the effort." Her words lacked conviction. She hadn't been faking how turned on she was, that I was certain. The air was still scented with our mingled musk.

"What are you? Think you can fuck with me like that?" I demanded

Her eyes narrowed. "I don't have to tell you anything, slick."

But she looked nervous now, licking her lips with her pink tongue that had been damned beguiling not five minutes ago. *Naked. Unarmed.* She was no longer a threat to me.

I let her go and stepped back. Though she was up to no good, I couldn't help but admire her beauty and proud look while caught in this desperate situation. This wouldn't go unpunished. She had to know that.

She didn't argue her case, but stood defiant and naked before me, her dress shredded and incapable of covering her considerable assets. I reached down to retrieve the knife.

"Silver," I hissed as pain burned into my palm. I threw it into the farthest corner of the elevator car.

"What are you?" With my lust eased, my mind cleared. I suddenly knew what she was. "*Witch*," I growled.

"What if I am? What you did to my sister deserves retaliation." She glared at me with defiance.

"What did I do to your sister? Who is she?" I wanted answers. The elevator was still stuck between floors, but that could wait.

"Elena Champagne. My baby sister. You threw her away like a piece of trash."

The name didn't ring any bells. *So many one-night stands. How could a man or wolf remember?* But I never made any promises, no matter what they said afterward. At least I hadn't been a mutt about that.

"Who are you?"

"Isadora Molay Champagne and I proudly bear the name of the last Templar Knight Grand Master who died on his funeral pyre cursing his accusers in 1314. And, if you know your history, it proved to work very well indeed. Pope Clement V a month later and King Philip IV within the year."

The last part was said with a smugness that grated even as my interest was aroused by her appearing so sure of herself in such a dire situation. She was at my mercy, in my casino, and she had to know there was no escaping.

"Jacques de Molay's curse may have worked, but it took its bloody time. If you intend to try to do me harm, I suggest something that's not so slow acting or it could just be placed in the coincidence column of checks and balances."

She straightened her spine, making her breasts jut out, her expression one of controlled anger. She was a magnificent sight as she spread her arms wide, my excuse for not taking more seriously what happened next. "Be reassured, this will work far too quickly." Her tone shifted to one of immense power, sending chills down my spine. Was that my hair she held between her fingers?

"I call now upon the powers of the east wind and the west wind, the north wind and the south wind to curse you, Lucius of the House of Luceres, with—" She hesitated, a look of indecision fleeting in her eyes. I could still detect hints of her arousal and the thought of her being conflicted at this moment struck me as interesting. "With the physical inability to have any more one-night stands." She gave a merry laugh filled with derision. "Try getting it up now, slick!"

My cell phone rang, interrupting the show. The elevator started to move again as I answered the call.

"Lucius," I barked into the annoying device.

"Emily's gone missing," Cristaldo said, his voice tightened by worry.

The elevator stopped and the doors flew open.

"Hang on," I said, pulling off my jacket one-handed and tossing it at her. I couldn't have her walking through the casino half-undressed.

Isadora gave me a final glare before strutting away. My mind roiling from the impact of my twin's news, I let her go. The time for play was over. Someone in my pack needed my full attention.

Chapter Three

Lucius

"When was she last seen?" I asked Cristaldo. Striding across the casino floor, I was pissed I hadn't gotten laid, but even more upset that a pack member was unaccounted for. *Damn it, on my watch too.*

"Her mother said she didn't come home last night. She thought she was staying with friends, but then she didn't show up for work this morning. She's already called all her known contacts. Emily's always been a responsible girl until now, so we have to take this seriously."

"Okay, I'm on it."

I signed off and headed to check the eye in the sky, to see if surveillance had caught anything.

A couple of hours later and I was still in a quandary. No footage existed of Emily ever entering or leaving the casino, and no one on duty last night had seen her. *Where are you, Emily?*

I headed for the casino floor. My thoughts were so totally focused on my missing cousin that I bumped into Veronica without realizing she was standing right in front of me, blocking the way.

"Careful there, you almost knocked me over." The woman I had made the mistake of bedding more than once held on to my sleeve like a terrier, all bark and no bite.

"What do you want?" I asked. Seeing her, I was once again struck by how little we had in common. Zero outside the bedroom. And right now, I couldn't even see that being a possibility.

"That's not very nice," she said with her signature pout, her suffocating perfume surrounding her scantily clad body in a cloud of desperation. "I came to see if you'd like to spend an hour or two upstairs." She waggled her brows, just in case I didn't get her drift. Never had I wanted her less. She must have caught my look of disdain, because her eyes narrowed.

"No time for any dalliances. A pack member's gone missing."

"Oh, can I help?"

"Do you know my cousin Emily?"

"No." She shook her head.

"Then you can't help me." I strode away, leaving her before she had a chance to answer back. *Hmm, I could use some specialized help in finding Emily.* A vision of Isadora came to mind. Her and her ridiculous curse. Hot anger bubbled up again at her thinking she could do such a thing to me, Lucius Luceres. *But then again, on second thought, witches can be useful. They're known trackers.*

Yes, and she owed me big-time for her slur on my name. And the House of Luceres had a pact with the coven that called themselves the Circle of Wisdom. *Wisdom indeed.* I snorted, thinking how the witch had come at me with her charms and her foolish revenge curse. *Considerable charms though.* My pace quickened now that I had a destination in mind and a debt to collect.

I jumped into my sleek Lamborghini Roadster, top down, and turned up the sound on the CD player. Filling the air with the strains of pulsing rock, I headed out of Vegas on the I-15. Tapping the steering wheel to the rhythm of the drumbeat of the song, I kept a lookout for the turnoff that led to the compound. It was home to the most powerful coven in North America, thanks, no doubt, to High Priestess Meredith Crane and her old family money.

Spotting it on my right, I turned down the hidden laneway that only supes knew the location of and drove past the ancient rockface that lined both sides. The powerful protection wards that guarded the area raised the hair on the back of my head.

The desert rock finally gave way to a center courtyard surrounded by a series of low-lying adobe-type buildings that shone white in the harsh Vegas sunlight. The place looked peaceful enough, but since the location was situated on a convergence of ley lines that the coven swore increased their magical powers exponentially, I doubted it always was. I shrugged. *Whatever.* I just wanted help and payback for slander.

Striding up to the main office — easy to spot as it had an image of the third eye over the doorway — I went in the front entrance to the ringing of the overhead bells that announced supernatural visitors.

"Lucius of the House of Luceres. We've been expecting you." Meredith Crane came forward gracefully, her long chiffon skirt making her appear to float toward me. It was an effect I was long used to. Witches loved to play dress-up, in my experience.

"Meredith, good to see you. If you knew I was coming, then you know why I'm here?"

"Yes, unfortunately I do. One of our members has overstepped. I do apologize." The woman's thin lips disappeared, her expression not boding well for the errant witch. *Excellent.* "She will be held accountable, have no fear."

"Yes, she even carried a knife made of silver."

Meredith's widened eyes meant she wasn't aware of that little fact. I went on before she could manage a response.

"Actually, I was wanting some assistance. One of our pack has gone missing. I thought I'd call in our marker. A little pro quo in addition for you on any future needs." That should be sufficient to get the wise woman totally onboard with any and all of my demands. *It's an uneasy alliance between all the supes of Vegas, but we make it work.*

Meredith nodded her head, making her chandelier earrings dance against her tan skin, her coal-black hair framing her pretty face. Her dark eyes glittered with interest. "That is gracious of you. Isadora is an excellent tracker. Let me summon her. She needs to make *full* restitution to you. You can have complete access to anything she has to offer you to assist you for as long as required."

"Splendid. You have my thanks and a future favor granted. Whatever you need." I piled it on. I wanted Isadora at my beck and call. A ready smile sealed the deal.

Isadora

Savanna, my favorite lab partner for the preparation of concoctions our coven prescribed, came sashaying up to me. I was busy grinding ingredients by mortar and pestle on the pristine white marble countertop in one of the adobe huts that our High Priestess, Meredith Crane, had had specially built for the purpose. I worked five days a week at the Circle of Wisdom compound hidden in the desert near Las Vegas. It was stimulating and satisfying, especially when I could help a fellow witch with a problem like the one Savanna had come to me with before the weekend break. I was dying to know the results of my aid.

"So, your roommate's boyfriend was up to his old tricks?" I had to ask, impatient sort that I am, though I stood behind my handiwork one thousand percent. When Savanna had caught the perp on live feed raiding her underwear drawer and doing the nasty, she'd come to me for help. After all, I was the resident encyclopedia of useful knowledge for striking back at disgusting human behavior. And my lips were always sealed. *Promise.*

"Uh-huh. And guess what happened when he used my underwear to jerk off?"

I gave an over-the-top villainess chuckle, pretending to twirl my invisible mustache. "He ran screaming into the night? Never to be seen again?"

Devious really, but it was very effective to dust undies in ingredients guaranteed to cause delicate tissue to burn like mad. I found ground-up rose hips and *Mucuna pruriens*, a member of the legume family, especially useful as an itching powder, what with their needle-like hairs. *But not to worry, it wears off in a day or two with no residue effects except for mortification. And if the rash lingers, I have a balm available for a price.*

"So, he's out of your life now?"

"And out of Jo's as well. When he let it slip what had happened—I guess the agony loosened his tongue—

she threw his ass to the curb." Jo was Savanna's roommate and too naïve by half. *Protect the innocent* was my motto.

We shared a conspiratorial smile. *Nothing better than keeping the male of the species in check.* Though the jury was still out on whether I would get away with my most recent stunt with Meredith. *Ah, but it's good to be badass.* And at least Lucifer didn't charge a surtax on such small endeavors. *Probably beneath his notice.* "Glad I could help."

"Okay, let me get my lab coat on and I'll pitch in."

"Isadora, your presence is required *immediately*." Meredith's voice resounded over the loudspeaker. Her tone did not bode well. Really, she only used the annoying system that interrupted everyone's work when she was angry at one of us and was making a point.

Granted, she had a point to make. I had screwed up royally with my transaction at the Glitter Palace with the world's most annoying werewolf. I set aside my tools that I had been using in grinding up some necessary ingredients for a special balm to aid in the healing process and took off my lab coat.

It was the yin and yang of things I subscribed to. One concoction to annoy a cock, the other to fix it. *Works for me.*

"Time to pay the piper," Savanna quipped, though her eyes expressed sympathy for my plight. We made a good team, Savanna and me, while Meredith and I tended to bump heads more than not. Unfortunately, being high priestess, she had the final say. Oh, and the fact that her family's money paid for the start-up capital for our online business had been a deciding factor. *Sucks to be poor.*

"Yeah, well, I'd do it again to put that piece of work in his place."

Straightening my dress, I glanced in the mirror over the sink. I looked a bit pale. Picking up a tube of pink lip gloss, I slicked some over my lips. Yanking the elastic tie out of my hair, I smoothed my hair over my shoulders and took a deep breath. Okay, I was prepared for the punishment that she had promised would be meted out once she had decided what it was.

"Good luck," Savanna called after me.

Walking toward Meredith's domain, the largest building on site, I worried a bit about what she had decided. I mean, really, had what I'd done to Lucius Luceres been all that bad? He had it coming, breaking hearts. *Well, best to get it over with.* I strode a bit quicker, noting the expensive cherry-red convertible parked out front. I wondered who it belonged to as I entered the office.

The first thing I saw was my nemesis smirking at me, looking as smug and relaxed as ever, all perfectly creased pants snug at the thighs and obviously designed to draw a female's attention to his very considerable assets. *Lucius Luceres. Oh. Hell. No.*

"What are you doing here? Come to break another heart, like you did Elena's?"

I could see it in his eyes. He didn't even *remember* my sweet baby sister. But the memory of his full lips drawing on my naked breasts seared me to the core. All the growing arousal was accomplishing was to anger me even more. I pressed my lips together tightly then glanced over at Meredith and found her glaring at me. *Figures.*

"Isadora!" Meredith's tone had the lash of the whip attached. "I've assured our guest that you will be *totally* available to see to his needs in an important pack matter. You have much to make up for and I'm absolutely certain you are more than prepared to assist him. Correct?"

It wasn't a question judging by her ominous expression.

I narrowed my eyes at Lucius who appeared even smugger now if that were possible. I hadn't intended to harm the wolf, of course, just give him a reminder of his vulnerability. Besides, werewolves were notoriously hard to hurt. But I wanted to make him think twice about how his actions affected the innocent, determined to stand up for all those women who had been bedded and forgotten by the big bad wolf. I had tasked myself with enacting the little revenge scenario at the Glitter Palace. Easy enough for a witch of my well-honed powers.

But I had not meant to curse him with loss of libido—that had come to me unexpectedly. Serendipity? But it was a sure-fire way to keep other women safe and off his rampaging cock. For his lethal weapon was as impressive as his reputation had promised, I could attest, having experienced it poking at me through his pants. Because whether I liked it or not, the only one not protected from the curse? Me.

"Since the curse you inadvisably chose is going to cause you grief as well" — Meredith paused to give me a speculative look—"I'll leave it to the Goddess and Lucius to restore harmony on this matter. When you've made it up, you'll be welcomed back."

Unfortunately, a curse works against *outside* forces, but doesn't protect the giver. One of the more annoying rules of the otherworldly universe. In other words, I was the only woman he could get it up for until the curse was lifted. On second thought, maybe this idea was about the single worst one I'd ever had? But it was done and no changing it. One per customer was all that same annoying universe allowed. Sort of like a double indemnity clause that doesn't allow double conviction of a crime. Which meant I was effectively in charge of whether the bastard got any nah-nah. Which meant...he'd better have a strong right hand.

"Isadora, you've been warned about this kind of behavior before. You dishonor our coven with your focus on revenge," Meredith continued in her no-nonsense tone. But pointing out my past transgressions didn't help the situation. My spine stiffened with outrage. I tried a new tactic.

"An eye for an eye, a loss of libido for being an out-of-control tallywacker. My way of balancing the books."

"Isadora!"

Hmm, guess she doesn't appreciate my idea of the scales of justice. Though I was being light-humored, I felt something else going on behind the scenes that sent a shiver of disquiet through me. What was up? It felt like too much energy was swirling around a vortex and it made the hairs stand up on the back of my neck. Something was stirring in the universe today and it would be wise to pay close attention.

"I don't believe in curses. It takes belief to make them effective and I have none," Lucius scoffed, making me and the head witch stare at him in disbelief. *What an imbecile!*

The annoyingly attractive werewolf stared me down, his dark brown eyes momentarily flashing blue. Why did all the Luceres men have such amazing builds with wide shoulders and narrow hips, handsome old-world Romanesque countenances and enough testosterone onboard to cause a Vestal Virgin to forgo her vow of chastity? *Damned if I know.* But it didn't stop me from taking a deep, appreciative breath of the arousing fragrance of mint and musk that made every part of me tingle. *With disgust!*

"Time will prove me right." I shrugged. I'd never let him see just how much he was disturbing my world view.

"Isadora, Lucius has come here for your help. I've promised it to him, not to punish you, per se, but to allow you to achieve proper karma with the Goddess. You are to leave with him immediately and provide any and all assistance he requires. That is, if you still want to be part of the Circle of Wisdom? You know we pride ourselves on rising above things whenever possible. It's what we have all sworn to do in our journey. As to your punishment, I think banishment for a time will give you reason to reconsider your commitment."

I swallowed. This was hard-core. When Meredith Crane warned a witch, she'd better listen. I was on thin ice. I didn't want to be banished—I loved everyone in my coven. The sisters were my family, my life. To be tossed out would be the worst thing to happen, maybe even worse than owing Lucifer.

"Can't we come up with another punishment? Something immediate, like a short, sharp shock?"

Lucius moved closer to me, his eyes narrowed. I'd got him off-balance. *Good.* "What do you suggest? Or more to the point, what can you handle?"

Reckless with worry and pressed against the ropes, the very first thing that came to mind spilled from my mouth. Something I'd often fantasized about…and that might shock him. "How about a spanking? Something quick and over with. In lieu of banishment." I didn't see him able to carry such a thing through. Then I'd be off the hook. *Ha!*

"Works for me."

That was not the answer I expected, and every fiber of my being screamed in dismay. I forced myself to nod and tilt my chin up. I was going to take the moral high ground, even if the wolf had no idea it even existed.

"Go, now. Have done with it." Meredith waved her hand at me in dismissal. "And don't come back until you've made things right with the universe."

"Okay, but I already made things fine," I grumbled. What part of the importance of not being walked all over by a man did she not get? I stomped out of the office, the werewolf hard on my heels, making the tiny golden bells over the door bang noisily.

"I'm still rock-hard. Your curse didn't work, witch." He breathed down my neck as we approached his vehicle. "Guess you might be needing some more precision with your spell-making endeavors, you know, to make them work on the Big. Bad. Wolf. Doesn't get any badder or harder than me, babe, if that's what you're looking for. Because I'm more than willing to let you practice on me—any time you like."

I whirled around shocked at his blatant disregard for decorum considering the situation we were in and tried shoving him away, but it was like trying to move a standing boulder. "It's not me you have to worry about. It's other women. Try getting it up for them, slick."

He glowered down at me, his eyes narrowing in thought. "What's this? You mean I can still get it up for you, but only for you? Rather selfish, don't you think?"

Heat suffused my body, and I knew my fair skin was turning beet red. I hate that my embarrassment shows with a vengeance, and it made me angrier, but I needed a clear head now more than ever. I counted to three. "It was not my intention. That's just how the universe works. I gave life to the curse, but it only works on others to save them the grief of you. I prefer to think that pretty *selfless* of me."

"So, you're in charge now of making sure I get fucked every day. Excellent. I'm up for it now if that helps you out any?" His eyes narrowed with devious thoughts, because what other kind of thoughts could the Lothario have? *Smoldered* might be more accurate, as they flashed bright blue once more.

"You disgust me! Never going to happen, wolf! I'm not going to fuck you today or *any* day for that matter." It wasn't often I used the *F* word out loud, but I needed to give back as good as he gave, or lose face with the shifter.

He laughed, a sound that rumbled up from his mighty chest as he stared deep into my eyes. "I think you want to be with me right now." He inhaled a deep breath and let it out with a smug slowness, his full lips curving upward with approval, then trailed a finger down my lips to my neck.

"Do you want me to cast another spell to nip those errant fingers? Turn them to stone?" Of course, I couldn't do that, but he didn't need to know. However, I could bite them off if pushed too far. Then offer a healing balm. *Just sayin'.*

He stilled, his eyes smoldering with the promise of retribution far more than I might have bargained for. The kind of dagger-over-my-head scenario that my nemesis Lucifer kept in his arsenal when he demanded my help, seeming to gift me nothing in return except more compounded debt. Just thinking of him brought a flash of his wickedness and the underworld to the forefront of my mind. *No. Not now. One asshole at a time.*

"You cast another spell my way and I won't answer for the consequences of the hellfire you'll rain down on that pretty little head of yours. As it is, you have a punishment coming. Here or back at the Glitter Palace — you choose."

"Let's get it over with right now." Righteous anger fueled me, not to mention the heat in my belly that was maddening to my sense of fair play. Why on earth was I attracted to this uber-bad shifter? I flipped him the bird to cement my position.

"Yes, please," he whispered, his mouth so close to mine my lips quivered with ridiculous anticipation.

"What?" My brain capsized and I shook my head in disbelief. Of all the responses know to giving the middle finger, this one was off the charts. *So hot.*

"I think I've made my intentions clear."

"Seems we've hit an impasse." I moved away. "Since only one of us intends to do that."

He moved so quickly to follow me that all I saw was a blur of light and shadow. Damn, a very, *very* fast werewolf. He loomed over me once again. Not as a man. This time as a werewolf!

I stood perfectly still, his paws on my shoulders, his eyes having turned a constant bright blue. I shouldn't have moved. What was I thinking? Wolves loved to chase down their prey. And I had no place to run, no place to hide. I had to go with him today or lose my standing in the coven that I revered more than any other on earth. I had to take what I'd told him he should dish out or risk losing it all. *Double fuck.*

The wolf growled, his size intimidating. If he was magnificent as a man, he was even more so as a wolf. I could only imagine what it must be like. To have that power and size. To fear no one.

"Stand down, Luceres." I swallowed, my voice sounding far calmer than I felt. "Okay, I've decided. I'll take my punishment right now." *Best to get it over with, give a little.* I mean, what could he really do to me surrounded by my coven members? If he got too far out of line, they'd help me in a second. *That's if they could?* I licked my lips. He was so damn fast and so virile.

He blurred a second time, naked. Then he took his time to re-dress in clothes I had not seen him shed. *Adonis body, built for speed and endurance, too beautiful by half.* All the parts were at the peak of perfection. Wow, I'd never seen a man built that well before in my life. *Never will again, is my best guess.*

"Good, then I think we know each other well enough for first names, since I've had my hands pretty much all over your body, *Is-a-dor-a*. What other gifts are you endowed with?" His eyebrows quirked upward with interest. It was like what he had displayed just now was nothing out of the ordinary, when for me, it was as surreal as it got.

I licked my lips again. The way he said my name, drawn out and with such feeling, caused chills to break out all over me. I hugged my arms to my chest, trying to calm myself. I had to be too young for a heart attack. This was definitely *not* going the way I'd planned it. It had seemed so simple in my mind, attract the wolf to get him off-guard, enact revenge, then beat it out of there.

But instead of being free of him, I was once more trapped with him and a raging libido. How long could I fight off the attraction? My legs were turning to limp noodles propped up by only a thin edge of willpower as I stood there, doing my best to stare him down. Goddess, but I hated his power over me at that moment!

"What kind of powers do you possess?" he asked. "Other than the obvious?"

"What's that supposed to mean? Can't handle the eye candy?" I scoffed, crossing my arms over my chest. Fine, so *I* couldn't, but I'd never share that.

"Just answer the question."

"I'm a remote viewer, if you must know, and can call upon the weather when needed to do my bidding, along with the excellent gift of divination. And I cast a mean spell of invisibility and a host of others. What can you do besides hound-dogging and menacing everyone as a wolf?" *If it's a competition, bring it on.*

A sudden tremor, a seismic shift deep in the ground beneath our feet, made me sway forward in response, reaching out and grabbing hold of whatever was nearby. *Bad idea.* Because he grabbed me right back and I was once more enthralled by a tantalizing cloud of raging hormones, my breasts pressed hard against his broad chest. *Fucking betrayed by my own damn body.* It wanted this man to take me over, ravish every square sensitive inch of flesh. I shook my head with denial, stars dancing in front of my eyes. I had to fight this attraction with everything I had. Never would I let him know he was getting to me on such an elementary level. I bit down on the inside of my cheek, causing instant pain. *There, something else to focus on. The taste of metallic blood should sour things.*

He stood over me for far longer than necessary, a strange look in his eyes. He even leaned in closer and breathed in my essence, his nose twitching. What did he see? What was he thinking? Who was he listening to? All the energy of the time and place seemed to have converged in the here and now. Finally, he made some kind of decision, for he nodded at me and his expression changed to one of assurance and confidence. "Time for your punishment." He grabbed my hand and began leading me toward an ancient strand of Joshua trees that lined the edge of the property. I swore they leered at me as I was dragged in protest across the sandy soil.

I kept my mouth shut, though it hurt to do so. *Best to get it over with, right?*

At Summoner's Rock, he came to an abrupt halt. "This will work."

The waist-high saddle-like rock was built for cradling water on a midsummer's night, smooth and worn from centuries of weathering. We often used the sacred spot to perform rituals under the stars with all of us sky clad.

"Strip," he said, releasing my hand. My blood pressure soared. My mind rushed to make sense of it.

"No fuckin' way! This is a sacred place."

"Never stopped you at *my* place of business. Coming at me with a knife." His expression had turned cold as ice. My heart skipped a beat. This was going badly and I didn't know how to turn it around to save myself.

"I wasn't going to stab you for heaven's sake! Just teach you a lesson, you dumb ass." Maybe I could have chosen my words better, but I was between a rock and a hard place.

"Now it's my turn. And I want your bare ass over that rock."

Oh shit, that was so hot.

"I need your verbal consent before I begin, Isadora."

I stood there, chewing on my bottom lip. I had been so certain he'd back down. Now I was really between a rock and a hard place. Well, I had suggested it in a moment of weakness…and part of me was curious to experience it. *No going back now.*

"Fine, I consent to being spanked, okay, but I'm *not* stripping."

"I want you to feel it on your bare ass. Pull down those panties and raise your dress and we'll call it even. I think twelve strikes should be sufficient to teach you a proper lesson."

I gave him a look that told him in no uncertain terms that he was on very, *very* thin ice. I reached under my long cotton dress and tugged my underwear down my thighs, then hiked up my skirt and lay over the warm rock that instantly heated my nipples and groin.

Lying there, knowing I was exposed, made me want to enact an invisibility spell. But I knew better. Doing so would only prolong the punishment.

Waiting was the worst part. I turned my head to the side in efforts to see what was taking so long. "What's the hold-up?" I asked.

A loud slap resounded, heating one bare cheek. I pressed my lips together to avoid letting him know that it hurt like hell. No shifter was getting the better of me.

Then a second swat, on the other cheek this time. I was heated through and through, and not in a bad way, but in a far too enticing way. I shivered, trying to keep from getting any more turned on.

He slipped my panties down to hang off one ankle and tugged my legs farther apart as I hugged the boulder. The sensation of being exposed, the sun on my ass, was so damn erotically charged I was hard pressed not to come right there.

A harder swat. *Oh Goddess, please let this be over with. I don't want to embarrass myself.*

"Three," he said unnecessarily. Each and every spank was going to be stamped in my memory bank for all eternity.

By number seven, I was a melting pool of want and need. When had spanking become so hot? I had to blame it on the location, the sunshine, the ley lines, the having to do it whether I liked it or not. Me, a witch who always called my own shots, was enjoying something I would never admit to, even if someone pressed a gun to my head.

He ran a huge hand over my sensitized flesh and murmured, "So warm and inviting. You like it, admit it."

"I fucking hate it, you asshole."

"I don't think your asshole agrees." He dipped his fingers down between my exposed cheeks, gently massaging my anus. *Oh Goddess, give me the strength.*

Outraged, I grabbed on to the rock with all my power, digging my fingernails into it sharply and breaking a couple in the process. "Fucking get it over with!"

I was beyond humbled by this point. I wanted to slink away, find a place that served alcohol and drink my humiliation to oblivion. Later, I promised myself.

"Eight."

It was *never* going to be over with. My pussy was heated to the point I had no idea what I was going to do when I was finally released from the torture.

"Eleven."

You can do this, Isadora, one to go.

I waited, and waited. Fucker was the most annoying shifter in the entire universe. When I got my chance, he was going to pay. *Big-time.*

"Twelve."

The last one was the hardest slap of all, and my ass instantly heated to the boiling point. I groaned and shuddered against the rock, an orgasm coursing through me like a freight train out of control.

I came around to the sounds of a chuckle. "Now that's a sight I'd have paid a king's ransom to see."

Face flaming, I groggily got off the rockface with legs that could barely support me and yanked my panties and dress into place. I avoided his eyes. I would bide my time. *But isn't going after the wolf what got you in this insane predicament in the first place?* I had no answer for that.

"Let's go." I stomped back across the desert to the courtyard where the convertible was parked, the shifter at my heels still chuckling. I *never* wanted to talk or think about this day ever again.

Chapter Four

Lucius

My cell phone rang as I accompanied Isadora back to my vehicle. *Perfect timing.* I had accomplished the punishment of the witch with aplomb. She was obviously beyond mortified, which had begun to tilt the scales of justice more evenly. I had to give her credit. She'd more than piqued my wolf's interest as well, his wanting to shift held at bay only through sheer willpower during that erotic spanking session.

That spectacular moment in time had given me far more satisfaction that she would ever know. Not that I believed her for one second that I wouldn't be able to get it up for another female — the entire time I was spanking her I was hard as the rock she lay spread on for me. She had to be bluffing about the curse. She was the type to twist and turn things to her satisfaction, but she had met her master now.

I touched Isadora's arm to halt her in her tracks as I answered the call. No way was she getting away from me. A dawning of what it meant that I was feeling so protective toward her hit again at that moment. *Is this it?* Was this how it felt to have met her, the one I was meant to spend my life with? The earth had trembled with the rightness of our pairing, speaking to me, letting me know that big things were on the horizon. And now I burned with an intensity that defied reason as alive as if I was running across the desert on all fours tracking prey, making me fairly certain this was her. My very own Forever Mate. Which meant keeping on top of everything from now on of paramount importance. *Damn, but I am up for that.* My wolf fully agreed as well.

"What is it?" I growled into the phone, watching the gorgeous female lick her plump full lips, her eyes still softened from the orgasm I'd witnessed. My glance flicked to her nipples visible through her thin cotton dress. *Yes, hard as pebbles.* Like it or not, she was highly attracted to me as well on an elementary level. *The best kind and so rare. Worth breaking any rule for.*

"I need an update. Emily's mother is frantic. Have you learned anything?" Cristaldo asked, his voice tightened by worry.

I felt a slight twinge of guilt. But then, what had to be done *had* been done. Now I could focus better on the job. "I'm working on it. I've enlisted the help of a known tracker. A witch from the Circle of Wisdom. She's going to help us."

"A *witch*? Well, about now, I'd take any help we can get."

"I'll be right there and I'll be bringing her with me. She owes me."

Isadora and I shared another glance, though this time hers was fueled by a touch of curiosity. I opened the passenger door of my convertible and motioned her inside. She didn't know it, but she was never getting away from me now.

"What's wrong?" she asked.

"You'll know soon enough."

She glared at me, standing her ground.

"We need you to track a young shifter that's gone missing. Emily Luceres."

"Was that so hard to say?" She shook her head and slid into the vehicle, then winced. I understood her discomfort. She had my brand on her now. "As hard as it was to spank me, you oaf?

She was incorrigible, a lovely tall drink of water who would need many, many lessons on how to know her place. I took a deep breath of satisfaction and got in behind the wheel of the Lamborghini. We sped off in a squeal of tires back to the Glitter Palace. Man, with all that glorious Titian hair flowing in the wind, Isadora looked like a medieval princess of fairy tale fame come back to life. I admit, the woman intrigued me. If she could take a spanking with such aplomb, well, what else could she handle…

* * * *

The elevator came to a complete halt and I hustled her into the penthouse and down the hallway to Cristaldo's office. He looked over as we entered, his dark eyebrows rising an inch or two.

"This is Isadora Champagne," I said, thrusting her along in front of me.

"Stop pushing at me," she growled, her green eyes lit up like a cat's in the dark.

"Nice to meet you, Isadora," Cristaldo said, his voice strained. "You're a renowned tracker?"

She gave a nod, her eyes wary. She had the look of someone that would bolt first chance she got. I'd need to keep a careful eye on her at all times. *With pleasure.*

"A remote viewer, to be specific. I just need something she's worn, to get a sense of her. Then I can leave, right? I have work to do."

"You'll help for as long as we say if you know what's good for you!" I growled. Never had I wanted to tame a woman more. The *Taming of the Shrew* would pale in comparison if I had my way. And I always got my way. Oh yeah, thoughts of her being my Forever Mate were rising, and so far, she had passed every test with flying colors. From her incredible scent, the instant attraction between us, to the ground shifting and vibrating with the knowledge of the rightness of our pairing.

"Or you'll what? You can't do much now that I've cursed you, mutt!" She was in full attack mode again, her hair bristling with energy. What a magnificent sight she made. Someone who belonged on a throne with a crown on her head, anointing her followers with a sharpened end of a broadsword.

"Oh, we'll see about that," I growled back, narrowing my eyes at her. One spanking hadn't tamed her. Maybe the next one should be over my knee... Followed up with a good—

"Enough! What's this about a curse?" Cristaldo interjected, his expression somewhere between amused and annoyed.

"He'll never get it up for another female again. I've seen to that," she said, her expression beyond smug.

"Bullshit," I said. "I'm hard right now just looking at you." I pulled her against me to prove my case.

"You can get it up for me, remember, just not for others. Are you dim-witted or what?"

A surprised gasp from Cristaldo drew our attention.

Never had I been more incensed. She had gone too far this time, saying such crap in front of my brother. Sure, until she also knew she was my chosen mate, I would allow some leeway, but this was over the top. The edges of the room narrowed, everything gleaming blood-red. "You will pay for that!"

Cristaldo laid a hand on my shoulder, the voice of reason. "Stop! You said she can help us. She can't if you kill her outright."

He has a point. Not that that would ever be my intention. More like lock her up and have her every which way from Sunday until she agreed to behave herself. "I wasn't going to kill her. Just teach her another valuable lesson she has more than coming." She had just upped her punishment to the stratosphere. But somehow my brother had worked his body between us, the only thing that saved her.

"Okay, if you're quite done, Emily needs our help."

With that reminder I simmered down a bit, a streak of guilt I didn't like striking at my core. "Yes, of course. What do you need me to do?" I pulled on my enforcer shield, albeit with a bit more difficulty than usual.

As it was, she eyed me with enough passionate hate to burn an entire forest to cinders. Well, she would have to wait for the final shootout until later. *Bring it on. You'll be taken down another peg or two when I'm finished with you.* A paddling came to mind…

"You say you can remote view?" Cristaldo asked.

She nodded, her eyes still glittering with rage.

"Would this work?" He handed her a shoe from the top of his desk. "This was left at the festival. One of Emily's."

She took the red dress pump from him with a nod. "Yes, it should, and if she's still got the matching shoe, it will make it a much stronger reveal."

"So, what of it?" I asked, pushing her for answers.

"Give me a damn minute! It's not like there's no cost, okay? I have to call upon some — special help in the universe to hear my plea. Then I need to free my mind and read the vibrations. Let this object and its matching one spin and make a connection. Exactly like physics' Quantum Entanglement theory suggests." She closed her eyes, her expression calmer. She seemed to go into a trance, her body swaying back and forth.

"Oh, dear Goddess," she said, her face paling, though her plush lips remained deep pink.

"What is it?" both Cristaldo and I asked in unison.

"She's been taken."

"Where?" I wanted to shake the information out of her right then and there.

"Across the water. To Scotland."

"By who? Who took her?" I asked.

She frowned and closed her eyes. Her eyelids moved back and forth as if she was watching a movie behind them.

I'd have liked to be party to what she was viewing. A small twinge of admiration overcame me that I quickly stomped all over. First, I needed to get her in line before anything could be worked out between us, right? I had to admit I had no practical experience in this brand-new Forever Mate domain. Did any shifter? We all flew blind on this one, far as I knew.

"I'm getting the name Highland Heathens and some kind of ancient castle at the edge of the world. Does that mean anything to you?"

"The damn Wulvers!" I said, wanting to punch something. The Scottish wolves had been notorious since the early days of cattle and wife stealing for taking what they wanted *when* they wanted. Now they'd gone too far. Taking a pack member of the House of Luceres…

"Where are they now?" Cristaldo asked. "At Castlestone in the Shetland Islands?"

She rubbed her forehead. "I see stone walls all around her. And the sense of ancient spirits housed within the huge structure sounds about right."

"I'll be taking the largest helicopter in our fleet right away. And you're coming with me." I moved in close again, sidestepping my cockblocking brother, to show her I meant business.

"Like hell I am! You piece of…of…" She turned a charming shade of pink, her mouth firming into a line, like she couldn't find a big enough or bad enough word to describe me.

"You eat with that mouth? And your high priestess has already promised your complete cooperation, in case you've forgotten?"

"Would you two calm down! Isadora, we need your help to bring home a young girl. Will you help us to do that?" Cristaldo asked. My brother had never looked more exasperated, though it did bring back memories of his craziness during the time when he was 'courting' Everly, if the way he went after her with all guns blazing could rightly be called by that term.

The witch looked put upon, a satisfactory state, her eyes breathing fire. Figuratively, that was, though I wouldn't put it past her to actually manifest the substance like some kind of firedragon from myth and legend. Well, if she tried, I'd quench it for her…

Chapter Five

Isadora

Why me? All I wanted was a taste of revenge, setting the insufferable Lucius in his place, and I got pulled into the firestorm that the House of Luceres was so famous among supernaturals for creating. They had a well-deserved reputation as a lightning rod for chaos. So many volatile werewolves, too rich and too wild by half, and all in one huge extended family.

Mine seemed miniscule in comparison, just my younger sister Elena and my brother Ian. And now I had to stay, hang around with the very wolf I despised most on Earth? Not to mention that I had incurred another cost for using my remote gift that I preferred not to think about right now. My very blood seethed with indignation. Okay, someone was in need. A young girl. Something I could *never* let slide. I would do what I had to then get the hell out of there. And at least I'd have my coven to go back to.

"Okay," I said and took a deep breath. "For the young girl's sake, you can count me in. I'll do what I can, though I don't need to be in attendance to remote view. The very definition of the word is 'remote'. I can do it just as well right here." *There, suck on that.*

"Not going to happen. I don't trust you. You're coming with me."

"And I'm supposed to trust you? You who only think with that big strutting cock of yours? No, I'll *never* trust you. You take, take, take, and never give back. I may be the only woman you can get it up for now, but I'm—"

"How long until that damn curse you enacted wears off?" Cristaldo asked.

"There is no curse! She's bluffing," Lucius said.

"Pull it together. You're both needed by Emily. So take it down a notch or two and concentrate on getting our cousin home," Cristaldo said. "And you didn't answer my question, Isadora. How long?"

I pursed my lips, feeling a great deal of satisfaction at being totally in charge of this part of the equation. "No removing it without certain conditions being met. And definitely not before the next full moon. And only if I choose to."

"You'll do it when I tell you to!" Lucius huffed. "Not that I believe in curses. But I don't need bad mojo heading off to Scotland and dealing with those damn Wulvers."

I shrugged my shoulders. "It is what it is. And my number-one condition is that you tell every female you're with right up front that you will never commit to them—"

"I do that now. I *never* let a woman think otherwise. I always state up front that I'm a lone wolf, destined to stay that way as pack enforcer."

He stared me down, making me wonder for a second if I was not totally correct in my facts about his situation.

"And I have a condition of my own. You caused this mess so you have to do what you can to relieve my sexual hunger until the curse wears off. At least three times a day, morning, noon and night. That's the *least* you can do."

"If you think I'm going to relieve *you*, you'd better think again!"

A hand slammed on the desk, drawing both our attentions. "You two work this out. Now *go*, take the roof helicopter that's fueled and ready, and get the hell out of here. Argue on your own time. And for heaven's sake, bring Emily home safe."

"Fine." Lucius grabbed my arm and began to march me down the hallway.

"I can't go like this if we're going to be gone more than a day. I need to go home for some clean clothes at least," I protest. *Delay as long as possible, and maybe something will happen and change the course of events.*

"That didn't bother you in the elevator. Maybe I'll even keep you buck-naked and offer a straight-up trade for Emily. Or not. All wolves have a problem with witches. You're an enemy right down to your DNA. You know that, right?"

Enough is enough. "Sweet mother of the Goddess, you are the worst type of shifter I've ever met! I'll *never* lift that curse from you no matter how much you beg. Not if I live to be a hundred years old. Not even on my death bed."

Lucius

Her fragrance overtook me once more, making me rock hard. I admired her spunk, not that I'd ever say so. And I'm a gentleman in that I would see her dressed properly. But on some elementary level I was enjoying this. Never had I met such a strong-willed goddess before, beguiling and wicked in one enticing package. And I would have her all to myself on this trip. *Plenty of time to bend her to my will.*

"Sly, my brother's major-domo, will see to your needs." I hurried her quicker down the hallway, calling out for the man. "Sly, I need your assistance."

"Lucius, what can I do for you? And please, who do we have here? Welcome, darling girl." Sly suddenly appeared, looking as impeccable as always dressed in a deep-purple silk suit with a fragrant white carnation pinned to his lapel. His extra-high hair was gleaming with product, his expression animated and kindly. Everyone loved Sly. This would be an interesting test for my witchy mate.

"This is Isadora Champagne. She's in dire need of clothing for a trip to the Shetland Islands ASAP. Can we accommodate her?"

"But of course! Oh, *che bella bella donna adorabile*! You are so lucky, Mr. Lucius. To have this woman on your arm. *È magnifica!*" Sly reached for Isadora's hand and kissed the back of it in his usual old-world courtly fashion.

"Lovely to meet you, Sly. I love your suit. Perhaps you can find something for me in that gorgeous color? It's my favorite."

Where had the irritable, annoying persona vanished to? I narrowed my eyes at her, and she did the same back. I barked a laugh, taking us both by surprise, judging by the way those big eyes widened.

Sly ignored me, keeping all his elegant attention on Isadora. He patted her shoulder affectionately. "Of course. Purple would do all that lovely hair justice and make those beautiful eyes pop. Make our Mr. Lucius jealous with all the attention you'll be getting."

"Last thing I want in the whole world is to make *him* jealous," she said, pointing a finger at me. "I'd prefer a gunny sack if you have one available. Or a suit of amor."

"Careful," I warned.

The major-domo chuckled, sharing a speculative glance with me. "You will give the sire a run for his money, *bella*. Bravo! Now, follow me. I have a land of delight to share with you. We shall pack all the basics and some really scrumptious items cut down to there" — he pointed at her navel — "that will make your wolf drool and half-mad with the passion of a thousand suns."

"Not need for more passion, Sly, I think we got that base covered. More like a need for some magic to stop her bothering the hell out of me," I deadpanned.

Both of them ignored me this time, as they strolled away arm-in-arm, chatting like old friends.

I paced, waiting for them, ready to burst in and pack the damn suitcase for her. As I was about to pound on the door, it abruptly opened and the witch appeared, dressed in a flowing purple velvet gown that stopped at mid-calf and a pair of matching leather boots that actually looked rather practical for hiking.

Over the gown she wore a white cashmere sweater with pockets. She also carried a warm jacket I approved of. The Shetlands could get chilly. I grabbed the suitcase from her, grunted with pretense at its heavy weight, and began to stride down the hallway to the elevator to take us to the roof, expecting her to follow me. Of course, I had made an incorrect assumption.

Chapter Six

Isadora

"I'm not going until I have your promise." This was an important moment and I wasn't letting it pass without setting down some ground rules first.

"What do you want now? Have you forgotten we have a young girl to rescue?"

I swallowed. In my defense, I hadn't gotten the feeling that she was in any real mortal danger. Just that she was traveling in the company of the Highland Heathens. This wolf who right now confronted me and was offering a zinger of a look? I was a lot more concerned about him, because he was going to drive me insane. "Fine. We can set down the ground rules on the helicopter."

"Yeah, right. Only rule is you follow my instructions to the letter."

I didn't bother to answer him, but gave him my patented look of uber disdain.

I trooped down the hall after him, stood perfectly still and ignored him in the elevator, then turned away his help to get onto the aircraft. After awkwardly getting myself buckled in, I sat and watched him go about storing our luggage and the business of starting up the helicopter.

"Roger that," he said, speaking into his headset. "We'll stop on the way by and pick you up. Pack a bag. And be ready."

My curiosity rose a degree, but I made myself not ask. Goddess, why hadn't I brought a traveling spell kit and my emerald for extra power? This idiot still needed to be put in his place. Big-time. But without the necessary ingredients, it would be difficult to manage. Maybe some fellow witch in the Shetlands could lend me some supplies?

Damn, I didn't even have my cell phone. I needed to get my hands on one and search for my best options. A banishing spell right now to get the guy off my back would not go amiss. Too bad Meredith had banned poppets.

We flew a short distance, then landed in a large compound just outside of Vegas, setting down in front of a motel-like complex. Three very large men began racing from in front of the building toward us, each carrying a backpack. My, but the House of Luceres grew them big. Those fine specimens clamored into the back of the aircraft through the sliding back door, a boisterous mix of voices and friendly camaraderie.

"Hey, bro, who do we have here? You been holding out on us?" one asked, the biggest badass I'd ever seen next to Lucius. Oh, this was going to be fun. For the first time I regretted going after the wolf, because it appeared to have backfired. Now I was the one on the firing line being noticed by a pack of alpha males.

"This is Isadora Champagne. A witch and remote viewer who can help us find your sister. These are all my cousins." Lucius said the words with less grace than they were received by the men. They actually appeared to perk up and not be nearly as offended by my designation as 'witch' than he had suggested his pack would be.

"Hi, beautiful witch, I'm Gino." The one that had spoken first thrust an extra-large paw forward to grab for my hand. He was suddenly right there in my personal space as we shook hello. A giant wave of testosterone surrounded him like a ruthless magnetic storm — I'd gauge more than enough to start up an orgy in a convent full of devout nuns, if I was into such a thing. *I'm not. I'm stating that right up front. I'm a one-at-a-time kind of gal with a firm belief that the right one for me is out there somewhere. The kind of guy that's kind, and loving, and housebroken and sensitive...* My forever list didn't seem quite as exciting as it had in the past when I'd compiled it.

"Nice to meet you, Gino. Sorry about your sister." He would be easy to identify with those arresting dark eyes and long lustrous hair pulled back in a raw leather tie.

"Thank you. Emily's special. But don't let this mutt give you any grief over being a witch." Gino gabbed a finger toward Lucius. "I personally have no problem with witches. Now vampires, those cold dead soulless suckers make me want to practice target shooting."

"Well, if you do, make sure you stake them in the heart, remove their head and stuff garlic in their mouths. That is, if you never want them to rise and get their revenge. And a banishment spell would not go amiss before burning them and sending their ashes over a cliff on a windy day. And thanks, that does make me feel better," I quipped back.

I was rewarded with the big guy writhing with huge belly laughs at my remarks.

"You'll do just fine, Isadora."

Lucius growled. His expression had changed as well, his skin darkening with emotion. So, he didn't like that his cousin didn't find me nearly as despicable for being a witch as he suggested all wolves felt about females called upon by the Goddess to create magic. *Time to join this century. Witches are being more and more accepted all the time. We have gifts. Well, curses too, but one has to earn those fair and square. Ring any bells, mutt?*

"Hey, how about introducing the rest of us?" the only blond of the group asked, his hair swept back from his proud forehead, his brown eyes alight with keen interest.

"Isadora, meet Goldie. The only shifter with blond hair in our pack. We're still asking questions about who his mother is," Gino said, his tone taunting.

"Damn it, my mother's the same as yours, Gino. We're twins, by the way. Of course, we have the same mother!" Goldie said, obviously offended.

"Not necessarily. There have been cases of twins born to two different fathers." A new voice spoke up, the third member of their group.

"Right, heteropaternal superfecundation," I said. I regretted being a smart-ass know-it-all immediately. No one needs to think their parentage up for debate. "But it's extremely rare. And I can tell you guys are for real twins. It's obvious. You look very much alike. Dye your hair the same color and you'd see that."

"Yeah, let's bleach those long shiny locks, then lop them off," Goldie said with a bit too much glee. He got a punch in the arm for his trouble and a loud growl that made the hair on the back of my neck rise. These guys could be a lot of fun, but caution was always called for with shifters. *My Goddess*, they howled at the moon, fought, and marked and claimed their mates.

They were far too wild for me, though I had to admit there was something to be admired in their naturalness. They were far freer to just be themselves. Sometimes being an enabler of the magic arts was binding. Too many obligations and precise instructions. Not that I'd give it up, ever. I also enjoyed the control. Just sometimes, to run free and let all one's inhibitions out might be a glorious experience.

"And I'm Angelo. Nice to meet you, Isadora." The final cousin had short dark hair that might wave if allowed to grow longer. He was leaner than the twins, the expression in his eyes far more cautious. Maybe even haunted. What was his story?

"Would everyone just buckle the hell up so we can get out of here?" Lucius demanded, his tone impatient.

"You could have just said, bro. You get up on the wrong side of the bed this morning or what? Or maybe you never got to sleep because of the adorable witch here?" Gino said, settling down in his seat and doing as directed.

"Leave it alone," Lucius said from between gritted teeth.

"Then you won't mind if I court the beautiful lady?" Gino pressed, his grin exposing white teeth against the dark tan of his skin.

"Hell yes, I mind. She comes equipped with curses," Lucius countered.

"I thought you didn't believe in curses?" I called him on it.

I savored the sputtering that ensued. *Good.* It would only be the first of many. *There's a poppet with your name on it, and it's going to be crafted as soon as possible. See how you like it when I send a few pinpricks into sensitive areas.* Of course, I wouldn't really do that. But maybe I could play around with his doppelganger just a little…

Then suddenly I was accosted by a terrible, gut-destroying image from the past. My brother Ian, tied up and left in a closet. The helplessness in his innocent blue eyes, the bruises on his boyish face, the lack of a shoe, left at the crime scene…

He had deliberately sent me the piercing image in that split second that he knew would bring me to heel. An impossible-to-pay-off debt had been created by my now-deceased mother, needing his help once before to save my brother from a predator, and with nowhere else to turn since our father had abandoned us, she'd chosen to make a pact with Lucifer. *That's right, the damn devil.*

I'd inherited that debt, and every time I used my gift of remote viewing—the talent that had brought Ian home safe—I owed the maggot more time in his employ to do his bidding. What the hell did he want this time? He only showed me Ian's image in my third eye when he wanted something from me. He'd be following the picture up soon with a date and time to appear.

I swallowed hard. *Of all the days for him to send out a call after not hearing from him for months.* The fun and games of earlier came to an abrupt halt and I struggled to hide my agitation. No way did I want the wolf to know my business or feel sorry for me. I'd managed the heavy debt for years and I would continue to do so on my lonesome.

We lifted off the desert floor in one smooth move, breaking me away from painful thoughts. I was even grateful in the moment for the presence of the wolves, to take my mind off what I knew was coming — an invite no one could refuse from the master of the underworld himself. *And visiting hell is just so damn depressing. All those lost souls moaning and carrying on. The vile odors.* I just prayed I could find Emily first before the final summons was sent and I had to appear. Well, that, or be hauled before him by my hair. Yeah, there was precedence.

Lucius worked the controls, his expression grim as he headed the whirlybird east toward the open Atlantic and the Shetland Islands.

"How long is the flight?" I asked.

"About fourteen hours with one stop," Lucius said, giving me a piercing look, his brown eyes a bit too penetrating. "You okay? I felt a little something going on in the supernatural universe there for a second. Something that bothered you?"

It was the first time I'd seen that side of him, actually asking *me* if I was okay. I wasn't sure what I felt about it and I wasn't going to waste time thinking about such things. I had more than enough on my plate already, what with his royal evilness now on my tail.

"I'm fine. Wake me when we get there," I directed, snuggling down for a nap and turning my face away to hide my tears.

Why me? I know, I know, why not me? I had signed on to pay off the debt of family honor of my own volition, not been coerced by anything more than *somebody* had to pay. And I was the oldest. It wasn't like my father would step forward—he'd abandoned us years ago when he'd found out the cost for what mother had done. *Like she had any real choice in the matter.*

Chapter Seven

Lucius

A moment in time could change *everything*. Back at the coven's compound, when I'd felt the rumble of power under the earth, things had changed. And now I was absolutely certain that Isadora Molay Champagne was my Forever Mate. Everything added up, confirming it. It was the same as it had been for Cristaldo and his Everly last year. Overly protective, crazy with lust and obsessed by her every action. Even the earth agreed. I shook my head. The timing could be better, though I'd still have had to punish her, of course—I had to keep the upper hand with this one. Now and for all time.

When the flash of a young boy who resembled her had appeared in my brain, I recognized something deeper was going on with her. What the hell that was I had no idea, but it was important. And I would get to the bottom of it.

"You need anything? Something to drink or eat?" I asked the woman turned away from me, her posture suggesting the world sat far too heavily on her slender shoulders, which was kind of unexpected after all the accusations that she'd been slinging my way for the past hour.

"I just need to sleep." Her muffled voice came from inside the sweater she'd pulled up over her nose.

"Fine. Let me know if and when you need something. We've got supplies onboard." I surprised myself with the offer. Like I said, our situation was in a state of flux as we learned about each other. Normally, I let women go their own way. Sure, I could be charming when the need arises, but it was rare for me to care about their needs beyond the bedroom. And there, without a doubt, I make sure that their *every* need was met. Well, it was my obligation as the legendary enforcer of our pack. I did have a reputation to uphold. *Family honor and all.*

"Never thought you'd offer a female more than a roll in the hay," Gino said, the tease all too apparent. "Now, if Isadora wants some real action, some spectacular ways of being taken care of that will blow her mind, she should give me a call. My reputation is stellar on that account. I know how to take care of a lady!"

"Keep it buttoned, Gino. Isadora needs her rest. She's going to be on call soon enough when we reach the Shetlands."

"I think you protest too much, bro. The beautiful witch is getting under your thick hide, admit it."

I ignored the taunt. *Forever Mates always get under your skin. That's the whole point, bro.* But the thought of having her all to myself fired my blood, making my mind race with a wild passion. *Soon*, I promised myself. *Find Emily, then things will fall into place.*

"She's a human being. See that you treat her like one," I growled, keeping my voice low not to bother Isadora while she slept. If indeed she was sleeping. I'd swear those shoulders shuddered a bit from time to time. Could she be crying? The thought hit me like a thunderbolt.

What had I been thinking? Was she in distress? What had I missed? Was there more to it than being worried about that young boy? I could hardly ask her now. She was as curled up as tightly as a person could get strapped into a seat, obviously not wanting to be bothered. Fuck it, I'd ask anyway.

"Are you certain you're okay, Isadora?"

A few seconds of silence commenced, as if my calling her by her given name was over the top. *Hell, I'm not a monster, just a wolf consumed by this job of protecting my pack.* An image of my twin Cristaldo and Everly on their wedding day came to the forefront of my mind. *So much in love and so happy they were bursting at the seams.* I wanted that. And I would have that.

"I'm fine, wolf. Leave it alone."

Her cold words dismissed me. I hardened my so-called too-thick hide at that moment. She was right. I needed to leave this the hell alone. *Stay focused.* I had a job to do in bringing Emily home to her loving family. Get that over with first.

"You need to take a course on handling women, bro. You suck at it," Goldie chimed in.

I literally saw red, the color infused across the windscreen of the helicopter in sweeping waves. I counted to ten, my last recourse before my temper exploded. I now understood how a stack of dynamite felt before it exploded, destroying everything around it. *Fucking annoyed* didn't have cover it.

"He's not that bad at it," Isadora said in a quiet tone.

I swung my head around in her direction. What was this? She was defending me now? I wished I could see her face instead of that expanse of white sweater and those lovely red-gold locks that flowed around her with a life all their own. My fingers fairly itched to run through their silkiness again, and to drag that warm, full mouth up to mine, to test her willingness once more.

"See, I told you there was something going on," Gino said, his tone smug. Why on earth were my cousins taking an interest in my love life, now of all times?

"There's nothing going on," I said, gritting my teeth at the lie. Now was not the time to declare myself. Not while we were on a mission of rescue.

"You sure about that? Not many women defend you. Last I counted, one, your mother, on a good day when you haven't given her too much grief," Gino added.

"Keep this up and I'm dumping all your asses in the water. We'll soon be over the Atlantic Ocean. I suggest you not push this any further, any of you." I used my best alpha enforcer tone, knowing that would be the end of it.

A sweet silence greeted my words of warning. There's only so far I can be pressed, and today had exceeded all predictions.

I glanced over at Isadora. If only I could get her to open up, tell me what was wrong. I could be a lot of help if she were in trouble. With difficulty, I remained silent. There'd be time enough to get to the bottom of things when we were alone. Maybe she'd open up without the annoying audience? Sure, I loved my pack brothers, helped them with whatever they needed in a nano second. But what brother didn't get under another's skin once in a while? It was the nature of the beast.

Settling in for the long trip, I refocused my thoughts on how we were going to approach the damn heathens and get Emily back in one piece. But Isadora's soft breathing, the amazing scent that wafted into the air between us like an enticing cloud, kept pulling my mind back to her presence. Cristaldo couldn't come on this trip and I suddenly missed his thoughtful words of advice. Everly was pregnant with their first born, and of course, he had an empire to run.

But since he and his Forever Mate had hooked up pretty much immediately after only a few altercations and of course permanently—the only way shifters operate—my twin had learned things I could only guess at. Things that kept his mate, Everly, one of the happiest shifters I'd had the pleasure of meeting. But asking for his help via our twin telepathy would come with consequences. He'd never let me live it down. Especially since I'd not exactly shown my best side earlier in his office. So, I was on my own, navigating uncharted waters.

The image that had flashed through my brain earlier came back to mind. Who was the boy? Her son? She didn't look old enough to have a boy of around ten or eleven. Maybe a brother? Or was the image an old memory? Damn it, but I needed to get inside that mind and find out what was going on.

"We landing at Gander?" Gino asked, rolling his neck in a small circle having just woken from his nap.

All my passengers had fallen asleep or had been pretending to be for the past few hours while I'd flown us to the east coast. I'd planned a pit stop in Newfoundland, Canada, for refueling.

"Yeah, good a choice as any. Have you gotten any messages from Emily?"

Gino was Emily's older brother, which was why he still had a head on his shoulders after being a pain in my ass over his remarks about Isadora and I. *Hell, he's almost been flirting with her,* I thought, again feeling a renewed sense of righteous anger.

"None. She's gone off my radar completely. But it could be the vast distance and the fact we haven't been as close lately. Says I'm too in her face about her needing to get out into the world and make her own way. She's only nineteen, for heaven's sake! And turns out I was right. Got herself in a heap of trouble. My parents are beside themselves with worry."

"It's not as bad as it seems." Isadora spoke up, pulling the sweater back from her lovely face. She looked younger now fresh from sleeping, more vulnerable, and I felt a pull inside me unlike any I've felt before. I wanted to protect her from any and all hurts, in any way I could.

"How so?" I asked.

"She's not in any real distress. From what I've seen, she's being looked after really well."

"You absolutely sure?" Gino asked.

"I'm certain."

Gino let out an audible breath. "There's that then. But the sooner we get her home the better. I say let's storm the castle. Take them unawares. Just like they did when they took her, those damn heathens. The four of us is plenty of muscle to get her back."

"Five of us," Isadora said with conviction.

"No way! You stay where you're safe. I won't have a hair touched on your head on my watch."

She didn't say anything, but the mulish look on her face and the steely glint in her eyes didn't bode well. She waved a graceful hand in a sweeping movement at the windscreen.

"You listen to me. I won't have a female fighting—"

Suddenly it began to snow, a thick blanket that instantly obscured my vision from the cockpit. "What! Where did this come from? We were promised blue skies all the way to Gander."

Isadora snapped her fingers and the snow instantly stopped. The sky was blue again on a nearly cloudless day.

"What the hell was that?" Gino asked.

"A lesson in fighting," Isadora said.

"You control the weather?"

"Yeah, if I don't mind paying the toll." She turned pensive.

"What toll? What's that even supposed to mean?" I asked. I had nearly forgotten she was a witch, one that had cursed me hours earlier. Now I narrowed my eyes at her. This was a lot of power. Had she really done it? Made the snow instantly appear, then vanish? Or was it a coincidental freaky storm? Because if that was possible, bringing on a complete change of weather, what about the curse she'd hit me with earlier? Was it real?

The thought chilled my blood colder than the ice crystals that had just been falling. Just when I was softening in my thoughts toward her, she reminded me who she really was. A devious woman who I could not trust. Had a shifter ever had his work more cut out for him? Good thing I was Lucius, the pack's legendary enforcer. And of course, I would be given a Forever Mate of amazing strength and incredible powers.

"It means absolutely nothing. Forget I said anything."

"What else can you do? Can you do that inside?" Gino asked, his voice tinged with awe. That wasn't an easy feat to pull off—werewolves are hard to impress, what with our gifts of amazing hearing and eyesight, not to mention feats of inhuman strength.

"No, I can't make it snow inside the castle, but I can aid with our escape."

"Now that may just come in handy," Gino said, satisfaction coloring his tone. "Glad you're on our team, witch."

"No! Not going to happen until I understand more about this." The sense of being on the wrong foot that had been happening all day got the better of me once again. Until she explained things, I wasn't having any of it.

Chapter Eight

Isadora

Now I owed his royal evilness another debt, just because I'd wanted to show off to the wolf, give him another taste of my power. So, compounded at the interest rate the black angel always demanded for any display of my ability, I was pretty much screwed for life. In debt up to my eyeballs.

Ah, but it was worth it. The look on the Lucius' face had been priceless. His sputtering denials of wanting my assistance priceless. *Of course* they needed my help. What other witch in the universe could control the weather like me? With the Goddess's help, I might add. All that energy had to come from somewhere, and it came direct from Mother Earth. But still, it was some feat.

And to help Emily escape, I'd do whatever I could. Even if she wasn't in any immediate danger, that didn't mean that the tide couldn't turn. Kidnappings were volatile setups. If she began to feel closed in or turned away unwanted advances, anything could happen. My pulse jacked up, just thinking about the situation. Now I wanted to get there ASAP. Why had I not felt this push earlier? Oh yes, damn pheromones had gotten in the way. I was far too attracted to the wolf. He was like some kind of high-energy vortex, sucking me in. Well, that stopped now. I was my own person. I called the shots.

"Seems you and I have a mental connection. I caught a glimpse of someone. Who's the boy? Your son? Your brother?"

"What boy?" I turned my face away from his penetrating glance that threatened to light the air around us into a firestorm. He was the last person on earth I wanted to be able to read my mind. *Deny, deny, deny.* It had worked for Clinton.

"You'd win more converts with a little less subterfuge, Isadora, and a little more honey." He gave me the lopsided smile I was hard pressed not to return.

"Duly noted. But honey's only good for attracting flies." I wasn't known for giving an inch, even though he had a point. *Crap.* Now I was seeing some sense in the guy.

"Would you two settle down? I was trying to get some sleep here. You're driving me crazy with all this pent-up passion. Hell, let me take over the controls and you can go at it in the back of the copter," Goldie said. "Work it out of your systems already."

There was dead silence as his words sank in.

Was I being that obvious? Whoa. It was time to get a grip on myself. One minute I wanted to murder him, the next I wanted to be with him? *Not my usual MO.* Though a witch did need a lot of emotion to craft her spells, I usually had a way better handle on things than this. As soon as Emily was found, I was jumping ship. I'd get dropped off at the nearest airport and leave for parts unknown until everything blew over.

"I intend to get to the bottom of things, so be warned. You've met your match, Isadora. Might as well give it up," Lucius said, his tone like steel. Man, he was a handsome wolf, but I wasn't having any of it. *Maybe just a taste?* My other side spoke up, the one that always got me in trouble. *No, definitely not.* Now here I was talking back to myself like some kind of nutcase.

Fortunately, the radio erupted at that moment, needing Lucius' full attention.

"Come in, Gander. We're approaching the airport. Are we cleared for immediate landing?" he spoke into his handset.

Thank the Goddess. Something to take my mind off this ridiculously explosive situation. Me. Locked in with four werewolves was the ultimate test. Though the head wolf was my biggest and really only concern. Something told me he'd never let this go. He'd dig to the center of the Earth to figure out what was going on. Something he just might need to do to confront Lucifer himself. Now that would be some match. Not that that was *ever* going to happen. This was my problem.

The next few minutes were taken up with landing and coming to a complete stop on the tarmac near the service attendants for refueling.

"You want to stretch your legs, now's the time," Gino offered, advising me from the rear seat.

"I don't need to be asked twice. I need a break," I said.

No one said anything as we piled out of the helicopter. I took off toward the hanger at a fast clip, hoping for a bathroom and some snacks I could purchase. I had a terrible urge for chocolate and some salty chips, plus a liter or two of water.

Ten minutes later, when I was refreshed and consuming said snacks, his nibs came strolling into the hangar, his expression thunderous. *Uh-oh.* I'd better beat it back to the aircraft.

Too late. Suddenly he was right in my face, towering over me like some kind of superhero in a comic book. He did look good though, I'd give him that. All wide shoulders, narrow waist and long, sturdy limbs that a gal could swing from. But this wasn't looking like it was going to turn into something funny to share years from now. I could see this particular scene going sideways.

"I need some straight answers from you. And I need them right now."

"Couldn't this wait until we reach our final destination?" I sighed heavily, putting more emphasis on being put upon than I actually felt. Something stirred in me again. Something with a life all its own, and it wanted what it wanted. *To give this shifter a royal witchy fucking.*

I absently licked at my lips, imagining the huge shifter divested of all that annoying clothing and standing before me in his naked glory. He'd be an ancient warlord, no doubt about it.

I caught him studying my mouth before his glance shifted upward and he locked eyes with mine in a tug-of-war that left me breathless. "Well, what's the deal? Are you going to tell me or am I going to have to throttle it out of you? Because trust me, I will."

"I'd rather make love than make small talk." Knowing I had the perfect diversion to avoid questions,

I began to undo the buttons on the front of my dress, one by one, until I had reached my waist. I shrugged the garment seductively off my shoulders, along with my now too-warm sweater, exposing my see-through white lace bra. I unclasped the front of the undergarment, and drew it slowly away from my naked breasts, arching my back and leaving no doubt I was throwing down the gauntlet. I'd never been known for subtlety.

His eyes widened with intense interest, the heat that shone from those smoldering orbits enough to set my panties on fire — that was, if I weren't already soaking wet from my own keen interest in having a quick diversion.

He moved suddenly, wrapping his arms around my waist to draw me near enough that my sensitive nipples rubbed against the textured fabric of his jacket. I threw my head back to stare up at him, enjoying the delicious challenge that electrified the air around us. Tingles of excitement heated my blood, brought on by his closeness. All that hard man flesh pressed against my softer flesh stroked an itch that I needed taken care of. *Now.*

"Let's go. There's a bathroom around here somewhere." His deliciously low tone of voice vibrated deep inside me, putting us on the exact same wavelength.

"In the back," I volunteered.

Gino raced into the hangar and, spotting us, hurried over. "We got to get going. Forecast is for a real blizzard this time, riding the Atlantic up the eastern seaboard. No time to waste if we want to get going before they close the airport. Oh, did I interrupt something?" His teeth flashed pearly-white against his awesome tan. He wasn't one bit sorry at catching us in a now awkward embrace.

I pulled away from one very incensed shifter, though I was no happier at being stymied by the interruption than he was, and began to redo the buttons on the front of my dress. Gino dropped his glance from my face down to, as I'd been told before, my rather spectacular breasts. I heard the quick intake of breath as his eyes widened.

Men, they're just too easy. And if they're werewolves, it just doubles the fun.

A growl of warning from Lucius sealed the deal. He'd be far too worried about blue balls now than what was going on in my life outside this little side trip. I had hoped we would both gain from the encounter, and take the damn edge off what was looking to be a powerful physical attraction that could derail one or both of us if we weren't careful.

Chapter Nine

Lucius

I was about ready to put my fist through a cement wall. Of all the times to have a snowstorm.

"You didn't cause this, did you?" I asked, staring at the witch with enough intensity to make even a sociopath admit the god's honest truth before meeting his maker.

"Thought you didn't want me doing such things, so I haven't done anything untoward in the past hour or so. Standing by your edict. Okay with you?"

I'd never wanted to shake the truth out of anybody more than Isadora at this moment. As it was, I had to satisfy myself with glaring at Gino again. The wolf had the grace to back off, his hands raised in supplication, like he was staying right out of my business. *Good.* Dragging three pack members along right now was not helping my game. Certainly not the one I wanted to play with the beautiful witch.

"Let's go. I want us in the Shetlands and boots on the ground as soon as possible."

"Want me to do the honors for a few hours while you rest, boss?" Gino asked, in a careful, casual tone. "The rest of us have all had power naps. Seems only fair that you grab one too."

"Last thing I am is tired." *Not that I wouldn't mind being free to enjoy Isadora in the back of the helicopter.* But not with three other werewolves onboard. At least piloting the copter would keep my mind busy some of the time.

"Let's go," I said, taking the witch's arm to escort her from the hangar. For once she didn't put up a fight, just raised her eyebrows at me with a small smile as if she found me amusing.

"You're a funny guy," she deadpanned and rolled her eyes.

I just couldn't resist what I did next. Either she'd get it or she wouldn't. What did I have to lose? This day couldn't get much stranger and I sure needed some sure-fire way to release the tension. And she did like to play games, right? Otherwise, she wouldn't be here. So what the hell.

"'You mean—let me understand this, 'cause, you know, maybe it's me, I'm a little fucked up maybe, but I'm funny how, I mean, funny like I'm a clown, I amuse you? I make you laugh? I'm here to fuckin' amuse you? What do you mean funny, funny how? How am I funny?'" I recited lines direct from *GoodFellas*, one of my favorite movies of all time.

She blinked once, obviously confused which was satisfying in its own right. Then she delivered the magic line spoken by the actor Ray Liotta, "'Get the fuck out of here'."

I laughed, I couldn't help it, my good humor restored. Sometimes it doesn't take much to make the male of the species happy.

Both Isadora and Gino joined me in some honest chuckles. This time, when we all once again packed into the aircraft, the tension came down a few hundred notches. How long it would last, well, that was another thing entirely.

Isadora gave me a certain look, then began to recite, "'I know there are women, like my best friends, who would have gotten out of there the minute their boyfriend gave them a gun to hide. But I didn't. I got to admit the truth. It turned me on.'"

"The character Karen Hill," I said, snapping to attention, more intrigued by Isadora by the second. "What else turns you on?"

I asked without giving much thought to my words, a rare experience that seemed to becoming rather more common around Isadora. I also normally keep my sense of humor covered up to avoid any misunderstandings about my ability to turn on a dime when needed to protect the pack.

"You know, a werewolf with a great sense of humor…actually, I can't say I saw that coming." She pursed her lips at me. And not in a bad way. A quick memory of how amazing her body truly was fired my blood again. She fit against me perfectly. I tamped the image down with great difficulty, needing to keep my wits about me — something I'd been sadly lacking since the witch and I had collided like red-hot asteroids into Earth's atmosphere. It seemed our atoms might have gotten permanently intertwined in that wild encounter in the elevator. Bring it on. One thing was for sure, these next few days were not going to be boring, or any day in the future connected as I was to my Forever Mate. I'd bet my fortune on it and double it in no time.

"Okay, let's play another game. Truth or dare. I'll start it off," Goldie said.

"Now there's a great idea," I said with feigned enthusiasm, watching with interest as Isadora's expression changed to one of chagrin. *Wait until it's my turn.*

"Aren't we a little old for that game?" she asked, doing her level best to throw a cold blanket on proceedings. Of course it was juvenile, but it would also work for my purposes. I had an inkling that my pack brother had launched the idea knowing I had questions about the witch.

"Where's that sense of humor gone? Isn't turnabout fair play?" I chided.

"Right. Never too old for a little fun," Goldie said. "Okay, this is for my alpha. How many women have you flown across the water to Great Britain?"

My cousin couldn't have made the ice-breaker question easier. "Truth. One. Isadora."

"Yeah, but how many have you slept with?" Isadora launched the javelin right at my throat. Though I suspected she'd prefer a lower region to take a stab at.

"Someone sounds jealous," Gino remarked.

"I'm not jealous, okay! I'm just asking."

"You forgot to say truth or dare," I said, raising my eyebrows at an obviously very incensed Isadora. She'd better be careful or she'd have a coronary. Though in point of fact, she looked far too young and healthy for that outcome. She'd probably give death himself a dressing-down.

"Truth or dare, okay?" she sputtered. She was even more beautiful when she was pissed off. Though around me, it was looking to become a permanent part of her disposition. But she was also glorious in the heat of passion. I could only imagine what it was going to be like to bed her. We'd probably blow the lid off the joint. I'd better invest in a sturdy box spring and mattress.

"Dare," I said.

"Sweet, I *dare you* to tell me how many women you've slept with," she taunted.

"That's not how this works!" I protested. "Besides, we're all one-hundred-percent choice beef. Werewolves don't get any sexually transmitted diseases—our immune systems won't allow it. However, when it comes to potency, we're very, very fertile. You want a baby, you've come to the right place." That was complete bullshit, but she didn't need to know that. We're only potent with our Forever Mate, otherwise, no babies. Which was a good thing, because children were precious and deserved the best.

"Oh yeah? Good thing I'm immune to your come-ons, then."

"You didn't appear immune earlier," I murmured. "Or in the elevator."

"That was all a ploy!"

"Does a ploy make a witch that turned on? You going to deny it?"

She sat and simmered while I waited for the lid to blow. *One, two, three –*

"You were just as turned on! So much so you didn't realize I had a knife made of silver in my hand."

"Hold on," Gino said. "She held a knife to you? And lived to tell the tale?"

"She tried but it didn't work. Cursed me instead. Good enough for you?"

"Now that I would have liked to see," Goldie said with a chuckle.

I turned around and froze him with a full-on alpha stare.

"Or not," Goldie muttered.

"My turn. Truth or dare for Isadora. You have a brother or a son?"

"Truth. I've never had children." Her words were clipped and she wouldn't look at me. For a second I thought about skipping the interrogation — we'd finally found some common ground with our love of *GoodFellas* — but intuition also spoke up, saying the mystery was important and had to be solved. That lives might depend on it.

"So you have a brother?"

"Yes." Her tone turned colder than the weather system headed toward Newfoundland.

"And he's in some kind of trouble?" I pressed.

"Sort of. Let's leave it at that," she said in a flat tone, so unlike what I'd been subject to so far with her hot tongue lashings. Hmm. What I wouldn't like to do with that tongue of hers, and mine, for that matter. *Stay focused.*

"For a woman who likes to take charge, that's a lame answer."

"It means that if he needs me, I might have to be there for him. Okay? Good enough answer for you!"

"Is he ill?"

"Not exactly."

A gray mass, swirling and moving at a fast clip toward the helicopter, drew my attention. *Damn.* Had the weather system moved ahead of us now? The radar screen picked it up just then, pinging an alert and showing the scope of the storm front. Visible due to the type of precipitation the clouds contained.

"That looks like hail," Gino said, his tone now dead serious. "Any way around it? Man, that came up fast."

"You didn't have anything to do with this, did you?" I accused the witch.

"Of course not! Why on earth would I want to do that?"

I raised my eyebrows, but directed all my attention on the approaching storm.

Chapter Ten

Isadora

Crap! Had this storm been sent as a warning? It had an ominous feel to it, having appeared too quickly. And here I sat without sea salt, dragon's blood, willow, alder and laurel to grind in a mortar and pestle, which I also didn't have handy in my back pocket. What if I were responsible for these charming men being in trouble? Because in the past hour or two they'd kind of grown on me. Not that all was forgiven in Lucius' case. Far from it. But a fragile truce was holding. And now this. Maybe there were candles onboard? I could then at least start a protective chant.

"Does anyone have a candle and a match?"

"Why? Now's not the time to have something burning when we're about to get pounded by hail," Lucius said. "You'll set us all on fire."

"No, you don't understand. Maybe I can drive it away with a chant? But I need a candle to start the process."

"Fine. Grab the emergency kit, Gino," Lucius barked.

Angelo gave a long, low whistle. "That doesn't look good."

"Stop! Don't whistle. You'll just encourage it to come closer," I cautioned. I felt bad having to be so abrupt to the shifter. Angelo had been pretty quiet up until now.

"Yeah, that's a little too witchy for me," he muttered.

"But of course, how could you know that?" I said in a lighter tone of voice.

Gino handed a candle to me he'd rummaged up from somewhere in the back area of the aircraft.

"And a match or lighter?" I asked.

"Better hurry up. It's coming," Lucius warned.

I glanced over at him. His face was strained. He had a right to be concerned. If Lucifer was indeed behind this, it could be very bad indeed. And here we were over the vast, cold, Atlantic Ocean that had swallowed the *Titanic* whole. I shuddered with terrifying thoughts of freezing water rushing over my head. My heart began to pound. I was deathly afraid of drowning, right down to my DNA. Proof of innocence for witchcraft in centuries past had meant being tied up and thrown in a body of water to test a person. All my female ancestors and a male or two had failed. *Never lived to see another day.*

Was Lucifer done with me? Was this his way of signing off on our contract? If so, this was all my fault. I'd brought this curse with me. Their deaths would be on my head. Forever. An unbearable burden there was no coming back from. My soul would be imprisoned from this day forth in the underworld.

I lit the candle with hands that shook so badly I barely managed the simple task. I had maybe thirty seconds now before we were enveloped by the crushing hail. Closing my eyes, I began to chant over and over, "*This storm's intensity I seek to shake, calling for the storm to break.*"

The stirring of a sense of power in my blood encouraged me to keep going, even after the helicopter slammed into the storm and Lucius fought for control, nearly jerking the flickering candle from my hands.

The battle had begun. Only one question remained. Was this the final one?

The harsh sounds of heavy objects striking the windshield and roof of the aircraft were so loud I could barely hear my own voice. But still I persisted. I had no other recourse. No other defense between me and the ultimate evil.

A vision of an elderly woman appeared in my mind's eye. My great-grandmother had appeared only one other time. When I had worked to save my brother from the predator. She was surrounded as she had been then by other witches from the distant past, all of them joining hands in an act of supplication to the Goddess. They hovered at the threshold of entry into the luminal world that all witches can access upon their death, the glow of their spirits a sliver of hope.

I reached with all my might to connect with the women, to absorb the power they offered. I gave of myself as well. But with excess energy came huge pain. It slammed into me, set every nerve ending on fire as I struggled to redirect it against the storm. We needed to create an artificial bubble around the helicopter that would soften the blows of the huge ice crystals intent on destruction. In such agony that I could scarce draw a breath, I let it happen, let the burning sluice through me. The only way to save my mortal soul was to accept the torture, to use it to try to save the shifters from certain death.

"My God, are you okay?"

I had no way to answer Lucius, knowing any noise I made would come out sounding like a wounded animal caught in a death trap. When I was certain I could not withstand another second, when defeat stood before me, looking to swamp me, a slight shift of energy happened. Enough to make me redouble my efforts. *Take the pain*, I commanded myself, pushing it out against the forces aligned against us.

Slowly the bubble around the aircraft took hold until the brutal storm began to recede. Enough to lessen the possibility of us being struck right out of the sky. I didn't dare let up, but continued to monitor the danger. Finally, when exhaustion loomed so large that pinpoints of blackness threatened my vision, I stopped. My ancestors had vanished as well, all the positive energy they possessed now depleted. They exited back to Summerland to rest and recover. It was where I hoped to go one day, not to the terrifying underworld because of my unwanted and unwilling connection to the devil.

"Thank God that's over," Gino said, relief clear in his tone.

We now flew through skies devoid of dark clouds.

"How the hell did you do that?" Lucius demanded.

Depleted of energy, I turned and looked at him, too weakened to bother with erecting any kind of barrier between us. "With a great deal of help," I murmured, my voice strained.

"What kind of help? What does that even mean?" he pressed. He had a right. I had endangered his pack by coming along. I should have warned him of my situation.

"Give me a moment. Could I have some water, please?"

Gino passed me a bottle from the back seat.

I murmured my thanks. After slugging the entire contents, I took another deep breath, prepared to explain. "I'm not sure where to start —"

"We got time. At the beginning," Lucius said.

"When my brother was just nine years old, someone moved in next door to us." I stopped. The memory was just too visceral.

"And I take it this someone was a child predator?" Lucius said, his voice strangled by an emotion I knew all too well. Hot, undying anger at the evil that existed.

I nodded, my vision trained straight ahead, though it was not the clear skies I was observing, but the flashes of images that had scarred my soul.

"My mother, she found out what was going on, and in a moment of weakness called upon Lucifer to save her son." The words came out so low she wasn't certain that anyone had heard her until Lucius reacted.

"Is that what this is all about? Lucifer wanting something from your family in return?"

"It's a debt I've inherited as first-born, now that my mother is gone."

An outpouring of breath behind me suggested the other wolves felt the same. Shocked, upset and pissed off, I couldn't bear to tell them the worst part. That the gifts they depended on to find Emily just upped the cost each and every time I called upon the evil one for help. I'd never be out of debt if I lived to be a thousand years old.

"This has to be stopped!" Lucius said, his voice lined with righteousness.

"If you know of a way, have to it." I shook my head. "I've been caught in the quagmire for years now and I haven't been able to figure a way out."

"The sins of adults should never be visited on the young," Angelo said with a deep sigh.

I straightened my spine, thinking he referred to my mother's sin. "It's my debt. No need for any of you to get involved."

"You're with us now. We help our own," Lucius said, his words cold and final.

About to explode in anger but far too exhausted to do it properly, I suddenly understood that I had allies, that I wasn't totally alone in the world with an unbearable burden. Confused, I didn't make an instant rebuttal to Lucius' statement, but pondered the sense of change his words had brought. Uncomfortable as it was, the thought of some outside help called to me in an alluring way.

"I wasn't criticizing your mother, Isadora, only making the statement that so often the young inherit a world tainted by what's come before. It's not right that you've had this cross to bear. And not of your own making. Life's hard enough at times without that," Angelo said, his voice tinged by a hint of sadness.

"Sorry, Angelo, I know you're just trying to help. But really, guys, there's nothing to be done."

"There's always something to be done. Just a matter of figuring it out. Where there's a will, there's a way," Gino said, his voice filled with conviction and, even offering an old cliché, it still mattered that he wanted to reassure me.

"Of course. We've got this," Goldie chimed in.

"I'll make him an offer he can't refuse," Lucius said, his expression as bleak as I'd seen to date.

"What do you mean by that?" I asked. A sense of dread chilled me. The line from *The Godfather* movie had ominous overtones, and I was uncertain how he saw things unfolding. What were his *exact* intentions?

"Let's just concentrate on getting Emily home first," Lucius said in the same flat tone of voice. "Then I'll fix your situation as reward for helping us."

"I don't need you fixing things. I'm doing just fine as things are," I insisted with more force, staring at him with conviction. A frisson of fear mixed with anger at the loss of control held me in its sway.

The firm line of those full lips and his silence said it all. He didn't believe I was capable of dealing with my own life. Well, two could play at that game. When this was over, I was out of here so fast his head would spin like that girl in *The Exorcist*.

The quiet that descended next was unnerving. Hell, it was the aftermath of a storm that could have annihilated all of them, a time when normally in my experience anyone with one wit of sense joined in a celebration of still being alive. Discombobulated, I pulled the sweater up over my face again to gain some privacy. The heavy sense of dread didn't lift, not when they finally reached the shores of the Shetland Islands, not when we touched down a few miles from the fortress.

And certainly not when they began final preparations for storming the Bastille. Well, castle, but Bastille had more of a ring to it. Then I found herself praying that this wasn't the beginning of a revolution like what had ensued in France in seventeen hundred and eighty-nine.

Chapter Eleven

Lucius

"Can you try again and see if you can get an exact location on Emily?" I asked.

Isadora gave me a steely-eyed look. "Give it here."

I handed her the shoe and waited while she closed her eyes. I glanced at my crew and met looks laced with seriousness and concern. I knew what they were thinking, but I also knew they wouldn't interfere. What had to be done, would be done. The witch needed my help more than she knew.

The minutes dragged on while we waited for a response from Isadora. Her expression changed from confusion to interest back to confusion.

She handed me back the shoe and I tucked it into my jacket pocket.

"So?" I asked.

"Well, it's odd. She doesn't seem that concerned about her situation. In fact, she appeared to be enjoying herself."

"What the hell! Could she be drugged?" I asked. Did Isadora even know what she was talking about? No way Emily could be okay with the situation. But I had witnessed the witch's power first-hand, leaving little doubt she had to be picking up on something. She didn't give the appearance of being dishonest and a werewolf can sniff a traitor out easily enough. *Skin gives off an odd mix of odors when someone lies.*

As it was, the lovely fragrance that wafted around Isadora was stimulating and enticing. A little too much so, in my opinion. It just might be obscuring her real intentions. I had missed what she was up to in the elevator, though I could chalk that one up to her witchy powers.

"No, I didn't get the sense of that going on. Maybe she went willingly? You know, on a lark? Has she ever run away before?"

"Not that I know of." Frustration erupted at going into the situation blindsided with a lack of facts.

"Can you bring up a mist or fog and make us less visible?" Angelo asked, his expression pensive.

"Good thinking," I said and was rewarded with a tight smile from Angelo. His wolf's nature had always run deeper and wiser than most.

"I can do that," Isadora said, her tone of voice flat.

Where was the feisty witch that I had encountered in the elevator and that had been busting my balls every moment since? It had to be still under there, just waiting to erupt. The thought made me want to poke her, make her respond to me. The last few hours with her had made me feel more alive than I had in years.

"Okay, do it then."

I got a shot-across-my-bow look from Angelo for my curtness. *Fine.* "Would you kindly create a fog to hide our movements so we can reconnoitre Castlestone? Get through their security systems."

A bleakness came into her eyes that I immediately wanted to stamp out.

"Don't worry—whatever the cost, I will pay it."

She shook her head. "No, its fine. I'm just going to need to channel my energies."

I sensed there was something she was holding back, unwilling to share. It only drew me closer to her, wanting to know more of what made my newfound mate tick. Not that she knew that fact yet, that we were destined to be together. But now was not the time for long histories.

"How long can you make the mist last?" Angelo asked.

Isadora shrugged, pulling the white sweater closer around her body. I was once more reminded of how statuesque she was. *A perfect Forever Mate.* I quickly amended my viewpoint. She was also far too volatile at times, something I had to take to task before our final vows. Willingly, I might add. Though when she was on the war path, she was a sight to behold. A part of me actually missed the sheer craziness of our first meeting, which surprised me.

To date I had chosen shallower women that were far easier to deal with, though of course no one got to choose their Forever Mate. That was ordained. Isadora would never be easy to deal with, barring the current situation. *Hmm.* I seemed to be acquiring a taste for feisty. I'd better—she was my one.

"I can make the fog last about ten minutes before it thins. No more than that. So, we need to get as close to the castle as we can if we want to catch them unawares."

"Sounds good," Gino said. "What's the deal? How do you want to go about this, alpha?"

I quickly explained the plan I had devised during the long hours piloting the copter, having had access to a virtual, updated map of the castle and grounds from one of our satellites. *Money's only meant to be spent, right?* The whole world was mapped out now, making it impossible to hide anymore. I couldn't wait to see the Wulvers' expressions when we confronted them. My words were greeted with nods of approval all around.

"That'll catch them unawares," Goldie said with a wide grin. "Four giant wolves suddenly all up in their faces."

"Plus one witch," Isadora said.

I shook my head. "No bloody way! I'll not have one hair harmed on your head."

The three pack members looked from me to Isadora, an action I caught out of the corner of my eyes. I ignored their looks of supreme interest. This was strictly between me and Isadora.

Isadora

"I'll not be left behind! Not with the price I'm paying for this! Besides, I have to be there to create the mist. I can't do that from this great a distance." I worked very hard to hide the lie, focusing instead on thoughts of getting to our destination in order to help Emily. She needed another female to talk to. That was obvious. She was half in love with the alpha of the Wulvers and was worried about how her pack would take it that she was fairly certain that she had found her Forever Mate.

A stab of envy at her situation surprised me. I had picked up on a moment of pure bliss the young girl had experienced with the alpha that she had nicknamed *Sweetie*. My Goddess, really, *Sweetie,* for a werewolf? But then she was one too while I was a different supernatural entirely.

"We have to bring her. At least part of the way," Angelo advised.

I watched Lucius struggle with the idea. Why was he being so protective of a woman who had tried to pull a knife on him? It defied reason. In the end, his expression beyond annoyed, he realized he had no choice if he wanted to carry out his plan. Emily had to come first. Neither of us would have it any other way.

"Fine. But soon as you bring on the fog, I want you to stay clear of the action. You got that?"

I gave him my best *whatever* shrug.

"I need to hear you say the words, Isadora." His tone chilled me to the bone. The alpha was back stronger than ever, and he was a force of nature no sane person would dare to tangle with. I probably should be more careful not to piss him off so much. It did appear it was fast becoming my specialty around this particular wolf.

Okay, he's fascinating, I'll give you that, I argued with myself, *but for heaven's sake, be careful, Isa.*

Isa. My younger sister had always called me by the nickname since she was little and had trouble pronouncing my full name. The effect was sobering. I was here because Lucius had hurt my dear sister, whether he intended to or not. No backing away from that.

"I hear you, okay. I'll try to stay clear of the action."

"You'd better," he said. "Okay, let's roll."

I scanned the terrain, using my hand to shade my eyes. The northernmost island we marched across was dotted by ancient trees on land rocky and barren since time eternal, making them stand out like old soldiers needing the war to be over. We were headed for a promontory on the headland where an ancient ruin housed the Wulvers. Darkness was still an hour or two away, judging by the distance of the sun above the horizon. Lucius grabbed hold of my hand after a few steps, his expression inscrutable.

"When we get nearer, we'll be shifting to wolf form as you bring on the fog. Then you wait outside while we attack and grab Emily. You got no hint of their wanting a ransom for her return?"

I shook my head. "No. None whatsoever. I'd almost think she's here willingly if I hadn't heard differently from your alpha."

A sense of danger chilled me all of a sudden and I swung my head around, looking for the cause. Something or someone was tracking us.

"Act normal, but I think we have company," I said, striving to warn Lucius without alerting the enemy.

"Wolf. I can smell them. Stay calm. I'm here to protect you."

But as quick as it came the sense of danger defused, leaving behind the continuing foreboding I couldn't seem to shake. "I think whoever it was is gone. But keep alert. They know we're here now," I advised.

"We've lost the element of surprise. You'll need to raise a thick mist to cover us. You up for it?" Lucius asked.

"Yes." What was more compounded debt? I was more worried about being called away by Lucifer at any moment than I was about confusing a castle full of werewolves.

"It's not far now," Lucius said.

Indeed, a shadowy ruin was rising on the landscape, set firmly on a rocky peninsula that jutted into the North Atlantic.

"I know little about Castlestone other than it's a rare thing, a castle in the Shetlands," I said.

"It's got a long history of supes being attracted to its energy. The clan sells it as a tourist attraction. I would imagine it's fairly common for visitors to go off screaming into the night—that is any soul brave enough to test themselves by staying overnight," Gino said with a grin.

"Okay. Close enough," Lucius said.

We all stopped in our tracks, waiting for his next instruction. I had to admire how well Lucius got along with this pack, how they paid close attention to him. And I had to admit, they all seemed to look to him with good reason. He was attentive right back. I knew from experience all alphas were not created equal. Some were respected and feared, and a few bad ones were hated for their treatment of individual members. I had never heard any hint of rumor that the House of Luceres treated one another with anything but total respect.

"Time to bring on the mist, Isadora."

I closed my eyes, grounding myself with the earth and sky, allowing nature's power to flow through me, up through my feet and into my fingertips. When the energy hit a white-hot intensity, I released it. Sparks of light reflected in the sky before they blossomed into teardrops of mist that quickly spread out, covering the area in a deep fog.

"Now, don't be snapping those pretty little fingers and clearing the fog any quicker than necessary," Lucius said.

"The clock's ticking. Ten minutes is all this will last," I reminded him. His warning filled me with a new infusion of anger. Did he really think me capable of exposing his team?

I watched the four wolves turn as one, yank off their clothing, blessing me with an enviable and spectacular view of some very choice rear ends, before disappearing for a split-second into that dimension that wolves went to change their form. Their entry exposed us all for an instant due to the intense rays of light the shift created. Then they were back, swallowed up by the mist as they raced away.

"Be careful," I whispered. I didn't want anything really bad to happen to Lucius or the others, but damned if I was going to stand here like a ninny. At least if I was present, I could help Emily in some way. Then I would be free to leave before Lucifer demanded my presence, giving the entire game away. And why exactly had I brought this down on myself? *Right. My need to be badass. Well, I am who I am, no changing nature at my age. And badass rocks, most of the time.*

Chapter Twelve

Lucius

"Okay, you have your orders," I said. We all quickly shed our clothing. I couldn't help but feel Isadora's eyes on me for the few seconds I stood naked alongside the others. Then we entered the portal to the dimension where our atoms realigned, reappearing as gray desert wolves.

Back with four paws planted firmly on the ground, the scent of heather, the taint of wolf and a multitude of other scents bombarded me. It filled me with knowledge as we began to track toward the castle. The urge to howl was upon us and I cautioned my pack to silence. The sense of being touched by ancient energy channeled all my focus, kept me vigilant for attack from any quarter.

Even under the stress of keeping my brothers safe by paying attention to every single nuance, it was still great to be wolf. Running along the ground, the strength of ten men filling me with confidence, nothing could be better. I took the center position, a few steps ahead of the others, ready to do battle first. I would fight to the death for my pack. We all would. That was written in our DNA.

We approached the castle walls, a tight formation of wolves that would frighten anyone with a lick of sense. Castlestone was not a large structure and did not have a moat, making it a bit more vulnerable than some. I sent a telepathic message to my crew.

"Spread out and take your positions. Wait for my signal."

The three wolves moved away, silent sentinels that quickly vanished in the mist. I had chosen the most dangerous entry point, the front. Steep stone steps led up to an archway most likely guarded by one or two Wulvers. From there it would be a sprint to access the inside courtyard. But first I had to get through whoever was poised to stop me. The fog was holding as I sent the final message to the others.

"Attack!"

I leapt up the stone steps in a single bound, my claws grasping onto the rock surface to gain purchase. My fur stood fully on end to make me look an even larger threat, battle ready. I raced under the portcullis, thankful the grate was still up like in the live surveillance video I had researched a short while ago.

I growled with frustration. Where were those damn heathens? *Was that music?* I turned toward the odd sound, every sense strained by the waiting game. It seemed to be coming from an open door that led inside to the great hall. I rushed it, arriving in a split-second. No one guarded this entrance either. Were we going to be ambushed? Had everyone been alerted by the wolf that had stalked the heather earlier?

"Found anything?" I sent out another message.

"Nothing," Gino reported in. The others followed suit.

A sense of alarm froze my thoughts. We were expected. But why had they not attacked us immediately? It made no sense. I would have been on the defensive in their place.

It was then that I heard stealthy footfalls coming from behind me. *Ambush!* I whirled right around. Snarling, I attacked. I knocked the interloper to the ground and sank my teeth into their flesh. Then the fog lifted, making everything visible.

Isadora lay under me. Her special fragrance filled my nostrils. *My God.* I had bitten the witch! It wasn't a deep bite, more of a warning, but I had punctured the surface.

I instantly transformed back to human, lying naked on top of her. My wolf fought me, wanting to come back. He also enjoyed her scent and the feel of her. The perfect way she fit against me, all the lush curves rubbing against all the right places.

"What the hell are you doing here?" I pinned her to the ground, angry as hell. She stared up at me, her expression just as defiant.

"Get off me!" she demanded.

Her struggles only aroused me further. I could easily tear off that gown and be inside her in a second. Instead, I licked the wound to heal it. What would it mean for her, a true witch, to be bitten by a wolf? I had little knowledge of the effects of such an event.

"Get off me!" she screamed again.

Growls erupted all around us. I gave her a look that clearly stated this wasn't over. Not by a long shot. I got reluctantly to my feet. I gave Isadora a hand up, then confronted the alpha of the Wulvers, uncaring of my naked status. My own team was spread out around him, all dressed in different pants and shirts than they had arrived in. All seemed far more relaxed than I felt. What was going on?

"Welcome to Castlestone, Lucius of the House of Luceres. Where are your trousers, man?" The huge alpha, with a wild mane of black hair and a matching beard, gave a louder shout. "Manus, bring Lucius a pair of your best trousers. Now where are my manners? I'm Ronan Cameron, head of the Highland Heathen Clan."

The huge wolf stepped forward, offering a greeting. On closer inspection, he bore a long scar. It seamed his right cheek and looked like it had nearly cost him an eye.

Reluctantly, I shook his hand. A pair of pants were tossed my way and I pulled them on, zipping them up. A white silk shirt soon followed and was quickly buttoned up before I stepped into a pair of black dress shoes.

"And you must be the lovely Isadora Molay Champagne. May I offer you welcome and say how much I admire your namesake, Jacques de Molay. The courage of that warrior of Christ is legendary. His sacrifice did not go unchallenged. May one day the Templar Knights regain the power of their namesake."

Isadora allowed the alpha to take her hand. Having him touch even that little part of her made my wolf stand up, pushing to be free to set upon him. With great difficulty, I held him at bay.

"Will someone please explain?" I growled with a nod toward my pack.

"We've been expecting you. Care for some food or drink after your long trip? We make our own beer and whiskey right on site." The alpha had a growly voice and rolled his words, looking like he enjoyed his profound Scottish accent, which seemed a bit exaggerated to my ear.

"Where's Emily?" I needed answers.

"She's fine," Ronan said. He nodded with his head toward the great hall. "She's inside, dancing with the others. She's taken a fancy to Jamie, my brother, the enforcer of our clan."

"You bit me," Isadora accused, her eyes flashing bright green sparks, her hands braced on her hips. *What a woman.*

"You're lucky I didn't do more. Sneaking up on me like that after I warned you to stay put." It looked like being wolf-bit hadn't slowed her down any.

"Of all the nerve! I came to help *you*," she fumed. "Who was it called upon the fog? Do you have any idea what you've done by biting me? My coven mates will have your hide for this, mark my word."

"You're a powerful witch, you are. Come. You are our guests for as long as you can be persuaded to stay," Ronan interrupted, admiration coloring his tone.

The alpha then took her arm. I growled louder this time, and he let her go.

We ended up striding into the great hall in pack formation, everyone careful to keep their distance from one another.

Inside the largest space in the castle, a huge celebration was in progress. Dancing, bagpipes, banners, tartans all screamed the local color around the huge stone space that had room for dozens of guests. And where was cousin Emily? Seeming to be having the time of her life, the center of attention as she danced with a huge wolf that looked very much like Ronan, alpha of the Highland Heathens, minus the scar.

The music stopped and the young girl looked our way, catching sight of her rescuers. She gaily ran across the floor, cheeks flushed, and greeted us.

"You're here! My goodness, how did you get here so fast?"

"We're here because we thought you were kidnapped. Is this any way for a pack member to act? Worrying their family like this? Running off and not leaving word that you're all right?" I asked with all the power of the House of Luceres behind me.

The young girl blushed a deeper red. "I'm sorry for that, okay? I just got caught up in things. And you know how Mom and Dad are. They'd never have let me come here on my own. And I've met someone very special. Someone I was destined to meet."

"Doesn't excuse your behavior, young lady. You need to come with us now. You can settle this with your family once we've got you home." I kept my expression cold, knowing everyone was watching. *An alpha enforcer needs to be certain of his words.*

"No! I won't go! You can't make me leave. Jamie and I are meant to be together. It would break my heart to leave him."

"You have no choice in the matter. Come, we need to get going," I commanded.

"Please, Lucius, let Emily enjoy her evening. Let's have some food and drink. I'm starving, for heaven's sake," Isadora said, her expression softened for the first time since I'd met her.

It took me by surprise. She was beyond gorgeous with that angelic look on her face. My thoughts stumbled and I took a sharp intake of breath. I wanted to keep that look on her face — maybe have a dance with her in the moonlight?

Against my better judgment I found myself giving in, quickly coming up with a compromise. A first, no doubt, but I wanted my Forever Mate to be happy. To glow like that forever. "Fine. But she calls her parents right now. Let them know she's safe. Explains what's going on."

"Sure." Emily was about nodding her fool head off in agreement.

"Come. Let's have some food and drink, man," Ronan said, his voice even more cordial than before. It somewhat pacified my need to be alpha.

We sat down at a long banquet table obviously reserved for us, each spot pristine with unused plate and silverware. So we *had* been expected. I narrowed my eyes at our host.

"I want the full story and I want it now," I said.

Isadora sat on my left and placed a hand on my forearm, nearly burning through the flesh. As it was, the undercurrent of electricity that shot through me was impossible to ignore. Whoever said patience was a virtual never wanted to bed his woman.

"Of course, you shall have it. Gwen, pour our guests some ale and bring out the food. We celebrate tonight. The meeting of two great packs in the world. To the House of Luceres," he said, raising his tankard of ale.

The young woman immediately did as he commanded, filling everyone's drinking vessels before heading off to the kitchen, I presumed. The fragrant scent of the alcohol brought on a fierce thirst. I did need to eat and drink. It had been a harrowing day, far too busy to tend to physical needs. Though there was one physical need that burned brighter than any other — taking Isadora to bed.

My pack raised their frothy mugs and waited for me to raise mine. I glanced around the table, seeing expressions filled with hope and expectations. Emily's was particularly poignant. She was in lust or love with Jamie, who sat by her side, that was apparent in the looks of admiration she kept sending his way while Jamie's features remained contorted into one of prideful concern. I got it. Well, when in Rome, as they said.

I raised my tankard amid looks of supreme relief. "To the meeting of two great packs. May this day be one heralded in legend of bringing about a union worthy of the Highland Heathens and the House of Luceres. Amen."

"Amen," a chorus of voices from around the table chimed in and everyone pounded their tankard on the table.

Spontaneous applause then broke out about the hall, an added blessing I presumed for the couple. Well, it was what it was. Right now, I wanted a few moments of peace to consider my next move, a precious commodity in an alpha world.

Chapter Thirteen

Isadora

I couldn't believe I had been bitten by a wolf. And not only that, but by an important wolf of the House of Luceres. He didn't seem to realize what it meant. How connected we would be from now on. How very much I needed to get away from him to stop things from progressing any further. Soon as things calmed down, I was hightailing it out of here.

The merriment grew louder with each gallon of beer consumed. I had my fair share of food and drink, enjoying the show. In truth, I found the party to be more fun than I'd had in ages. The warmth of the heathens was legendary and they more than lived up to it, toasting and laughing at shared jokes until it hit a crescendo of activity. When it did, I got up, intending to slip from the room.

A hand grabbed at me and I stopped in my tracks. Apparently, it wasn't going to be so easy.

"Dance with me, beautiful," Lucius asked, or more like demanded, a bit of a slur to his words.

"I can't. I have to check on something." I tried pulling my arm away, but he held on tight. I didn't want to make a scene, especially under the vigilant eye of Ronan. His thick black eyebrows pulled tighter together as he watched us over the brim of his mug of beer. I sensed others watched us as well. Maybe their merriment was a cover?

"What's more important than us having a da — dance?"

"I thought werewolves never noticed the effects of alcohol?" I chided, adding a smug smile. I shrugged off my sweater, the heat of the hall and the moment making my skin perspire freely.

His eyes narrowed in concentration as he watched me. "Well, I admit I've had a bit more than my fair share. This has been one thirsty day. One you make far thirstier with your presence."

He got up abruptly, pulled me to my feet, and gave me a quirk twirl with his strong hands. It was a true pleasure to feel the light graceful movements he enacted so easily, and the air rushing over my body. And damned if he didn't manage to dance me right out to the crowded mass of bodies, moving at a brisk pace around the huge stone floor. Well, I might have let him. Really, what harm could one dance do?

And oh boy, how that man could dance! We gyrated, we dipped and he spun me at all the four corners of the room, dancing as if our lives depended on it. His touch fired my blood. Adrenaline poured through me, making me feel more alive than I had in such a long time.

Finally, with the music paused and my breath sounding ragged in my ears, I shook my head. "Enough. I'm dizzy with it."

"I can make you dizzier still. Come, let's find a room all to ourselves. Or better yet, let's head back to the helicopter and fly to our estate in Scotland."

I was so tempted. There was nothing I wanted more at that moment. My blood was up, my lust burning brighter than the waxing moon peeking in one of the stained-glass windows. The lovely scenes of knights of old and fair ladies posing with hunting dogs banked one wall of the great hall. But I couldn't. My life was not my own. I owed the devil his due and I sensed with every fiber of my being his calling in a favor was imminent. And if I didn't go quick enough, I'd be a dead witch walking. I had best put an end to this right here and now.

I gave Lucius my best smile and stepped back out of reach. "I wish I could. But duty calls. Can I have a rain check?"

His instant scowl didn't bode well.

And certainly not Ronan Cameron's arrival on the scene, his expression one of expectations that we would remain his visitors. I had to give this group of wolves their due, they were friendly as hell.

"I've got a suite with your name on it. If you'll follow Gwen" — he pointed toward the waitress — "she'll direct you there. A nice quiet, private section of the castle. I've taken the liberty of having your luggage brought from the 'copter there as well."

"Sorry, but I can't. I have a pressing appointment back in the States." Or anywhere outside the wall of this castle for that matter, because I didn't want what I was going to have to do to become apparent. Not that I couldn't access the underworld from anywhere on earth — it would just be best to keep the visit quiet from a castle full of wolves.

"Thank you, Ronan. That's very welcoming of you. We'll take you up on that generous offer."

And before I could say another word, Lucius bore me up into his arms and over his shoulder. He began to stride across the stone floor behind our guide Gwen. Meanwhile, I beat ineffectually at his back with my fists. "Let me down!"

A swat on the backside that brought heat to my loins seemed to be for the merriment of the crew. I swore we'd regressed to the times of the clans when cattle and wives were stolen as marks of courage between warring members. My thoughts went back to my punishment, the heat of his hand on my ass, bringing even more desire to my loins.

"I want to talk with you alone."

"Oh, it's *talking* you want now," I said, scorn lining my tone. What was it with this place? Even my word choices had shifted slightly, like we had entered a time warp and were really back in the seventeenth or eighteenth century.

From my upside-down situation, I could see the wide hallway floor and the stone steps that led upward in a spiral configuration.

"You're in the tower, the pair of you. Best place to — ah — sleep in this place. No one will bother you," Gwen said. She opened a door and stepped back, the bottom of her legs the only thing visible from my undignified position. "Get up when you want. We have an all-day breakfast available for guests. Join us any time. Sleep well."

And with a giggle, she scampered away.

Lucius kicked the door open wider and bore me inside, setting me down inside the spacious chamber. I spun around, taking in the room. High narrow windows, a skylight over the bed allowing moonlight to spill in, all push brocaded fabric hangings, *and yes*, modern conveniences, by the look of the adjoining bathrooms. How perfect was it that there were two facilities?

Our luggage sat on a low table to the side of the room, ready for us. I grabbed my case and called over my shoulder. "First dibs." I headed straight for the one with all the amenities. A lovely warm soak was just what was needed while I waited for the quiet and privacy I needed to access the underworld.

Five minutes later with the door locked — though I truly didn't think it would hold against the alpha if he really wanted in — I sank into a deep tub scented with lilac bath beads. I let out a deep sigh. Now *this* was heaven.

Letting the warmth of the water seep deep into my bones, I reviewed my day, wondering how in hell I had ended up where I had. Here I sat, in the tower of a castle from days gone by at the far end of the world, wolf-bit. I knew I should have run sooner, but something inside me had kept me prisoner. First revenge for my sister, then worry over my status in my beloved coven, then this thing with Emily. And now I had to extract myself from this situation without letting Lucius know where I was going. Because the gleam in his eye told me he was taking far too acute an interest in my case. Well, I had the solution for that. One I'd enjoy as well — exhaust him with a round of sex he'd never forget. All I had to do was pray I had time to enact my scheme before being called away.

Mind made up, I stood up and grabbed the softest lilac-colored bath sheet imaginable, blotting off the water drops and squeezing the excess moisture from my long hair.

I took my time anointing my skin with fragrant lotion, drying my hair, then brushing it to a sheen. Donning a lovely royal-blue robe with embroidered white roses all down the front of it, I strode barefoot from the bathroom, ready to do battle.

"You took your bloody time," Lucius remarked. He was fresh from a shower and lying on the king-sized bed. Sky-clad. Long and lean, with powerful muscles that gleamed golden in the moonlight, he brought an instant sheen of perspiration to my flesh. I let out a whoosh of breath, brought on by the lust that stirred deep in my loins. Hungry, I approached the bed and let my robe flutter to the thickly carpeted floor.

I stood and waited, watching for his reaction. It was instant. He rose from the bed, his cock heavy and engorged, hanging between powerful thighs. I salivated looking at all that man flesh before he was upon me, his arms like steel as he pulled me against the heat of him. It seared, our naked flesh touching and sizzling with power. This was not going to be any ordinary mating, but one right out of myth and legend, for every cell in my body stirred with extreme interest.

"I want you, Isadora," he said, his tone raspy and fueled by raw desire.

In response, I pulled him tighter against me, the flame of passion seeming to scorch my very flesh. I was tall, and we fit together perfectly. We stared into each other's eyes. Waited. What did he see? For I saw myself reflected there, a mirror image of my own soul. I trembled, unable to say a word as I stared back at him in wonderment. *What is this?* I felt a pull toward him, a rush and a sense of something releasing, and I fell as if slipping into a deep pool, the water closing above us and around us.

We kissed.

But it was no ordinary kiss. The touch of his lips, the heat of his core pressed against me sent delicious waves of pleasure coursing through me, each nerve ending awakening to a burning sizzle. My breasts pressed into his hardened flesh, my sensitive nipples furrowing into points of intense longing.

As if he understood my need, he drew his mouth from mine and searched out a nipple, tugging it deep into his mouth. When he sucked on it, my pussy wettened and clenched around nothingness, wanting everything, unable to wait.

I moaned aloud, the sound so unlike me. A terrible yearning fired deep inside me. I needed more. So much more.

"I want you *now*," I said.

"Not until you're crazy with lust, witch." He pulled me down onto the bed with his strong hands, making his intentions clear.

"You want to go downtown, be my guest," I said, licking my lips. My limbs were heavy with desire, a throbbing pulse beating between my thighs.

Oh. My. He used those talented fingers to spread me wide before him, then used an even more talented tongue to lick a wide swath along my pussy. The sensation stopped my breath, waves of incredible pleasure streaking through me. When I was too aroused, when I was certain I could take no more, he took mercy on me and thrust his tongue deep inside my channel. Over and over until I was screaming aloud, clutching at the bed coverings with my clenched fists. Never had I been more turned on.

"Enough foreplay. Fuck me, wolf!"

"My pleasure, witch," he growled back at me, a grin on his face as he swiped at the wetness on his lips with one hand. "You taste of sunshine."

"What on earth does sunshine even taste like?" I asked.

"Like the birth of new life. Time to do this thing." And with that he tugged me toward him and in one thrust of his powerful thighs, pushed his huge cock up inside me. I squirmed trying to accommodate his immense size, needing to have all of him. To be complete.

The room spun in a dazzling display of sparks of firelight as we coupled. Was it real? Or an imagined hallucination? I couldn't tell. All I knew was the incredible sensation of his body stretching mine, pushing against sensitive tissues that ached for more. So. Much. More. My lust, it consumed me. His heat and passion, they drove me senseless. We were a machine, our healthy bodies taking what they needed. And yet, they gave back as much as they took. A shared passion that left me breathless, yearning to have it all.

A crescendo of white-hot energy flashed and he swelled even further inside me. I knew it when it happened. The knotting. The locking together of two bodies into one. There was no going back now. The pleasure was half pain, half ecstasy, my body struggling to accept his full knot. It sent me over the edge, into a wonderland of sensation that became indescribable, a place I had never been or knew existed. I went with it, accepting the incredible sensations.

My heart thudding loudly in my chest, my breathing in tandem with his, I began to wish it would never end. That this feeling could last forever. We were a mated pair at that moment, the lust too strong and true to be called anything else. The knowledge bore through me that this mating was far more than just lust.

Why now? I had no idea. It had come right out of the blue, no warnings, no preparation for having myself stripped bare. Lust and need consumed me and something more I could not, would not, define.

And just when I was nearly unconscious with the overwhelming pleasure, he came, filling me with hot fluid that my body hungrily claimed. I absorbed his seed with what seemed an ancient purpose.

What is this?

I had been told I could never bear children, so it had to be something other than being fertile. But knowing and feeling are two different things. I would have sworn on the Book of the Seven Secrets that my body started a new life at that moment, though it was an impossibility. Along with my tenure, the devil had taken that as well for payment — no babies until I'd paid my debt. For a witch in my bloodline slowly lost power as the child grew older until she was eclipsed by her offspring.

Then my mind spiraled away as a powerful orgasm claimed me. Waves of increasing joy that never seemed to end sluiced through me. Lucius collapsed on me, his hard body pressing mine into the thick mattress. The sensation was electrifying. Sweat pooled between us, and his musk filled my nostrils. I breathed deep of the scent that now marked me. And I took it in, wanting for a time to feel this closeness that I had never experienced before. *Never knew existed.* It was illuminating, grounding, and more than anything it made me feel right. Like for once my needs had come first, that we had shared a special moment in time. A time that could never come again.

I cuddled against him as he rolled off me and spooned me from behind, holding me close. It was almost like he truly cared for me as we lay there together. I closed my eyes, enjoying the unaccustomed sensation. Just a power nap then I would leave. A terrible sadness at the thought lingered as I drifted to sleep, wishing it could be different.

Chapter Fourteen

Isadora

I awoke from a deep slumber, hearing the all-too-familiar calling inside my head, the voice oozing evil and dripping with sarcasm.

Isadora Champagne, your attendance is immediately requested.

Damn it. The call had come and the devil awaited.

I listened to the steady intake of breaths from Lucius behind me, his arms still holding me possessively. *How to slip away without the wolf knowing I'm gone?* Inch by inch, I eased away from the strength of his touch, the heat of his body. And inch by inch I lost that warm sensation of someone caring about me. Real or faked, at the moment I didn't care, only that it felt awesome and I didn't want it to end.

"Where are you going?" Lucius asked, his voice sleepy and endearing.

"To the bathroom. Got back to sleep," I murmured. "It's the middle of the night."

"I have a better idea," he said. His hand moved upward and he tweaked a nipple, making it instantly harden, desperate for more. When he pressed his cock firmly against my backside, insistent and commanding, it was all I could do not to begin our lovemaking all over again.

The connection with Lucius was so vital, so life-affirming, that I could scarce believe my original reason for confronting him. Lying in his arms, being buffeted from the world, something I would treasure the rest of my days. But right now, I had a duty to perform, or cause my family grief. And that I could not allow — they had suffered enough already. Remembering at that moment that a part of the suffering was in the miscommunication between Lucius and my sister made it a bit easier to move away from him and get to my feet.

"I'll be back soon."

"Hurry up. I want to be with you, beautiful."

I swallowed at his term of endearment. That might be the first and last time I heard those words directed at me by the wolf after I left him high and dry.

Knowing my stinking of wolf would annoy Morning Star, the moniker the Prince of Darkness preferred, I didn't bother to shower, just pulled on some underwear, pants and a sweater I had left at the ready on a shelf in the bathroom. Dressed, I stood perfectly still and recited the words aloud, my palms upright raised in prayer.

"Underworld portal reveal and open, send me across the invisible divide. Keep me safe from harm and allow me back when I return."

A small round disc tore into the fabric of space and time, forcing open an entrance directly before me. I had no choice but to step into it. A painful surge of hot energy coursed through me, sending me flying through an opaque gray mist. Nauseous, my ears feeling like they were bleeding buckets of blood, I was hurled to the ground. Befuddled, I shook my head to clear it before scrambling to my feet. There was no time for hesitation—creatures lurked in the dark fog, some with bigger teeth than a werewolf.

I crept through the mist on high alert. My throat dry as the proverbial bone, I swallowed to relieve my anxiety. Each time it was the same thing. A test of courage before his unholiness would venture forth to inform his minion what he required in payment at this time.

Volcanic eruptions spewed forth hot lava in several different directions around me in a chaotic cycle, with no rhyme or reason. I shuddered, never wanting to get any closer to those pits of never-ending death. Or maybe they were an illusion? Scientists theorize that the whole world could be a projection. The creature I prepared to face was capable of most anything, creating illusions at will. I took a deep breath to steady myself, reminding myself that my magic was of use to the fallen angel.

"You stink of wolf." A raspy voice pierced the dimness. It echoed around me and through me, making it impossible to know from where it came.

I whirled around anyway, my ears and eyes seeking the source.

Then he appeared before me, his black wings outstretched to great effect. He folded them dramatically against his body and stepped forward until he was within grasping distance, towering over me. I kept my courage high, refusing to step backward.

I stared into his obsidian-colored eyes, once more wondering how much of his drama was an illusion, a projection on reality? His skin was dark and tight and smooth, stretched over high cheekbones. His face framed by thick dark hair that flowed to his shoulders, his lips red and sensuous, he appeared ageless. *Almost mummified.* Was he a reincarnation of the original fallen angel, or the supernatural creature himself? Each time I was summoned, it was the same thing. Questions that went unanswered.

"You interrupted me, you take me as I am," I said, scoffing at his comments on my hygiene.

"You take chances, little witch. Be aware to whom you speak," he said, his voice penetrating and oily, making me want to wash my skin clean of him.

I hid a shudder and stared him down, my arms crossed over my chest. "Why have you summoned me?" I asked, staying on point.

"Why? Do you have somewhere you need to be?" he said, his voice dripping vitriol.

"I have a life." I spread my arms to encompass his domain. "And this is just part of it."

"Perhaps you need a reminder of who you are and who I am," he said in the coldest tone possible and it wasn't a question he was asking, but a promise of pain to come.

"Prince Morning Star," I began and caught a glimpse of deep satisfaction in his eyes. For one second, the dark orbs seemed to reflect fire. I shook my head to dispel the image. "I've come to do your bidding. Is that not enough?"

He studied my face, his expression closed. What was he looking for?

"There's something different about you. Something I don't like. What has changed in your life?"

I shrugged. "Nothing's going on. Same old, same old. The magic business is rather predictable."

He pursed his lips, as red as a vampire's but appearing far crueler. "We shall see. I want a reading on you. You need to see the Oracle. Today. Find out what she has to say."

"I'm a bit busy. I can't be gone long, or my host will know something's up. I want to avoid exposure." Though I had no intention of going back to the castle, His Evilness didn't need to know that. The threat of others knowing his business should be sufficient to stop me from being accosted by the damn Oracle.

"Hmm. Soon then. Right now, I need to share what your new job entails. You know the female called Emily Luceres of the House of Luceres of Las Vegas, Nevada?" His eyes bore into mine. My chest squeezed with worry. What was coming now?

I nodded reluctantly. "We've met. She's a sweet young girl. What could you possibly want with her?"

"Aww, we come to the crux of the matter. She made a request of the devil. A wish for a coupling with a certain shifter—a love spell if you please. And, as you are well aware, nothing comes without cost. I need you to bring her to me. I wish to collect my due. A future favor for my granting hers."

No. The word rang harsh in my head. "Surely it was just a childish prayer, it couldn't have meant what you think it did?" The last thing on earth she wanted to do was to bring an innocent like Emily to the dark angel.

"Not your provenance to work out, witch. Just deliver her to me and we'll call it even."

"What? Call what even?" My pulse began beating too quickly, making me feel faint.

"All your debt will be erased. You will no longer be called upon or expected to appear before me."

"You don't mean that," I said, my voice sounding hollow even to my own ears.

"But I do. Even Prince Morning Star is subjected to the universe's rules when he takes an oath."

"But why do you want her? She's just a werewolf, with no particular powers that I am aware of?"

"That's none of your concern. Suffice to say she in one in a billion and doesn't even know it yet. And it was her that called upon my powers, using a Ouija board. She was serious and even signed the contract with her own blood."

"Surely she was just joking around?" Why did young people do that? Take such horrible chances with their lives and souls? There was enough information out there online to tell them to back off and leave the dark arts to those who knew how to control them. Oh Goddess! How was Lucius going to react to this news? No way would he allow this to happen.

"This is no joke. You want out of your contract, bring me the girl Emily."

"And if I don't?"

"You need to ask me that? Death awaits those who dare thwart my wishes. Is that enough reason for you to fulfil your contract with me?"

I shook my head, my lips pressed tightly together.

He eyed me up and down, like a human inspects an ant crossing their path. "It's not just you that will die if you don't do my bidding. Did you not feel it last night? The stirrings of new life?"

I froze, unable to move or think. Long seconds passed as his words penetrated my brain, then began to make some sense as they bounced around inside my mind.

"It's not possible." I shook my head with denial even while I remembered the night before, how different the lovemaking had been with Lucius. How it had felt real, the surge of new life inside me. How the connection between us had been overpowering, like it had been destined.

"Oh, it is possible. I removed all restraints. You will have the wolf's offspring in nine months, give or take a few days."

The smugness of his tone told the whole story. What he said was true. Oh, and how I wanted it to be true. I'd longed for a child for what seemed forever. But I knew it was impossible with the debt hanging over my head like a hangman's noose. No way would I have brought a child into the world when I was at the devil's beck and call. But if the debt was to be discharged…

No. I could never have Emily take my place. A beautiful young innocent girl. Torn asunder with the most horrible decision that even Solomon would have had trouble dealing with, I found myself feeling helpless for the first time in my life. What the hell was I going to do? I was damned either way. And why on earth did he want Emily so badly? What was her power?

"Now. Head back and do your duty. Protect your child by turning in the she-wolf. Then all will be well."

I shook my head. "Nothing will ever be the same. You've damned me either way."

"I do believe that's in my job description." He dismissed me with a grand wave of his hand. "You have your orders. Go. You have one week to conclude this business."

Chapter Fifteen

Lucius

"Where have you been?" As soon as Isadora appeared in the doorway of the bathroom, I pounced. I'd been waiting for her to come back for some time, impatient for us to make love again. And when I'd finally checked on her, she was nowhere to be found. Worried that something had happened to her, I'd been pacing up and down for the past half hour.

She stabbed me with a look of such sadness, such poignancy, that I was struck anew at the influence the witch had achieved in such a short period of time. "What's wrong?" I asked, rushing to embrace her.

She stared into my eyes for a long moment, then appeared to make some kind of decision and suddenly her expression shifted, smoothed over. I didn't like it. I wanted her back. That feisty spirit that called out to me on every level.

"Nothing. I'm fine."

"You're not fine. I'm not falling for that. Where were you?" I had to get to the bottom of things. I wouldn't beg, of course, I'm a Luceres, but I could demand to know. Surely, she understood the fragility of a beginning of a relationship? Lies now could end things before they were properly rooted. Then I realized what I was saying, that this *was* the true beginning, destiny aside.

Something had happened to me that I had never experienced before. I wanted this witch, this woman in my life, whatever the cost. And I wanted to be part of making it happen *correctly*, with an understanding that things couldn't just be swept under the carpet. That everything between us from now on *mattered*. No going back, and no holding back.

She pressed her lips together, a dark shadow coming over her that I desperately wanted to shake away. Instead, I pulled her into my arms, took her face firmly between my hands and made her look me in the eyes.

"Whatever it is. You can tell me. I'm here to help."

She shook her head. "You can't help me with this. You have no idea what's going on."

I wasn't making myself clear, I realized. *Try harder.* "Something powerful is going on between us, Isadora. Something so powerful it has us in its sway. Do you really not feel it? It's magical, far more than two horny people falling into bed together. I believe it's destiny at work."

Her expression stilled. Yes, she had to know my words were true. But something was making her hesitate.

"Is it the devil? Is he demanding something of you?"

She looked away, but not before I detected a gleam of guilt in her beautiful green eyes. "I'm fine. Leave me alone, okay? I know what I'm doing."

"What are you doing? And what about us?" I pressed.

"What about us? There is no 'us'."

Pain struck me in the gut. "You're lying. You know as much as I do that last night was something special. Something more than a night spent in lust. Tell me you didn't feel the connection?"

"What if it was? Are you ready to settle down and leave all those one-night stands you're so famous for?" She hit back, her expression tightening.

"Yes. I'm willing to give us a try. Unlike humans and other creatures, werewolves can cut through the bullshit and go after what we want. And I want you, Isadora. Only you."

She froze in my arms. "You can't be serious. After only one night?"

"I'm dead serious. Last night was special for me. And I believe it was for you too."

"You're just worried that you can't get it up for anyone else. That I'm your only option."

The tease in her voice, the odd look in her eyes, all convinced me I had made a terrible mistake. I had allowed myself to be open and honest for once in my life, and this was what I got for it? How could I have been such a fool? A shifter with all the power imaginable at his fingertips, and I had let in a woman who did not appreciate what I had intended to offer, a life built on being a chosen pair, the golden ones, with everything possible ahead of them. Instead, I get it thrown back in my face. Like it meant *nothing*.

"I need to eat," she said, pulling away. I let her go. My life had taken another spin, but this time it had landed me alone on the other side of the abyss. Why was she denying us? A bitter taste in my mouth made me want to spit. I needed to run now, race across the highlands on all fours, forget what had just happened. If I ever could.

"Of course, doesn't mean we can't enjoy our nights here together," she said.

"Right. I don't intend to be here long enough for that. I'll be leaving today." My mind made up, I strode from the room, relieved to get away from the one person that was causing me the most pain I had experienced in my life.

I felt her eyes on me, but I didn't look back. What was the point? The witch had proven herself to be a cold creature, uncaring. It didn't get much worse than that. How could she be my Forever Mate? Was I wrong? Had I read the signs incorrectly?

Isadora

I dropped to my knees, an unbearable pain slicing through me. I'd had to do it. Pretend that last night had been just fun and games. If we were meant to be, how could I ever destroy that later? Better now, while he still had a chance to move on and find someone else, though I knew I never would.

A terrible need to eat something — anything — made me get up off the floor. I pressed my hands to my belly, knowing that cells were busy inside, growing and sub-dividing with profound energy, capable of creating an amazing creature — my daughter. How I had wanted to share that with Lucius. To think of our two powerful bloodlines coming together in such a rare event...

But this child would have to be protected. She would inherit the family debt and that I would never let happen, even if I had to take out Lucifer myself. And I certainly couldn't have Lucius involved. He didn't know the devil like I did. He'd only get himself harmed in some way. Yes, I needed to hide somewhere safe until she was born and probably for decades to come. I felt I knew her already, for my line always had a female child first. But first things first. The Emily situation had to be resolved. *Soon.* The clock was ticking.

I raced through a five-minute shower, redressed in a lovely calf-length royal-blue dress with bell sleeves and a low neckline, soft suede knee-high boots, pulled my hair up in a messy bun and charged down the spiral staircase, intent on finding food and eating my fill.

The great hall was filled with wolves, each concentrating on eating his or her weight in food by the looks of things. It should be easy enough to slip amongst them and fuel up. A feast was laid out on long catering tables, and I joined the queue at the end of one of them.

"Morning, Isadora," Emily said. She was in line just ahead of me and seeing her there, her fiancé, Jamie, by her side, made my stomach hurt all over again.

I gave her a forced smile of greeting, my throat tight with grief. "Morning." I couldn't think about the decision I had to make yet. I had to eat first.

Picking up a white plate from the large stack, I began filling it up with an assortment of delectable choices, doing my best to ignore furtive looks sent my way by a number of the shifters present. When my dish couldn't hold any more fluffy scrambled eggs, crisp bacon, fat sausages, honey ham, buttered toast, hash browns, English muffins or jam, I balanced the feast carefully over to a side table that was nearly empty of occupants and sat down, ready to dive into the biggest meal I had ever assembled.

Two bites in and someone chose a chair across from me. I looked into the concerned eyes of Angelo, then away.

"Morning, Isadora," he said.

"Morning," I mumbled over a mouthful of spicy sausage that made my mouth water with extreme interest.

"Something wrong?" he asked, making his point with a nod to my over-heaped plateful.

"No, I'm fine." I continued to eat like a person possessed, like I was worried something or someone was going to pull the sustenance away. This was a fragile moment in my baby's development. She needed all the nutrients she could get. This at least I had under my control, since my whole life was in shambles. From now on I lived for the unborn life inside me. That was a given. Everything else was pushed aside.

"That must have been some night the way you're going at it." He gave me a strange look. "Did you and Lucius have words this morning?"

"Why?" I asked innocently, more intent on my food than the conversation I didn't want to be having. I took a huge bite of the buttered toast and blueberry jam, releasing a sigh of extreme contentment.

He shrugged.

I shoveled more hot food into my mouth, feeling the overwhelming urge to eat everything in sight.

"Good food?" he asked, a teasing light gleaming in his dark brown eyes. He was such a handsome devil that if I had met him first, I might have been interested. Now, not so much. One guy for me and I couldn't have him. The thought finally turned off my appetite and I pushed the nearly empty plate aside.

"It was all right," I said, downplaying my keen interest.

"Would you like some coffee?"

"No, but a glass of milk would be perfect." *Calcium for her bones.* What else did she need? *How about a father?* The thought made my head ache, and I rubbed at my forehead, wanting it gone.

"You're sure you're okay? I'm a good listener."

I nodded. *Right.* Like he'd want to know his cousin had somehow gotten herself involved with the devil and I was holding the no-getting-out-of-jail card pressed to my bosom. "I'm fine, thanks."

He raised his dark brows, but only ambled off to get my beverage, giving me time to look around. The room was beginning to empty, groups of shifters heading out. What would be on the agenda for this day? Now that I was full, I needed to make a game plan. *Seek out Emily again and find out what her deal is?* Had she really made a damn pact with the devil she was avoiding payment for? Would she admit it? I'd try the direct approach first and see where that led.

I got to my feet, but swayed dizzily and held on to the table's edge for support. That was strange. I was never unwell. It must be the extreme changes my body was undergoing. Or the emotional turmoil the past twenty-four hours had dumped on me.

"You okay?" Angelo asked, setting the milk down.

"I'm fine." I picked up the glass and downed it in one go. "Thanks." I swiped at my lips with the back of my hand. "I need to talk to someone, if you'll excuse me?"

"Sure. I'll catch you later." I felt his eyes boring into my back as I walked carefully away, my mind focused on my target. Emily. I caught a glimpse of her across the hall and made a beeline for her.

"Emily, if I could have a word?" I asked, catching up to her. "Alone," I added.

She frowned. "Okay, I guess." She kissed Jamie on the cheek and walked obediently beside me over to a quieter part of the hall.

"What is it?" she asked straight away.

This wasn't going to be easy. "You upset a lot of people with your actions," I began, watching the girl closely for her responses.

She pursed her lips. "Couldn't help it. I fell for Jamie first time I saw him in the casino. Love at first sight." She signed with deep pleasure, her face beaming with joy. "The most handsome shifter ever. It was meant to be."

"Why didn't you tell your parents right off? Instead of running away?"

She gave a shrug. "It all happened so quickly, I wasn't thinking straight."

"So, it was all an accident? His being there?"

"What do you mean?" Her eyes turned wary with my question. "Why wouldn't it be? Lots of people circulate through our casino. It's very popular — sooner or later most werewolves make their way to us."

"You didn't ask for a little assistance in having him come to you?"

She startled, her eyes darting to the side while she licked her lips. So, she had done it. Asked for help from the wrong *freakin'* guy. Now that I was expecting a child, I would have to watch my language more carefully and quit swearing. I didn't want my daughter to begin life like a salty sailor.

"What if I did? It was all meant to be. Jamie and I are perfect for each other." She was defensive now, being called out.

"Did you promise anything for this help?" I pressed. This was the crux of the matter.

"What if I did? The devil's not real, right? Just a myth. If you don't believe in him, he can't harm you, at least that's what my friend, Tiffany, said."

I shook my head. "Did Tiffany ask for anything? Make a deal with Lucifer?"

"I don't think so. She kind of egged me on. Asked if I had the courage. Well, duh, of course I do!"

"You are aware that a pact with his evilness obliges you to pay up?"

"*Phttt.* Why? Like I said, it was just a game."

"I hate to spoil this, but Prince Morning Star is very real. And he expects his due."

"Prince Morning Star?" she asked, frowning.

"His favorite moniker. Now, he's waiting for you to come across with your promise. The one you made over the Ouija board and signed in blood." I hated having to share such a stark fact with Emily. I pressed my hands to my belly, feeling the upset right down to my toes, trying to protect the fragile life within from the truth of such things. A witch's baby deserved being born out from under a cloud of anger. Especially one not of their choosing. We were white-magic witches, only trying to make the world a better place…though not adverse to doing what had to be done if called upon.

"How do you know this?" Her eyes held suspicion now as she locked glances with me. "That's right! You're a witch!"

"Witch or not, it's your deal, not mine. You need to straighten things out. Settle up. Lucifer never lets things like this go." My warning fell on deaf ears.

"It's all your fault! If you weren't a witch, he wouldn't be able to call me now! I'd be free of all this. You brought him here!"

Emily's irate tone was drawing too much attention now. I cringed. This had taken a bad turn. Angry eyes seemed to follow me from all directions, making me feel even more protective of my unborn daughter. I swallowed hard. I needed time to think. Obviously, Emily was not going to step up to the plate. She had what she wanted, a new love and a new life. While I would once more be the outcast. It didn't take a crystal ball to know that outcome.

"Are you okay, sweetheart?" Jamie asked, rushing forward to stand at Emily's side like the protective wolf he had been raised to be. He looked me up and down, his brows coming together into a righteous scowl.

She nodded. "I'm okay. I just need to sit down."

She favored me with a glare and I stepped back in dismay. Where was my protection? I had eliminated help from any of the wolves now, and especially from Lucius. My heart sank. I missed him already. His presence had been reassuring and stabilizing. Nothing for it but to withdraw and seek another way.

I stumbled from the room and took the stairs to the tower bedroom where I slumped onto the bed, breathing in the wonderful fragrance of Lucius that lingered on the sheets and longing for him with every fiber of my being. Tears prickled behind my eyelids and began to flow down my cheeks. I cried for what could have been. What could never be now.

When I was empty, unable to release any more emotion through tears, they stopped, though my mind and body remained saddened. If only Emily hadn't called upon him. She was so young, so vulnerable to the sway of the master of deceit. And if only I weren't pregnant. Then I quickly corrected the thought, not wanting the growing fetus to feel my worry. I wanted my child, more than anything on the Goddess's green earth. But I wanted her father as well, an impossible wish I would have to accept would never happen.

I had to give this some sober considerations. This situation didn't make a whole lot of sense on a logical level. My biggest unanswered questions were, why Emily? What did he want with her? What was her power? Nothing seemed special about her, well, nothing more than the usual powers of a werewolf — superhuman strength, excellent eyesight and hearing. Oh yeah, and the ability to turn into a giant wolf at will. But I knew he had a few wolves amongst his minions. Which kept leading me back to the same question. *Why does he want Emily?*

Chapter Sixteen

Lucius

I shifted into the multiverse as I ran full out, re-entering earth's dimension as wolf. I needed to run until I was too exhausted to think, too exhausted to feel, then run some more.

Hours later, after racing around the island and checking out every nook and cranny, my body finally succumbed to the inevitable. I collapsed onto the cool fragrant heather near a pool of water. I fell fast asleep, unable to take one more step, my paws tucked under my massive head.

How long I slept I didn't know, but when I awoke the moon had risen, revealing more of itself tonight. Good hunting moon. I was still wolf, and I got up and shook out my fur. No one had bothered me during my sojourn, a fact I was grateful for. I had needed this time alone, time to start to heal my broken heart, if that were bloody possible. No turning away from the stark fact —

my Forever Mate didn't want me. Had thought me a plaything, unworthy of being with her. *Why?*

That was the burning question. Last night, in my arms, she had given me all of herself. I felt it in every fiber of my being. Then this morning she had vanished, coming back changed. For the worst. What had gone on during those missing minutes? I set aside my anguish to consider a direction to go. If I could figure where she went, maybe this would make some sense? Maybe she had been threatened by something or someone? The thought sickened me. Though we couldn't be together, I still didn't want to see her harmed, the urge to protect burning strong as ever in my chest.

Time to go back. Find out what the hell is going on. Put aside my personal interests. Isadora might be in trouble. The wind to my back, I began to loop across the moors, feeling the power of the moon flowing through my system, charging me with energy.

When I arrived back at Castlestone, I shifted to human form before redressing, intent on knowing all the facts before leaving the Shetlands.

"You need to do something about the witch," Jamie said, hurrying up to confront me. He was alone.

"Why, what's going on?" I demanded, returning his frown with a darker look.

His Adam's apple bobbed up and down nervously as he realized I had far more power than he did. But he held his ground, which I had to give him credit for. I could tear him apart with my bare hands if I wanted. *Stand down. Think of Emily.* She'd fallen for this wolf.

"She's been badgering Emily. That's just not right," he said. "Emily's innocent in all this. It was her friend who started the whole thing."

"Started what? Spit it out, man. I want the facts and I want them *now*."

The younger shifter was quaking in his boots at my frost-edged tone, shifting back and forth from one foot to the other. I could almost feel sorry for him if I weren't so incensed by all that had happened in the past twenty-four hours.

"It was just a silly thing, really. Her friend Tiffany said she could help Emily get what she wanted. It never meant anything. They were just playing around, having a little fun." Jamie shrugged, trying to make light of it.

"And what did they do?" I asked, wanting the wolf to get to the damn point.

"Just used a game board to ask for a favor."

"A Ouija board? Is that what they used?"

I hauled the young wolf up by the shoulders, his feet barely touching the ground. "What else?"

Jamie, bright red with embarrassment, tried pulling away, but I had a solid grip on him. He wasn't going anywhere until he admitted all he knew of the situation.

"Hey, what are you doing?" Ronan demanded. He'd come up without either of us noticing. "Let him down. Now."

I held on to the wolf an extra few seconds to make my point, that dropped my hands away. Jamie stepped backward soon as he was free, watching me with narrowed eyes. "Your brother is holding out on me. I need to know what he knows about things."

"What things?" Ronan barked. His patience appeared scant this morning. Too much indulgence last night? He'd been a fine host, partaking with the best of them in a drinking game that would have put any other supernatural being under the table.

"I want to know what Emily and her friend Tiffany were up to with the Ouija board. Was there a blood oath involved?"

"It was just a lark. They didn't mean anything by it, Ronan," Jamie said to his brother in a weaselly tone that turned my stomach.

"Blood oaths are not to be taken lightly. You know that." Ronan's expression turned sour. "Was there blood involved?"

Jamie shrugged. "I guess. But Emily says —"

"This is serious. I want all parties involved in this affair to convene in my office right now." Ronan turned on his heel and strode away.

"Where's Isadora?" I asked.

"How the hell should I know? She confronted Emily then disappeared. She's your problem, not mine," Jamie said.

"She better be fine, or you'll rue the day you tangled with me, wolf," I said, giving him a look that would make better men quake in their bootsteps.

As it was, he sidled around me and made a quick exit back into the castle, most likely looking to round up my cousin Emily, who had some explaining to do if she knew what was good for her. Even family has to follow a moral code or endure the wrath of their alpha.

I strode into the great hall, keeping a sharp look out for Isadora. Gino stood with his twin brother, Goldie and cousin Angelo with a small group of female shifters. It didn't take a science degree to see the group was involved in some social interactions that should result in bedpartners later in the day. Protecting the pack and making money, feasting and mating, all prime directives of werewolves, and not necessarily in that order.

"Alpha, we were wondering what you've been up to," Gino said.

"I was looking for Isadora. Has anyone seen her?" I asked. Until this mystery was cleared up, I had no other directive than seeing to her wellbeing. She might never consent to being Forever Mates, but that didn't change our blood chemistry one bit. We would be in each other's lives from now on either way, though estranged from each other was the most painful existence of all. She'd come around to see that, given time.

"No, sorry, not since breakfast," everyone said.

"Damn it!" The words exploded from my lips. Where in hell had she gotten to?

Isadora

It was time to get out of here if Emily wouldn't take the heat for her rash promise. But where to go? I needed refuge until my daughter was born, somewhere the devil wouldn't think to look for me. Or the wolves for that matter. The one place I most didn't want to go in all the universe. But I was backed into a corner and they owed me a favor. And I could provide valuable services for them for forever if need be. Anything to keep my child safe. Even going hat in hand to the coldest beings on earth — the Egyptian vampires of Alexandria.

A chill in the air made me shiver uncontrollably. Was it the sense of being unwelcomed at the castle after confronting Emily or knowing what I had to do?

No point putting it off. The sooner I stated my case to the last pharaoh reigning over the oldest group of vampires in existence and asked for her mercy, the better.

And for that I needed to head to an actual airport. No portals existed that led to that part of the world. Long ago the Egyptian Queen had destroyed them all in her grief over losing her lover. It was probably a wise decision. Who wanted to be constantly called upon for favors? Assaulted by the modern world? Everything had changed around the clan and the vampires preferred to keep the old ways, an ancient hierarchy still existing inside the group. Though they were known as Egyptian vamps, their leader wasn't really Egyptian at all but Greek Macedonian, as though it mattered when confronting the ice queen who'd sooner bite a person's head off than grant a favor. *And I mean that literally.*

Mind made up, I threw a few things into a carryall bag, then looked for one last time at the bed where my life had changed forever, thinking of what could have been if only things had been different. But they weren't and I had to think ahead. Protect the tiny creature growing within me. At all costs.

It was easy enough to creep down the stairs, keeping a careful watch for the enemy. The wolves had earned that label in my mind when they had aligned with Emily, setting me free to do what I had to do. I was used to being the outsider anyway, as witches so often are. Misunderstood for centuries, hounded and driven from their homes by those who sat in judgement of their healing arts and gifts. And I knew the wolves were the eternal enemies of the vampires, like lions and hyenas, so they'd leave me alone where I was headed. I'd raise my daughter alone. It happened all the time, women being the unsung caregivers of children more often than not.

At the bottom of the stairs, I took sharp left and headed back toward the kitchens, instead of the great room. A bowl of apples had been set out on a counter and I grabbed a few and thrust them into my pockets, nodding at the women busy cleaning up after breakfast.

"Thanks, I thought I'd head out for a walk. Don't expect me back any time soon," I said. No one said anything or tried to stop me, but one of them nodded slightly, her expression cool and watchful. It was obvious my reputation had taken a beating as my altercation with Emily had made the gossip rounds.

I turned and slipped out the back door of the castle. Before I began my journey, I needed to leave a spell that would obscure my scent trail, make it impossible to follow, in the unlikely event anyone followed me. A small rhyming one would do as I didn't want the devil to know I was using magic or he'd add another toll to the ledger.

"Heaven and earth, hear my plea. Let my scent be obscured from thee."

Protected from tracking, at which the wolves were experts, I began to make my way across the landscape at a brisk pace. It was a lovely day for a stroll, but I ignored the beauty of the countryside, too intent on getting to my destination to take time to enjoy it.

The Scatsta Airport was only just over three kilometers away and I wanted to be on a flight before anyone realized I was gone. Though most likely it didn't matter. My chest squeezed at thinking they'd all be happy for me to be on my way. Would Lucius even care? Now that he felt betrayed, when I didn't share how much last night had meant to me, the look in his eyes would haunt me all my days, without question.

Don't go there. I had to keep my mind busy thinking ahead. *Do everything that needed to be done, one day at a time.* I quickened my step, visualizing boarding a plane that would whisk me to Alexandria, Egypt in mere hours. Queen Cleopatra was my best hope for sanctuary. I would have my baby, then deal with Lucifer. A terrible realization overcame me, stopping me dead in my tracks. What about my sister and brother? They would go unprotected now that I would be no longer available. The dilemma froze my brain. What to do?

I stood and stared down at the ground, my mind a whirlwind of seething emotions. *Think, Isadora. There's a bit of time before everything comes crashing down. One week to be exact. Okay.* One thing I could do was ask the wolves for help in looking out for my family. Surely they would at least keep them safe since one of their own had caused this terrible mess? But I wouldn't approach them until I was nearer my destination. Then I'd send a message with all the stark facts laid out for Lucius, care of the Glitter Palace casino.

I'd compose it while I flew to Alexandria and there should be time to buy a new cell phone at the airport. My mind relieved to have found an answer, I resumed my journey. *Please forgive me, Mom, wherever you are, for what I need to do,* I prayed. A part of me was pretty sure she'd understand looking down from heaven as I always had envisioned her. Look what she had done to protect my brother. Of course, that was the beginning of all this turmoil. Would it never end?

I ate all the apples as I hurried along a path that had seen many footsteps or paws before me by the look of it, the powerful urge to get away driving me onward.

Finally, the airport proper came into view. I needed money. *Fast.* Hopefully from a good Samaritan. I strode through the electronic eye and the front door whooshed open for me, revealing a busy international airport. Who to approach? A businessman in a tailored suit and wearing a gold Rolex looked promising, his attention focused on his iPhone. He wasn't in line, but standing off to the side, apart from other people. I strode up to him, a smile on my face.

"Hello," I said. "I wondered if you could help me?"

When he looked up, annoyed by the interruption, I used my body language to suggest I found him intriguing by making my muscles relax into more sensuous lines, my eyes widening with keen interest. Sure, it was a bit of a ruse, but perhaps forgivable knowing the situation.

His eyes expressed pleasure at my appearance, a small smile playing over his features. "Certainly, if I can. Miss?"

Great. His accent was American. This should make it easier for him to relate my needing a bit of help here.

"Please, just Isadora. And you are?"

"Samuel. What can I do for you, Isadora?"

He used his eyes to check me out from head to toe. I hid my chagrin—after all, I was the one who had approached him. I just needed enough money to make a quick call to my home bank and have funds sent directly to the airport to purchase a phone and a ticket. I had made arrangements for such an eventuality from anywhere in the world. A gal can never be too safe or too prepared. Now my forethought was about to pay off dividends.

"I wondered if you could help a girl out? Seems I left my wallet at home and I need to make a call and have someone bring it to me. I can pay you back soon as my bank sends the money. It shouldn't take long," I said.

His eyes narrowed. "What do I get for my trouble?"

"The satisfaction of doing the right thing by a stranded person. And my forever gratitude. Where are you headed by the way?"

"I'm already here. Just waiting for a pickup that's been delayed." He gave me another calculating look.

Please, please be a nice guy. I didn't want to cause a scene in the airport. Just make a more than fair proposition and get on my way.

"How much do you need?"

"Enough to call home to Vegas."

"In the States! That's an expensive call," he said, dithering.

"Like you can't afford it."

His look of exasperation softened my next words.

"Sorry, I would be ever so grateful though. Even give you double your money back," I said as sweetly as I could. Only for my baby would I put up with the likes of this guy.

"Okay, but I think I would need a little bonus for my trouble. Say fifteen minutes in the men's bathroom."

Eww. Did he really just say that?

I swallowed my disgust and gave him a bright ultra-fake smile. Two could play this sordid game.

"First I make my call."

He handed me his cell phone. I quickly keyed in the name of my bank, worked my way through the endless security questions, then had an electronic transfer of funds sent to a bank listed inside the Scatsta Airport.

"There. Now I just need to collect the money and I'll pay you back straight away."

He grabbed at my arm. "In the meantime, let's you and me get better acquainted."

I shook my head. "I'm getting my money first. I'll pay you triple what that call was worth, no questions asked."

"No way. I have a better idea. How about you don't pay me *any* money, but let me take it out in trade. You've a fine-looking woman, Isadora. Gorgeous really. I could make it worth your while. Say add a few hundred dollars to my proposition." He lowered his voice, his expression confident to the supreme.

"Thanks, but no thanks, Samuel. I pay my debts in good old hard-earned cold cash."

"You were just cock-teasing me then? You bitch." His eyes expressed his anger at being thwarted.

"No need for name calling. You made good on the deal." I pulled away from him, my sights on the name of the bank my funds should be arriving at shortly. It was just a hundred yards or so away from where we stood. I would be in and out and on my way in no time.

"Not so fast. I'm going to report you. This was all a scam. Admit it," he hissed. All sense of decorum had vanished.

"No scam. Come with me. I'll hand over the money I borrowed in spades. Besides, who are you going to call? I've done nothing wrong. You gave me your phone freely. To a stranger in need of assistance in a foreign land. You look like a hero. Don't spoil the illusion now." It was all I could manage not to cast a curse on this poor excuse for a human being and turn him into a full-fledged eunuch. That would be far worse than I had done to Lucius. *Oh Lucius, how did we end up here?* I swallowed my anguish. No time for regrets.

"Fine," he said, coming around just in time. I was getting prepared to blast him one. Let out all my channeled energy. Well, I might have gone overboard, so it was probably fate making this work out and come to a proper conclusion.

We walked stiffly together over to the bank, our postures probably not concealing the dislike we felt for each other. It was then that I had an epiphany. Before Lucius and the baby, I would have used my feminine wiles to make all this happen in a far more congenial atmosphere. But now all blinders were off. And I had one purpose driving me.

"Wait here. I'll be right back," I said, moving away to approach a teller's cage.

"Don't worry. I intend to collect every last dime you promised," he muttered.

I held my displeasure in and donned a fresh smile for the woman who greeted me at the customer counter.

"What can I do for you, hon?" she asked. Middle-aged, she was the perfect example of bank employee to the outside world. Friendly and professional and well-groomed. I particularly liked the genuineness of her greeting. Perhaps I should have approached her first, asked for help? Well, too late now. Just finish the transaction with disgusting guy and get a move on.

"I just had funds wired to this bank from Vegas and I need to collect them. I'm stranded here without them."

"We can't have that. Okay, what's the transit numbers of your bank and your accounts, please?"

In a matter of minutes, she handed over the money, counting it out for me on the wooden ledge situated between us.

"Thanks a lot."

"Anytime, hon. Be safe now."

"You too."

I hurried over to the man with a scowl and paid him the cash, keeping the curse I so badly wanted to bestow to myself.

"Here. This should more than cover it," I said, keeping my tone neutral. I just wanted this over with so I could be on my way.

"I should warn others about you. Promising more than you give," he growled. And before I could stop him, he snapped a photo of me.

"You had no call to do that. I paid you more than your time was worth. I didn't take advantage of you in anyway. In fact, I should report you!"

My hands itched for a phone to take his picture.

"Heaven and earth, bestow a curse, give this man the gift of empathy. Make him experience walking in the other person's shoes until the sun rises nine days hence."

It was the most power I could safely use without Lucifer being alerted to where I was and what I was up to. A small curse really, and one that might turn into the biggest blessing the man could ever experience. Not that I would be around to see it.

"What did you do? Are you a damn witch?" he demanded, his eyes nearly bugging out of his head.

"Of course, it rhymes with bitch. Thanks again," I said, gaily waving him off. Major karma points for me.

Which meant the same for the tiny life I held in the palms of my hands.

Ignoring the man's continued cursing droning on behind me, I made a beeline for the ticket counter stationed outside the bank. The time spent with the not-so-great-a-Samaritan had eaten into the day. *Ticket, buy phone, then get the heck out of here.*

Did anyone know I was gone yet? Did anyone care? The last question hurt me to the core. The looks on the werewolves' faces when they thought I had harmed one of theirs still burned, a festering emotion that I had to let go of.

After using a slight glamour to make the agent think she'd seen my nonexistent passport and purchasing a ticket that fortunately departed for Alexandria, Egypt, in two hours—fate really was on my side at the moment—I made my way toward the Apple Store to replace my cell phone. Things were falling into place. Then why did the back of my neck suddenly tingle with apprehension, like someone was watching me? I kept a sharp eye out, turning and scanning the area frequently before I went inside the commercial business, but nothing seemed out of the ordinary.

"What can I help you with, miss?" The male salesperson bestowed a professional smile, wearing the ubiquitous black tee shirt, Apple logo and gray pants.

"I need a new phone. Mine's kaput. And I need one fully charged. Is that possible?"

He frowned. "Hmm. That's a bit difficult. They all need charging when you buy one. Are you incoming or leaving?"

"Leaving."

The young man's face cleared. "Just charge it on the plane then. That should be no problem. Then when you get to your destination, you're all set."

"Great. I'll take one."

Within twenty minutes, I was striding back down the tiled corridor, newly purchased phone tucked in my carryall bag. My stomach cramped, making me bend over mid-step.

"Hungry again, baby?" I asked, rubbing at the pain as I carefully straightened up. Was it my imagination or was my stomach already a bit rounder? Nah. That was impossible twenty-four hours in. I wondered at what she looked like right now. Just a blob of cells, I imagined. But soon some definition would arise and her tiny heart would begin beating in about four or five weeks.

An urgent, overwhelming feeling of the need to provide protection about her took my breath away. I couldn't wait for my flight to be called and be on our way.

Chapter Seventeen

Lucius

Where the hell has she gotten to? My mind darkened, anger growing with every step and place I checked. The chat with Emily in front of Ronan had not gone well. She had done what Isadora had pointed out—made a blood oath with the fucking devil. Now I was on damage control, seeking my mate to let her know I understood and was on her side in this thing, and that she was more than welcome here.

I finally make my way to the kitchen. Maybe she'd gotten hungry?

"If you're looking for the *witch*, she went for a walk," the head chef said like she had something distasteful in her mouth.

"She's my intended, so best keep a civil tongue in your head," I growled. Apparently, Ronan hadn't spoken to this member of his clan yet.

The woman's eyes widened and she pressed her lips firmly together.

"Anyone see what direction she was headed?"

No one said anything and I shook my head. "If this is how you treat guests in your house, I'm not impressed."

Guilt turned the woman's face pink. I stalked out of the back door of the castle, intent on following Isadora's trail.

I took a deep breath, checking the air for her unique scent. Finding none, I stood and considered things. Had she enacted a spell to keep me from following her? Okay, logically, where would she go? Her feelings had been hurt by Emily's attack on her. Had she gone somewhere to lick her wounds? Back home to Vegas? Yes, she had probably headed for the airport. It was close by.

And if she did, someone would have seen her. She stood out in a crowd. A beautiful woman like Isadora could run, but she could never hide. And certainly not from me. I had the money, the wherewithal and the superpowers to track her down, more than anyone else on Earth. I would find her and bring her home.

I began to run across the ground, staying in human form because, when I got to the airport, I unfortunately required clothing. The sun was about to slip below the horizon when I strode quickly through the front door of the airport. A quick check around provided no clue to Isadora's location. I raced up to the ticket counter and confronted the clerk.

"Have you seen this woman?" I held up a Facebook photo of Isadora, her face wreathed in smiles that took my breath away.

"Yes, I think so. Why?" The female clerk opened her eyes wider at me, obviously checking me out.

"Has she left yet? Taken a flight?" I bestowed as charming a smile as possible, considering my agitation. Her next words abused me of all thoughts that it had appeared the correct note to manipulate her into coming across with the intel I required.

"That's privileged information. Are you family?"

Crap. I was losing my touch. I dug into my pocket and pulled out a few large bills and handed them across the counter. "I need that information and I need it now. The woman is my fiancée and she's in some kind of trouble."

"No need to pay me," she said in a prim tone.

I ignored the money and gave her a steely-eyed stare.

She gulped, her eyes widening farther. "I sold her a ticket to Alexandria, Egypt. It left an hour ago."

* * * *

Isadora

"This is your captain speaking. We will be landing shortly. The time is coming up on ten o'clock in the evening and the temperature is a balmy thirty degrees. We hope you enjoy your stay in Alexandria."

Finally. The flight seemed to take forever. We were landing at the Borg El Arab International Airport, less than an hour from my final destination. I drummed my fingers on the armrest, impatient to get off the aircraft. When the seatbelt sign thankfully flashed and dinged off, I got up with the rest of the weary passengers experiencing jet lag, grabbed my carryall out of the overhead bin and followed the slow-moving line to exit the plane.

First order of business was to exchange some money. Twenty minutes later, fortified with Egyptian pounds, more than enough to travel by cab to the outskirts of Alexandria where I would need to make the final trek by foot. In the thousands of years the whereabouts of Cleopatra's tomb had never been discovered, I wasn't about to be the one that got blamed for that era coming to an end. No bigger disaster could possibly rain down on my head. Even my connections with Lucifer couldn't save me then.

The heat of the desert assaulted me soon as I stepped outside the airport. After the coolness of the Shetlands, the hot dry air overpowered all my senses, making me yearn for a long, refreshing shower. But that would have to wait. If I was being followed or watched, I had scant time to get where I needed to be.

A long line of bright yellow cabs stretched curbside near the front doors. I hurried to the first one and hopped in, sank gratefully back against the seat, my carryall at my side.

"*Ayn trade al-dhabe?*" The man asked for my destination, turning around to face me.

"Do you speak English?"

He nodded, his dark face beaming. "Yes, good English."

"Please take me to the town of Abusir." The original name of the town was Taposiris Magna, meaning great tomb of Osiris. I was up on the history of Cleopatra's own tomb site. And the fact it had never been found in two millennia. All supernaturals kept the secret, to stay one step ahead of humans, either through fear of discovery or fear of the great lady herself.

"Long way along coast. Over fifty kilometers," he warned.

"Not a problem. I'll pay double if you get me there quickly."

He nodded once more and gunned the motor, heading the cab into traffic. Alexandria, located on the Mediterranean Sea, was popular with tourists. I would have to be careful to avoid scrutiny. But this late in the day, most people would have retired to dine in restaurants and visit nightspots. My stomach rumbled, liking the idea of a meal.

"I need to eat first. Any suggestions of where I could pick up some take-out food along the way?"

"No food in cab." He shook his head vigorously.

"Fine. I'll wait." Tell that to my stomach that instantly turned up the heat, clenching into a tight fist, apparently wanting to be the one in control. Hungry baby? Or the fact that werewolf DNA even now was surging through my bloodstream, wreaking havoc with my chemistry?

My teeth ached, my muscles in knots by the time we arrived at the outskirts of Abusir.

"Hotel?" the driver asked.

I had to have some calories. No way could I arrive to speak with one of the most powerful beings on earth without some sustenance easing my belly pain.

"Where do you recommend? I need a hearty meal," I asked, chewing on a fingernail.

"No problem. I take you to my cousin's. She has good food and clean beds. Nice respectable place. Say Gurmeet sent you. Give you good price."

"Great, that sounds fine. Thanks."

A few minutes later, he dropped me off in front of a low-riding complex built of cement cinder blocks. The streets were nearly deserted so late at night, but the welcome mat was still out when I walked through the front door. A middle-aged woman strode toward me, all smiles. In the background, the soft sounds of a song played. The singer sounded as full of longing for something being over as I felt about what I was about to do.

I swallowed over the lump in my throat and gave her a smile in return. "Your cousin Gurmeet brought me here by taxi. He recommends you highly."

She gave a slight bow of recognition. "You are welcome. What can I do for you?"

"I know it's late, but I'm famished. Would I be able to get a meal?"

"Of course. You will be staying with us?" The woman's eyes glittered with keen interest.

Hmm. I might need time to talk Cleopatra into helping me. "Yes, just one night for now. I may stay longer. I don't know yet. Is that a problem?"

"Not at all. Come. I'll seat you in the restaurant. Make sure you are taken good care of."

I followed the slim, elegantly dressed woman across the foyer to a side room. She directed me to a small table, then clapped her hands. Out popped a young woman from behind a counter, her expression quizzical.

"Take good care of your guest. She requires a meal."

"Of course, ma'am," the young woman said.

Half an hour later, fortified with a huge plate of meat, rice and vegetables washed down by two large glasses of cold milk, I got up from the table.

"You like so much food?" the waitress asked, eyeing me with interest. "You have baby?" She rubbed her stomach, smiling.

I returned her smile. "Yes, I need to eat well now. Thank you for a good meal."

I paid the waitress, adding a generous tip, then ventured back into the main section of the hotel. The décor was soothing, light colors and simple lines.

"The food was to your liking?" my hostess asked at the reception desk, looking up from dealing with her iPhone. I could only imagine the hours the woman worked to make her business successful.

"Very good, thank you. Could I get a room now, please?" I was suddenly too tired to just head back out onto the darkened streets. A shower and a powernap would take the edge off and still allow me to see the queen before the sun rose.

"Yes. I just need a credit card and signature and you'll be all set."

"How about cash? My wallet was stolen earlier today, and I have to replace it."

"I'm sorry to hear of your misfortune. That will be fine." Her expression did not change as if she'd heard that line too many times to be at all surprised by it. *Wise woman to not make a fuss.* Cash was always a useful commodity, anywhere in the world.

I gave her the money and took the key she offered.

"We serve breakfast from six until nine," she said.

"Great."

"You're just down the hallway, last door on your right."

I followed her instructions and was soon safely inside a sparce but clean space. The room featured a small door to the outside, perfect for my needs. I could come and go undetected anytime, day or night.

Quickly stripping off my clothes, I headed for the small shower, soon emerging clean and refreshed and dressed in a bathrobe. Setting my phone to wake me up in twenty minutes, I fell instantly asleep.

The sound of a buzzer brought me slowly out of my dreamworld. Groggy, I made myself sit up. I needed to get moving, but first I had to send Lucius a message to look out for my family.

I leaned against the headboard, considering my words, keying them into a text message.

Lucius, I had to get away. My presence was not wanted at the castle – old prejudices were once more at work. But where I'm going, I can't look out for my family. I beg you, please take care of my sister and brother. They are all alone in the world and they need you. The devil has threatened their lives. And look out for Emily as well. Lucifer is too interested in her and I don't know exactly why. I promise, one day, I will pay you back for keeping Ian and Elena safe.
Isadora.

I held my thumb over the word Send, uncertain if I should proceed, my breathing far too rapid for comfort. Should I really do this? Was it the right thing? I did trust the wolf would look out for Ian and Elena. Werewolves were very protective by nature and his would be aroused by thoughts of my siblings being accosted by the evil one. Yes. I hit Send. *Oh Goddess*. No going back now.

To avoid thinking about it anymore, I got off the bed. I picked up a hairbrush and pulled my hair back from my face in long strokes of the bristles, twisting it up into a bun, then pinning it in place with a clip I had left on the dresser. Dressing in a pair of beige linen pants and a loose tunic-style peasant blouse in deference to the heat, I opened the door that led to the street. Time to meet my destiny.

Chapter Eighteen

Lucius

My phone dinged with an incoming text, and I read the stark message as I piloted the helicopter. I was alone in the craft, having left all the cousins in Scotland to attend to their own love lives. I was stymied, disbelieving of what the witch was asking of me. Of course I would look out for her siblings, but what in the hell was she playing at? It sounded so final, like she would be gone for a long time, if not forever. And caring so much about Emily.

I cringed, thinking about what the young girl had said to Isadora. Frustration at the situation didn't cover it. I wanted to hit something to release the instant anger that flooded through me with its seething toxic chemicals, but I was trapped in the cockpit, needing to keep my senses about me as I flew over the Mediterranean Sea.

Was Isadora *really* going to Egypt to ask for the help of the House of Luceres' most ancient enemy? I could come up with no other reason for her being in the country. Especially since her bloodstream was even now being flooded with werewolf DNA, putting her in terrible danger if the Vampire Queen turned on her. Why would she do that? I rubbed my aching head in complete mystery and misery. The witch was impossible. Something more was going on here, something more than just trying to escape the devil's clutches. She'd been in debt to him for years, so why leave now? She could have run years ago.

Or maybe it was because she had met me, trusted me to help. Yes, that I would most certainly do. But why the enemy? Why ask for sanctuary in Egypt? Just because Emily lied, blaming her? Certainly, it was bad, a terrible way for Emily to act that she would be held accountable for, but it didn't warrant trying to disappear.

Damn it! I needed to find Isadora and shake some sense into her. Find out what was really going on.

I checked the readings on the digital gages of the cockpit. *Less than an hour before I set down in Abusir.* I prayed like I had never done before in my lifetime. *Where are you, Isadora?* I put all my anguish, all my fears, all my longing to keeping her safe into asking the simple question. The silence and darkness outside the copters cabin mocked my need.

* * * *

Isadora

I scurried down the side streets and alleyways, staying close to the buildings and in the shadows, the heavy night air oppressive. I made my way toward the outskirts of town, keeping a sharp look out for any surveillance. It was not unusual to be followed to the tomb of Cleopatra and Mark Antony. And I wanted to get to the Vampire Queen first, before I had to answer to one of her minions.

Where are you, Isadora? Come back to me.

A voice slammed into my head, making me reel in acute dizziness. *Lucius.* He was nearby. I had to hurry to the queen of the damned before he found me. I wanted my baby's daddy to be safe, to stay as far away from me as possible. Maybe later, after our daughter was born, then I could see him again. That was if Emily stepped up and made it right with my nemesis, for there was no way I could turn her in.

And there was no other way out of this mess that I could come up with. I would never allow our daughter to inherit my debt. Thoughts of Lucifer turned my stomach and I swallowed to keep the bile down. I rubbed my stomach. *We've fine, sweetheart. Soon I'll have you somewhere safe.*

I resumed my trek, anxious to get to there and get on with things. The moon had risen and my skin began to twitch as the glow bathed me between the buildings. Finally, I reached my destination, stopped and took a few cleansing breaths. Was this the last time I would breathe the fresh air and feel the sun or the moon on my skin? Watch the stars and the planets in the sky as they made their ancient loops around the ever-expanding universe, sharing their splendor and reminding us of our humbleness? Our insignificance in the face of eternity?

I placed both hands out, palms up and head bowed in the formal greeting, asking for entrance. When a surge of energy emanated from the rockface, the ward enacted to obscure the entrance vanished. I stepped through the stone portal that had turned to membrane then into the chamber beyond.

"You stink of wolf," a voice called out from the darkness. Vampires didn't require any light source with their spectacular vision, which was why they lived in tombs, crypts and inside pyramids…which was why I floundered around in the darkness for a few seconds, looking to find my bearings. Then something changed. I could see as my vision adjusted far more quickly than usual. The werewolf bite had added one good thing to my repertoire of abilities. What else would the venom cause in my system? I had heard Lucius clearly, meaning telepathy had also made its appearance.

"I am Isadora Moray Champagne, here to call in a favor of your highness."

"Isadora." The cold, cultured tone filled my ears, echoing inside my mind. "Why do you stink of wolf?" she repeated her question with less patience this time.

"An unfortunate accident, one quite beyond my control."

"Yes, unfortunate." The voice came nearer. Queen Cleopatra came into view. She was memorable, with her long, sleek black hair, high cheekbones and well-rounded lips. Not beautiful, but striking. Tall and slender, she wore a gorgeous filmy gown of red chiffon, floating about her like she existed on a cushion of air. Behind her nothing was visible to the naked eye, giving a surrealness to the experience.

"Why are you here? Explain." The tone was colder now, her lips twisted into a cruel line. I focused all my energy on her, wanting desperately to persuade her to help us.

"I need sanctuary, for me and my child. Until she's born."

Honor

"A daughter. How fortunate."

I nodded. "We're in danger. Lucifer —"

"Don't speak his name here! He's an abomination. As bad as the wolves that roam the upper world." She watched me closely after her comment about the wolves, looking for my response. Cleopatra and every wolf ever born had an animosity that ran deeper than eternity. Something to do with an ancient feud, I think, and that was something I kept my nose right out of.

I swallowed. "Yes, he's constantly upping the debt I owe him without regard for my being able to pay it off."

"What does he want you for now? Still trading in bartered or lost souls? So old-school."

"Yes, and I can't bring in the one he's asked for. A female werewolf who had no idea what she was really doing. Just having a lark." I had to tell her the truth. She would pry it out of me anyway, and being up front with the most intelligent vampire in existence was always the best way to go.

"He threatened you? Promised harm to your child?" She looked pointedly at my middle, as if expecting my pregnancy to be more visible.

I instinctively placed my hands over my stomach. "Yes, he said that the shifter was important to his plans."

"Odd." Her eyes surveyed me with a dark stillness that gave nothing away of what she was thinking. All I could do was wait. "And now you want sanctuary? But that is a risky business for me. The evil one will dislike my harboring a fugitive."

"But you owe me a favor. Anything I asked for after I brought you the Ark of the Covenant to add to your treasures. That's what you said at the time."

166

"But it didn't work!" Her words lashed out at me like a whip, as if I was directly responsible for the failure. "Antony is still lost to me."

Her voice filled with a terrible yearning, replacing the anger. Cleopatra had been collecting any known artifact that might bring her lover back for centuries. Her tomb was filled with them, everything from the Ark to the Holy Grail to the Philosopher's Stone and even the Elixir of Life in her efforts to raise her dead lover. Bringing her a new one to test was how one coveted favor with her. I had been guilty of it in the past, wanting a future favor in case of the exact kind of situation I now found myself in.

"I hear that the Lupus Sanguis Chalice has been recently located by the House of Luceres. Where you aware?" she asked, her bird-like eyes watching me without expression.

"Not really, just heard rumors." *Goddess, don't let her ask the next question.*

"Which house does the wolf who bit you belong to?"

I stood still, a sick feeling coming over me knowing exactly what she meant. I couldn't betray my baby's father, could I?

"I need that chalice. It might be the thing that brings my lover back to me. You get it, I'll grant you sanctuary forever, for both you and your daughter."

"Couldn't this wait until she's born?" I made a last desperate plea.

"Did the monster who asked for this Emily give you a specific timeline to rectify the situation?"

I reluctantly nodded. "A week. But it's not much—"

"Plenty of time to use your wiles to get what I need. Go. I will honor my words. Bring me the item by whatever means necessary and you will be offered sanctuary for as long as you wish."

"Would we be living here with you?" I needed parameters on how this would work.

She laughed, a sparkling sound that calmed my nerves somewhat. I'd always believed that inside everyone was a spark of goodness, even if it was buried under a ton of evil intentions. I prayed it included the vampire standing before me. And maybe even Lucifer. Could love change that psychopath?

"No, not if you don't want to. I have many safe ports in the storm if need be. I prefer this one with my love waiting nearby. His aura, even in death, sustains me. You know, love is the only thing eternal – the only thing worth fighting for," she mused, her expression vulnerable for a split second before it hardened again. "Bring me the chalice before it's too late."

I didn't ask about the *too late* clause. I already knew what she meant. *Lucifer calling in my debt.*

Reversing my earlier actions, I made my way back to the hotel, thinking of how to deal with Lucius, a wolf I was beginning to respect and certainly one that I was extremely attracted to. *Six days to locate and steal the chalice from his pack. Oh Goddess.* I broke out in a cold sweat just thinking about it and all the ramifications if Lucius found out before I could get away. This was going to be the hardest thing I would ever have to do in my lifetime. I could only pray I was up to the challenge.

I slipped inside my room and froze.

"Isadora. Nice to see you," Lucius said, revealing himself by turning on the light over the chair he was sitting in. He held a glass of something golden in his hand that gave off the fragrance of high-end alcohol.

He took a sip of it and set it down on the night table. The room was entirely too cramped, his presence filling it to bursting.

"Lucius," I said. I wanted to turn and run, observing the predatory look in his normally creamy brown eyes.

"Care for a drink?" He wasn't asking my permission but filled two glasses from a bottle of bourbon.

I shook my head when he held out the offering. "No, thank you."

"Why are you not drinking? You should, you know, to calm those nerves. You smell nervous to me, among other things."

I stayed silent. I was damned if I did, damned if I didn't.

"In fact, your scent has changed a great deal since last we met, under that stink of vampire. I had an interesting talk with the owner. Something the waitress shared with her had her quite enamored about you. Something you want to tell me?" He swallowed the last of the liquor and began on my glass.

"I know you don't trust me," I began to buy time. The fact he knew I was pregnant was obvious and it almost swept the legs out from under me.

"What? Don't trust you after you run away without a word? I need to know why, Isadora. Was what I offered you not enough? A new beginning for us, a chance to become a mated pair. And whose baby is it anyway?"

"I ran away because others were setting me up. Blaming everything on the witch."

"Nice try. But it was more than that. Emily's situation has been exposed. She came clean after you left. Everyone knows now that she started things, that you had nothing to do with it."

He got up and approached me, hovered over me, a darkness expressed in his eyes that took my breath away.

"Why did you leave me?" he asked, his tone sharp with impatience and what sounded like hurt. "Was it because you were pregnant with another man's baby?"

My stomach took a somersault. *Breathe, just breathe.*

"I had to. I was upset, confused, I felt I needed to hide. And Cleopatra owed me for something I had gotten for her. I thought to stay until — things got better." I was about to say until the baby was born, but stopped just in time. "And whether you believe it or not, it's your baby."

"Impossible, how could you know you're pregnant so soon? No. There's something you're not telling me. The story just doesn't add up. You're too strong to need to run from a small thing like Emily's indiscretion."

"I know, okay, I'm a witch, damn it!" I rubbed my belly and murmured, "Mommy didn't mean it." I turned my wrath back on Lucius. "And it was hardly an indiscretion! She has no idea of the cost!" The words tumbled out of their own volition.

"What cost? Is Lucifer pressuring you over Emily?" His eyes changed then, as if he were considering my previous words, his glance landing on my stomach.

I turned away, unable to answer. It was on me to figure a way out of this labyrinth, not a young girl who had no idea of how serious her actions had been.

"If he is, I will take care of it."

"There's nothing you can do. Just give me time. I'll figure things out." *Give me time to figure out how to steal the chalice, that is.*

"I will protect you. No one will cause you harm, understood?"

I nodded. My take was that werewolves just did not take this situation seriously enough. *No one wins with the devil.*

Though his words came from his heart, he didn't need to know that it was something beyond anyone's reach to fix. It was my burden to bear. I would stay with this amazing man until I had to go. I almost collapsed then, told the full truth. That I intended to betray him by stealing the chalice to gain sanctuary. But Emily was still at risk, which put my baby at risk when Lucifer called me in for not handing the young girl over.

"Just protect Emily. That's all I ask. I can take care of myself." Maybe I could even persuade the girl to ask for sanctuary from Cleopatra, though a vampire helping a wolf was almost never done, even if the young girl could be persuaded to give up her highland lover to hide from the devil. My head began to spin at the pressure of trying to figure a way out of the horrible situation that kept everyone safe.

"And our baby, if what you say is true? I will be in this child's life. Full-time. I want you as well, Isadora. Very much, if you'll just give me the chance to show it. I believe you're hiding your true feelings about us even from yourself, about how that one night meant so much more than you could ever have imagined. That's normal for Forever Mates at first. It even explains how you got pregnant in that whirlwind of passion."

His voice changed, grew husky with emotion. I swallowed my unshed tears.

"Of course, it meant something to me." The words spilled out before I had time to consider my response.

"You are aware that if you continue to fight this—what's going on between us—that you will stay in pain?"

His words cut to the bone. But I had to fight this, for the sake of my child. He had no idea what was going on behind the scenes. And I didn't want him to know — it would only put him in mortal danger too. "Doesn't matter. I have to do what I think best."

Then I told the biggest lie of my life, one that would scorch my soul for all my days, that was even worse than the soul debt I owed Lucifer. And one I could never take back. Heartsick, I said what needed to be said. "But okay, for the next few months until the baby is born, I will live with you. Then we'll see how we're doing."

In reality it would only be a few days until I could locate and steal the chalice and take it to Cleopatra. *And please, please let that be before the devil calls me in.*

He gave me a look that said he was unconvinced of my sincerity. He was right not to trust me, but I also saw a rawness in his eyes that said he wanted to believe. And that hurt the most of all. I had to turn away, sickened to my very soul.

Chapter Nineteen

Lucius

Reluctant to believe her – it being too obvious she wasn't telling me everything – but needing to get her to safety to protect her and the baby I was more and more certain was real what with her supernatural power of divination, I went against my better judgment and nodded my acceptance of her terms.

I had been waiting to hear the words she was coming back to be with me forever, but nine months was long enough to persuade her that she wasn't going anywhere. No one could love her or take care of her and our baby like I could. She would soon know that. Then she would never leave me.

"Fine. Let's go. I want to get you home as soon as possible and away from this damnable place." I disliked the cold ones of Egypt as much as any shifter, maybe more now that my Forever Mate had turned to their queen for help. I swore under my breath that that would never happen again, no matter what I had to do to stop it.

"Yes, that would be for the best," she said. I sensed a change in her, one that confused me. Thank God, I had months ahead to figure out how to break down all her defenses, find out the entire truth. I swore then and there I would do it. Soon she would be mine to the end of days.

I picked up her bag and offered her my hand. She looked torn before finally accepting my help. When our hands touched, a spark sizzled across the space between us, making her eyes open wider.

"No denying fate, beautiful. Time to come home."

She remained quiet, locked inside her thoughts, and I reached out to her on a primal level. She needed me, so much more than she knew. Abused by family with their connections to the evil one, her sense of persecution that lingered from centuries of the unfair mistrust of witches, the lingering effects of my having inadvertently bitten her, and now her pregnancy that she could not have seen coming.

"Fate can be a bitch," she finally said as we walked down the street toward the waiting helicopter. I had parked the craft on the edge of town in an open field ready for take-off at a moment's notice.

"True, but it can also direct the way to a better life. How can you appreciate what you get if you don't know the alternative?"

"When did you get so smart?" she asked, demonstrating a bit of her old spunk when she gave me a teasing look. This was the way I liked to see her, sure of herself and taunting the world with her actions. Quite the opposite of what I'd thought I wanted in a woman in my past when my objective was just getting them into the sack. Isadora was the real deal, a woman who would be an amazing life partner, in this one and the next. That is, once she settled down and found her footing. I already knew precious time spent with her was making me a better man.

"You're just now noticing?" I responded in a lighter tone over the sudden lump in my throat.

"Hmm, not like I have that much to go on."

"Isadora Molay Champagne. If you weren't pregnant, I'd bend you over my knee."

"Try it and I'll bite you back."

I snorted, though her words brought me up short. In all that had happened, I had nearly forgotten to ask how she was coping with the effects of being wolf-bit. "How are you doing? I have little experience in how a wolf bite affects a witch. Are you okay?"

She shrugged, like she had bigger concerns. She surprised me. I would have thought she'd be incensed by the situation. "So far, so good. I did notice the moon called to me."

"It's going to be full in a couple of days. Then we'll see how it goes — how it affects you. You might feel out of sorts, but because of your pregnancy, you won't be able to shift. Female werewolves can't change into wolves during those nine months while they're pregnant."

"Because it's not safe?" she asked, her expression changing to one of deep concern. I knew then and there she was going to be a great mother. Her protective instincts were already on a high setting. The thought made me relax a bit, giving me time to explain what turning into a werewolf was all about.

"Yes. We change at a cellular level. Since energy is never lost and can only be altered, we shift at the quantum level as we go through a portal where our special DNA allows us to reform into a new entity. The bite you endured is even now changing your genetic code, turning on genomes that will allow you to change one day. Become a wolf. But like I said, not until the baby is born. You'll have months to get used to the idea."

What I didn't say was this whole thing blew me away. *Me, a father? Good thing I have months to get used to the idea as well.*

She gave me a speculative glance. "I think it will be awesome to shift into animal form, to see the world from a different perspective for a change. There's a part of me really looking forward to that. Oh, one thing I've noticed—I can see better in the dark."

"That's good. Soon you'll be aware of odors more as well. Of course, being pregnant, you'll find some of them nauseating. Have you been hungry at all?"

"Hungry? I've been eating like a bloody fool!"

Her words hit home. They came out so spontaneously, giving me renewed hope that this thing between us had promise. That she was going to give us a chance.

The helicopter came into sight. I quickly hurried her along and ushered her inside. The sooner I got her home safe and sound, the happier I would be.

"Will we be picking up Gino, Goldie and Angelo?"

I buckled her into her seat in the cockpit, making sure she was properly secured. "No, they'll have to make their own way home. We're not waiting around for them."

"Found some females of interest among the Highland Heathens Clan, have they?" she asked, her lips twitching.

"Definitely. We might not see them for some time." I leaned forward to kiss her, so pleased to have her in my sights. She'd never be out of them again, if I had my way.

The heat of her lips, so soft and yielding, brought my cock to instant attention, the blood rush nearly making me faint. My wolf also took notice, wanting to ravish her on the spot.

When she sighed with emotion, seeming to fully enjoy the kiss, it was all I could do to pull away and buckle myself in behind the controls. But I wanted us out of Egypt and home. ASAP.

"I've packed a cooler of food. It's right there between us. Eat and drink whenever the need or mood arrives. A werewolf pregnancy consumes an enormous number of calories."

"What? You want me fat?" she asked. Her rosebud lips were still red from my kiss and all I wanted to do was to have her again, and again. But it would have to wait.

"You'd look good anyway. And it's hard for a werewolf to get fat. It would take up too much time in the day."

"You know, that's about the best thing I've heard about being a shifter. All you can eat and you don't get fat. You could sell the life on that fact alone."

"It also comes with stringent responsibilities. Rule number one, the existence of our kind must never be revealed to humans. Rule number two, the alpha always protects his mate and his offspring with his life."

"What about the female? Doesn't she get top billing for protecting her own child?"

"That's not how it works. Think of it as co-parenting. Both male and female protect their offspring — to the death if necessary."

Silence. I glanced over at her. She had gone white as a sheet.

"What's wrong? Is it the baby?"

When she didn't say anything, I reached across the space between us and touched her hands lying limply on her lap. "You know you can tell me anything, right?"

"I'm fine. I just want to get where I'm going."

Isadora

Of course, I was not fine. I was as far from fine as I could get. Worries spun round and round in my head, threatening to spill out at any moment. I clamped my mouth shut, determined to keep it all bottled inside, pregnancy hormones be damned. *Oops, sorry, baby.* At this rate, my little one was going to be a salty sailor. I had to be more circumspect.

Food. Then sleep. With that in mind I tackled the box of sustenance that Lucius had packed. I was halfway through a second meat and cheese bun supplemented by two packs of chips and a large refreshing container of full-fat milk when Lucius chuckled.

"If I didn't believe you before, I do now."

I ignored the dig and finished my delicious bun, then dabbed at my lips. "Wake me when we get there."

It came on quick. A dark, dreamless sleep that felt more like quicksand slipping up and over my head. Too exhausted to fight it, I fell under its sway and knew nothing more until Lucius was gently shaking my arm, his warm breath fragrant as he leaned over me.

"Time to wake up, sleepyhead. We're home."

The time felt lost, as if only a minute had passed in reality. I rubbed at my eyes, trying to get my bearings. That it was dark outside only added to the discombobulation.

His strong hands took care of unbuckling the safety harness, then he picked me up in his arms and bore me from the craft over my not-so-loud protests. I did feel off, more tired than I should be for having slept so many continuous hours. Too much had happened in the past couple of days, and I enjoyed the precious sensation of someone actually taking care of me for a change.

Don't get too used to it, Isadora. Soon you'll break his heart all over again. The memory of the morning after our lovemaking roared into my head, the look of betrayal on his face after I told him it had meant nothing to me. The thought made me whimper in emotional pain.

"Are you okay?" Lucius' voice filled with concern. "Is it the baby?"

"I'm fine. Just an old thought resurfaced. Nothing to be worried about. Everyone has baggage, right?" *Yeah, but not the amount and kind I do.*

"You might want to see a therapist about that? Or spend time bending my ear. I'm always open to listening, especially over a nice meal." His volunteering himself only hurt more. Oh *Goddess, I'm going to need all your help to carry me through these next few days that will no doubt be the hardest of my life. Please be there,* I prayed with all I possessed.

"You just want to get me into bed," I teased over the impossibly large lump in my throat.

"Well, that too. Not like we're not perfect together," he said, his expression shifting to one of pure unadulterated lust.

It was then I began to pray that the Goddess cast a spell on him to make him either less attractive or less thoughtful. Or both. A few days of this kind of treatment and banter was going to do me in, I swore it. Then thoughts of us being together in bed took hold of my mind and it was all I could do not to jump his bones in the here and now.

Like he knew what I was thinking, or maybe he smelled my arousal, suddenly the air between us electrified. His arms tightened around me as he strode across the roof of the Glitter Palace casino that we had landed atop of. Seconds later, we were inside the massive structure and going down the elevator.

"I have a private suite that I stay at when I'm working. I'll take you there. Or if you prefer, we can go to my compound outside Vegas? Plus, there's a number of choices—"

"Here's fine." *It will be easier for me if Lucius was distracted by work.* I was only going to be staying a few days anyway. I ignored the pain that thought brought on and kept my focus on what needed to be done—find out where the damn Lupus Sanguis Chalice was hidden.

"I heard something about the House of Luceres. That a special artifact was discovered in Barrow, Alaska, recently? I've forgotten what they call the town now."

"Utqiagvik. Where did you hear that?" His expression sharpened as we left the elevator and headed down a hallway with carpet so thick that his footsteps were virtually silent. Being held in his arms was so incredible that when he finally put me down, it left me cold.

"Where do you think?" I said with a hopefully realistic snort of condemnation. "Lucifer. His evilness seems to know all."

"Hmm. Well, it won't do him any good. He'll never get his hands on it, if that's his intentions."

"Good. Though I can't imagine he has much use for it. He only wants to torture and tear down and collect bartered souls. Helping a human endure the change to werewolf would not be something he'd be remotely interested in, is my guess."

Now, Cleopatra, that was a whole other ballgame. She'd give it a try to resurrect Mark Antony then toss it aside when it too didn't work. No way was what she wanted to happen going to happen. Nothing could come back from ashes. Well, maybe in old *Dracula* movies, but this was real life.

"He's never asked you about it? This is important, Isadora. I need you to be completely honest with me." He stopped me from analyzing the situation, taking my full attention up with his intense presence.

"No, never." My confident reply reassured him.

"Good. And it's best you don't know where it is, either. Then no one can pressure you."

The words chilled my soul.

"Has there been much of that? You know—other werewolves trying to steal it?"

He shrugged and began escorting me down the cream-colored hallway, his hand at my elbow. His momma had raised him well. "Not really. The House of Luceres is willing to help other packs if something goes astray and someone gets bitten. There's no charge for using it either, which keeps down the envy. It's not as common as you might think, humans getting bitten. We like to keep to ourselves and stay out of the public eye. Well, except when it comes to making money. But then that's accomplished in our human form."

"Your house is richer than anyone's, I've heard. And growing more powerful by the day."

"Guilty as charged. Are you wanting anything? A bath? Food? What can I do for you, beautiful?"

My stomach grumbled, instantly settling what was first on the agenda.

"Food, then a shower."

"Come. I'll show you the kitchen."

"You expecting me to cook?" I said with a half laugh, expecting that to be the truth of it.

"No, actually, I'm a fairly decent chef. One of my hobbies."

Now that floored me. "Really?" I didn't see such a hot stud being at all interested in cooking. "Thought you'd have live-in help?"

"I like my privacy too much for that. Steak and eggs okay? I always keep the ingredients on hand."

My mouth watered. "Perfect."

He swept me past incredible pieces of artwork I couldn't wait to check out more thoroughly at some point. His domain even featured life-like statues of ancient warriors of both the male and female variety. One stood out—a pair of lovers holding swords, seeming to have each other's backs.

We turned a corner in a flash and headed into a huge kitchen that looked equipped to feed an army, yet intimate enough with its seating arrangement to provide space for a couple to enjoy a meal.

"Come. Sit. I'll cook for you," he commanded, pointing at chairs lined up along an island featuring a cooktop and chopping area.

"I'll help."

"No need. But you could pour us a drink."

"Sure. What do you want?"

"A cold beer."

I laughed. I liked this brand-new side of him. So domestic yet in charge. And beer, typical North American male.

"But no beer for you. It's milk from now on."

"Yes, sir," I said, adding a salute accompanied by a wide grin before bumping him out of my way with a hip to access the refrigerator.

He chuckled. "I think we must have skipped about ten steps to be getting to this point in our relationship in a matter of days. From fighting to domestic harmony. Go figure."

Oh my. No, don't think about it. Live in the now, Isadora. Enjoy this brief time. It won't come again.

I poured his beer and my glass of milk with fingers that trembled slightly. He took the mug of alcohol and clanked it against my tumbler.

"To a new beginning for us," he said, a wonderful look of trust apparent in his dreamy brown eyes.

"To us," I said back, swallowing my tears, wishing I could stay. *No.* I could never tell him of the danger to him and our child. I had to face this alone.

He turned back to chopping red peppers and sweet onions while I dabbed at my eyes. Soon the delicious odors of sirloin meat frying and French toast baking in a hot pan with cream, vanilla, sugar and raisins mingled. It about turned my stomach inside out with want, making me forget everything else.

We sat down to a feast. When the first piece of perfectly cooked steak hit my tastebuds, I moaned with pleasure.

"This is so good," I raved, before nabbing another delicious selection of meat and savory peppers with my fork.

"I intend to make you moan like that in bed," he said, his eyes alight with keen interest.

"Think you're up to it?" I taunted, knowing damn well he was. *Oops, sorry.*

"Finish your food and we'll talk. I'll not have you hungry on my watch."

"You'd have made a great army drill sergeant, you know that?"

"So I've been told. Most likely due to my role as pack enforcer. Otherwise, some of our wilder-natured wolves wouldn't toe the line." He took my comment in stride, a teasing smile playing around his awesome lips.

I cleaned my plate, even going so far as to rub the last bit of toast in the gravy. When I jumped up, he got to his feet as well. "I'm good. Thanks for the food. Now I need to shower."

"Want some help with that?" He raised an eyebrow, his eyes filled with devilish merriment.

"Sure, why not. I never seem to get it quite right," I quipped back.

In that moment I knew that if I only had a few days to keep me going for a lifetime, I was going to make full use of them. *Make every precious minute count.* In my mind's eye, I could see an hourglass filled with sand, each grain a new priceless memory as it slipped down through the neck into the looming chamber below.

Chapter Twenty

Isadora

He came closer, tugging me into his arms and seductively swiping his thumb across my bottom lip. I took a deep breath, his tantalizing fragrance filling me with a sense of giddiness.

"You are so beautiful, so alive, Isadora," he murmured. "I want to kiss you from head to toe."

"I have no problem with that." My breath hitched with anticipation. *Oh my, this man has it going on. Alpha in charge, sexy hot man and so incredibly intriguing.* I was such a goner, knowing I was going to give in to all my wildest dreams and fantasies. Then my thoughts ceased as he once more bore me up in his arms and strode from the kitchen, holding me as if I were the most precious thing on this Earth.

He set me down on my feet in the spacious bathroom and began to strip me of my clothing, first tugging off my shoes. Then he slipped the blouse from my shoulders and pressed kisses to my throat, trailing his lips along my collar bone. He deftly removed my bra, letting the lacy fabric fall to the floor.

I moved in closer to his body and embraced him. My bare breasts rubbed against his warmth, peaked nipples pressing into him, begging for attention. My panties flooded with wetness, my sex swollen and needy. I ached for him with every fiber of my being.

He tugged at the tie on my linen pants before pushing them down past my thighs to pool on the floor. Pulling away from me just long enough to tear all his clothing, he embraced me again, crushing me to his naked chest.

He reached down and cupped my pussy with one hand, stroking me through the drenched fabric of my panties, softly at first, then with an intensity that made me rock against the delicious pressure of his fingers. His mouth devoured me and I moaned. *So. Good.*

He applied his mouth to my breast, tightening his lips around a budded nipple and licking all around the sensitive peak, then suddenly drew hard on the vulnerable tip, making me vibrate with need.

"I want to taste you. All of you," he breathed against my breasts, then pulled down my panties. When my underwear was free, he raised them to his nose and breathed deeply.

"You smell heavenly, like all things good." In a flash, he flipped me onto a padded bench so that my legs were braced on either side of his body, revealing my mound to his view. I let my legs fall farther apart. I wanted him to see all of me. To see how wet I was for him. How much I ached just for him.

"So incredibly perfect." He gazed hungrily at my nakedness before he dipped a finger between the folds, as if giving thanks. He found my clit and began to massage it in tantalizing circular motions.

I moaned, unable to deny how turned on I was. When he applied his mouth to my core, the nerve endings tingled and sprang to life, vibrating as I was thrust into a world of pure sensation. A world which was all about gratification and desire. I couldn't think. My clit was swollen and aching, my thighs slickened with the wetness that spilled from me.

He lapped it up, sweeping his raspy tongue along my inner lips, dipping into my channel and licking deep within me. Using his talented hands against clenched tissue, he stroked, working his fingers inside me as violent pleasure lashed me. All the while he sucked and nipped at my clit. It was too much pleasure. I went to push him away, but he continued, overriding my weak objections.

"Feel it all…take what you need, beautiful."

His voice threw me over the edge. I opened to him, let him feel all my pent-up desire. And when I could not take any more of his expert fingers stretching and rubbing against and in me, the throbbing increased to a crescendo and I spiraled into the abyss, falling completely apart.

I opened my eyes in wonder some time later. I blushed when I realized how wanton I had been. How I had let myself be so exposed to him. And how very right it all was. We were perfect for each other.

He smiled down at me as I still lay sprawled before him, unashamed in my nakedness. I glanced down at the apex of his strong golden thighs, where his cock jutted, begging to be kissed.

I smiled back. "My turn."

"Not until we've showered."

"Huh, like that stopped you. I love the way you smell by the way, Lucius." I treasured all things about him at that moment, wanting to share our bodies fully. Time was so precious now, and every second mattered, for memories that would have to last a lifetime.

I reached out and tugged him toward me, licking my lips in anticipation. He straddled my body and leaned forward on the bench before binding my long locks in one hand. I quirked a smug smile up at him.

"The perfect position," I said, guiding his cock toward my mouth. He grinned, his eyes smoldering as I lapped at his swollen member with my tongue. I kissed all along the extreme length of him, my tongue catching the essence of the pre-cum that continually glistened at the tip. My mouth finally closed over him, silk on steel.

A helpless moan escaped his throat as I sucked eagerly at his engorged hardness. I drew on it, my cheeks moving with the effort, giving myself up to the lust flaming through my body.

"That's it. Suck me. Take it all."

I tightened my mouth at the explicit language, reaching one hand down to cup his balls.

His huge cock filled my mouth and I pulled him in and toward the back of my throat. My hands busy with his balls, he reached for a nipple that jutted out from my swollen breasts. He took over the rhythm, thrusting in long strokes past my lips, knowing my expression was savage with lust.

When I moaned, he twisted my nipple, making me moan harder.

"I should punish you for running away from me." He let go of my hair and turned me sideways on the bench, smacking my ass the exact right amount, not too hard and not too soft, still playing with a nipple.

I arched my back, giving better access, and he hit the other rounded globe with the same perfect force. He reached between my legs and found me soaking wet, my lips extended and wide open, my clit swollen and defiant. He thrust two fingers into me, stretching me, making me moan loader.

"Take me, wolf, right now!"

Lucius grabbed my hips, straddling me. He teased my soaking wet lips and clit with the thick head of his cock, sliding back and forth down my swollen slit. My breathing became ragged, my skin hotter and more flushed. I was so ready that I was losing control.

I reached down and held myself open, pulling my lips wide apart, exposing myself. Heat pulsed as his pre-cum slicked my entrance, the elixir guaranteeing my nerve endings would burn with a desperate need to be touched, to be rubbed against. Submissive, I had no control but to give it all to him, my alpha. But it was my choice too.

When I whimpered in near pain, wanting him so badly, he relented and pushed as far as he could into me in one long satisfying stroke. His warmth surrounded me, hot and squeezing. Unbelievable pleasure roared through me, making my whole body vibrate.

"So tight," he murmured. I lost myself in the sensation. I was so aroused that it took a moment to recover before he began thrusting himself in time with my movements. A dream come true.

"Harder," I demanded.

He needed no other invitation, burying himself right to the hilt inside me, breaking through whatever emotional restriction remained.

I screamed and arched my back, holding on to him as his cock filled and stretched me to perfection.

"Are you okay?"

"Absolutely," I said, my voice low and throaty. He tugged on my nipples, making me squeal and push myself harder against him. Wetness flooded out of me, mingling with his juices. We smelled heavenly together, a perfect pairing on every level. He reached down and rubbed harder and harder against my clit, and I savored the waves of pleasure his actions brought.

Then I was spiraling in my mind, taking me far away from everything, the pleasure overwhelming and raw. *Almost too good to be true.* So uplifting, so capable of taking all my troubles away and leaving a new beginning in its wake.

When the waves finally eased, I discovered I was crying, of all odd things.

"What is it? Did I hurt you? Is it the baby?" Lucius was so caring as he cradled me in his arms that I just cried more, unable to bring myself to talk, to say was what wrong. That to betray this man, our destiny together, was the worst thing imaginable. Worse than death at that moment.

Finally, I grabbed a hold of myself, drying my eyes with my fingers. I could smell him on my hands, that fine fragrance that was all his, strong and wild and free. "I'm fine. Really. It was just so good, so overwhelming. So unimaginable."

He accepted my words, his expression tender beyond belief. I swear I wanted to lay down my burdens, share them with him. But I couldn't. I would be exposing him and all his friends and relatives to Lucifer's legendary wrath. No, better that I hide and allow him to live a normal life while I kept our daughter safe and sound from Lucifer's reach.

"I've been told that," he joked, making me feel teary all over again. But I had to stay strong. *Strong for our baby.* That would be my first and last crying jag while I was here, I vowed.

"Now, let's get you into the water," he said, pulling me to my feet.

He carried me across the room and tugged open a drape to a Roman-like spa area housed behind sliding glass doors. He slid one panel open to reveal a large sunken hot tub that would accommodate at least a dozen people. Crystal-clear water lapped against its tiled blue-and-white mosaic pattern, wisps of steam rising lazily off the surface. A chaise longue was placed between two lovely white marble statues of water nymphs at play. Stacks of fluffy white towels filled the shelves. *Definitely my idea of heaven.*

"I didn't know all this was back here. You certainly know how to live."

"There are lots of hidden secrets within these walls. As my mate, you will be party to all of them. Which reminds me, we have a party to attend tomorrow night. A chance for you to meet the family."

"Not everyone, I hope. You got a large pack, right?" Maybe this would be an opportunity to find out something out about the location of the chalice?

"Just the immediate members. Later this week you can meet the rest at our annual Summer Howl fest."

"Howl fest?"

"Just a day of sports and barbecues in reality. Fun for all ages. Nothing like the Lupercalia that's over for the season. That's strictly for consenting adults. Now, let's get you into the water."

Settling back in the warmth provided by the now bubbling hot tub, the heat soothing my body, I tried meditating to release the worries that threatened to derail the most important project of my life. *Breathe in. Breathe out.* I repeated the mantra a few times, grounding myself, a trick I'd learned early on for moments of unease or distress.

Not that being around Lucius was cause for concern. I opened one eye and peeped at him. Looking large and in charge, he placed his arms along the back of the pool, his expression one of supreme satisfaction. Oh, if only this were real. *A gal could really get used to such luxury.* And living with such an incredible man—he'd taken all the crap I'd given him and come back to me. That had never happened before. Not that I'd had many boyfriends, for one whiff of my being a witch and they deserted ship like pirates had set it on fire.

"Tell me about your family?" I asked.

"What do you want to know?"

"How many siblings, to start."

"Okay. We're four brothers. Cristaldo's my twin— you met him already."

"Yes, not that I think I made that great a first impression, with all the bickering we were engaged in."

He grinned. "Don't worry, he's seen worse. He's married to Everly. Then my mother, Sophia, had a second set of twins, Alessandro and Maximus, both married to Trinity. My father is Cesare. I have an uncle—"

"Hold on." I held up one hand, totally intrigued by the information. "Two men married to the same woman? Now, that's really cool, turning polygamy on its head."

"Yes, it's called polyandry."

I raised speculative eyebrows.

"Never going to happen. One man, one woman is the only way for me. But it works surprisingly well for them. Actually, there's a story that comes with their courtship. You asked about the Lupus Sanguis Chalice?"

I stilled, watching him closely. What was I about to learn? Just one tiny clue to its whereabouts, that was all I needed. Or at the very least, a lead to follow. I swear I could hear the clock ticking in my head now.

"The twins, both scholars, had been searching for the artifact for years, charged with finding it. It seemed like a wild-goose chase at times, but to their credit they followed the clues from Italy to Alaska, finally finding it hidden in an inukshuk. That's a manmade figure made of rock that's fairly common in the north. The trio—Trinity was also looking for it—went in by dogsled of all things, spending nights camping in the high Arctic. Amazing adventure by all accounts and one that brought the three of them together."

"An unusual set-up, two men and a woman," I murmured. "Happy for them though, that they found love together. So precious in this hard world."

He gave me an unfathomable look. "I'm sorry the world hasn't treated you better. But from now on all that changes. You're with me now, meaning you are entitled to the very best. I know no one can never totally make up for childhood traumas, but I'm going to try. That I can promise you."

"Entitled? That sounds a bit smug. I'd be happy just being thought of once in a while."

"For the past few days all I've thought about is you. And now I have a baby to think about. How soon until we know if it's a boy or girl?"

I laughed. I couldn't help it. "I guarantee it's a girl. The oldest female in my family always gives birth to a daughter first."

"A daughter. I have a lot to learn." His expression turned pensive.

Perhaps he was thinking of his past exploits and was rethinking them now? His telling his sexual partners up front that he had nothing else to offer them had helped, but still, the heart wanted what the heart wanted. I knew that some women had fallen for him on first coupling. I sighed inwardly, knowing I was one of them. The difference was, this time he wanted me too. This would be the ultimate revenge if I was still in that dreadful mindset. Thank goodness that was long gone. Not that the situation I had found myself in was any better. *From the frypan to the fire.*

A doorbell chimed, drawing our attention.

Lucius rose to his feet, blessing me with the glorious view of his well-developed pecs and stomach muscles, wide shoulders and narrow hips. *What a man!* The next second, guilt skittered across my skin. I shuddered. *Oh Goddess, what a horrible person I am. Leading him on and knowing nothing can come of this.* I was as bad now as he had been. Maybe worse because I was out-and-out lying to him. If only there was another way? But all I could see were sessions of torture scheduled for my immediate future.

Chapter Twenty-One

Lucius

"Now who could that be this time of the night?" I said with a grimace, annoyed at the interruption. Just when Isadora and I were beginning to find common ground. I was certain I could get to the bottom of what was troubling her with time. *But a daughter.* My knees weakened at the prospect. Suddenly, I wanted to be a better man for her.

I took a white robe off a shelf and pulled it on, then exited the bathroom. I jerked the suite door open so quickly that my brother Cristaldo, who had been about to knock, stumbled into the room, catching himself just in time.

"Welcome home to you too," he said, obviously annoyed. My twin hated looking uncool. *Runs in the family.*

"Sorry, Isadora and I were just having a soak. What do you want?"

"Isadora, is it now?" His eyebrows rose. "Getting along, I take it?" He snorted. "That's a change."

"We're doing just fine, thank you very much." I resented the implication that the pair of us were unsuited.

"I came to say thanks about Emily. She's apparently fine. Found herself a wolf."

"Yeah. She pulled the wool over everyone's eyes." My mood darkened. Something about the whole situation still bothered me.

"Yeah, she pulled a fast one." Cristaldo shook his head, chuckling. "The young today."

"Crazy thing to do. Calling on the devil."

"Yeah, well, it worked out fine. There's something else. It's about the Lupus Sanguis Chalice. The House of Anche has asked to borrow it."

"Why? What's happened?"

The House of Anche were the most neutral of the wolf packs, always helping to settle disputes. Far more likely that our rival pack, the House of Ribelle, had taken it in their thick heads to do or say the wrong thing.

"Apparently a human was inadvertently bitten during the Lupercalia and no one realized it until now. Too much horseplay combined with too much partying. I've been wanting to shut down that party for years." Cristaldo shook his head in disgust. "Nothing but trouble."

"Yeah, but the young need an outlet for their pent-up frustrations. At least now we have a solution for when things go too far."

I thought I heard something and turned to look behind me, expecting Isadora to greet us. But nobody stood in the hallway. *Strange.*

"Okay, well, we'll have to get it out of the vault. I'll head the delegation that takes it over to them. See that it's handled correctly then safely tucked away again." Both Cristaldo and I had to use our thumbprints to open the vault, our failsafe method.

"Good. That's what I wanted to hear. Tomorrow will be soon enough. We can do it during the party. Everly is so excited about meeting Isadora. I should warn you, there's going to be a few more people in attendance than I thought."

"What's a few more?" I was suddenly suspicious. Wolf parties had a way of getting out of hand quickly, with everyone vying for invites.

My brother shrugged and clapped a hand on my shoulder. "Best not to fight it, bro. Besides, Isadora looks like a woman who can take care of herself. She even had you going there for a while — the notoriously single I'll-never-need-a-woman brother." The accompanying grin did not cheer me up.

"Not for long. We soon began to find things in common."

"It's like that is it?" my annoying astute twin said, an interested gleam in his eyes.

I refused to get pulled into the argument. "Okay, was that all?"

"Yeah." Cristaldo turned to leave, then glanced back at me. "You know what they say about never trusting a witch, right?"

My ire burned bright and I had to stop myself from saying the wrong thing.

"Enough said on that subject." I pushed his words of warning away even as they resonated in a primal part of my brain I would never admit to.

"Fine, just know I warned you."

I stalked back down the hallway to the spa, but found it deserted. Where had she gotten to? I began a quick search of the kitchen, then opened every door down the long hallway checking for her.

"Isadora, where are you?" I shouted, worry making my shoulders twitch with annoyance.

A faint voice resonated and I hurried toward the balcony that overlooked the strip.

"What are you doing out here?" I demanded, worried about her catching a chill in the night air.

She looked so beautiful in the moonlight, her skin like marble, her hair flowing around her with a life all its own. She'd pulled on a white robe, her waist looking impossibly tiny where she tied the gown snugly around her body. It was the haunted look in her eyes that scared me though.

"What's wrong?" I rushed to her side, embracing her.

"Nothing. Just a touch of nostalgia," she said.

"You know there's nothing you can't share with me, right?"

She hugged me tighter, her words muffled against my chest. "I know. I just want to remember everything that happens now."

Maybe the pregnancy was already affecting her hormones, causing a touch of melancholia? "You should get some rest. Big day coming up."

"Good idea."

Taking her arm, I escorted her to the master bedroom and tucked her into my bed.

"Sleep now." I tenderly brushed a strand of hair away from her face, feeling an emotion I had never experienced before. I lay down beside her naked and spooned her from behind when she turned on her side facing away from me.

Soon her soft breathing told me she was sound asleep. As I held her close, I found that letting go eluded me. Instead, I lay and breathed in her essence, full of wonderment of how very much my life had changed this week. A twinge of fear course through me that this precious moment could disappear in a split-second if I didn't keep my hand on the throttle. Problem was, I wanted to let go, to enjoy this time. Did I dare?

Chapter Twenty-Two

Isadora

I awoke with a start, not knowing where I was. Too many changes of late messing with my brain? Memories of the night before came flooding back, bringing heat to my skin, remembering the wild passion Lucius and I had intimately shared. That was just before the wondrous fragrance of bacon captured my full attention, making me jump up and head to the bathroom to deal with nature.

Following the scent trail, I discovered Lucius in the kitchen again, expertly flipping pancakes and frying bacon. Glasses of orange juice sat at two precisely laid-out place settings, while a single red rose in a crystal vase added a sweet touch. The pure normalcy of the scene brought tears to my eyes I determinedly shook away.

"Morning, beautiful." Lucius' sexy and happy smile further unsettled me. "I thought you'd be hungry after last night." His eyes lit up with a passion that made my breath hitch.

"Morning, sexy," I said, savoring the view of him in just his boxer shorts. "Yum, you look good enough to eat. Not worried about that hot grease splattering you?"

"Nah, it wouldn't dare." He turned to turn off the elements on the stove and plated the food.

"Sit. Eat."

"Aye, captain," I teased, my mouth rising into a grin of its own accord. Could it really be this easy? Or was it just Lucius making me feel so at home? If I wasn't careful, I was going to get into such deep trouble there would be no way out. A slight fluttering in my stomach drew my full attention away from worrying and I pressed one hand against my body. But then I realized it had to be gas—no way would my precious bundle of cells be anything more than that yet, right?

"Everything okay?" Lucius set the two plates down in front of us.

"Of course," I lied. I picked up my fork and took a bite. "Heavenly."

He grinned, looking almost boyish. "Great. Eat up. We've got a busy day ahead."

"Yeah?" I gave him my most wicked smile, swallowing a morsel of delicious food. "And here I was hoping for more between-the-sheets time."

Sparks erupted between us, seeming to jump the distance and sear my very flesh.

"I think we can fit that it as well. Soon as you've cleaned your plate."

"What is it with you and feeding me?" I said in a lighter tone, my system bombarded with the urgent need to throw myself at him.

"I want you strong and healthy. You are my focus now, today and every day. Get used to it, beautiful."

My throat thickened with emotion. "A gal could get real used to that."

"Good."

I quickly finished my plate and held it out to him. I had about licked it clean. "Now can I have my dessert?"

In a flash we were in each other's arms, kissing, caressing, murmuring sweet nothings with hot, searching lips pressed against the other's flesh. My body lit up, desperate to be joined with this man. Dishes clattered to the floor as he swept them out of the way. He picked me up and sat me down on the tabletop.

Pushing aside my panties, he entered me in a single thrust, his huge cock instantly filling me and driving me backward onto the hard surface. The sensation of mating with Lucius was so intense I lost track of everything. Him pounding into me like he wanted to stay connected forever allowed me the freedom to just let go. To enjoy every single stroke of him. To feel my world aligning and making sense.

When we climaxed, it was as one. I took in his hot essence and it satiated me like nothing that could ever be described. I moaned aloud with the overwhelming lust that had consumed us. This was being alive like nothing else in the world could ever be.

With difficulty I kept my tears at bay. What was it with our mating? The sensations were too raw, too real, and tears seemed the only outlet for all that was consuming me.

"Dessert beats my cooking all to hell," he whispered against my neck, making me give a hiccup of a chuckle. The scents of breakfast still lingering in the air now combined with the spicy fragrance of our recent mating.

"I don't know. That was some fine feast," I countered.

He kissed me then, the raw emotion in his eyes taking my breath away.

"You are all the feast I need."

"Hmm, you can have all you want but I still think you'll need to eat real food from time to time."

"You feed parts of me that I never knew were hungry," he said with simple honesty.

Tears flooded my eyes. No. This was too much. *How could I lie to this good man?*

I was about to tell him. Spill all my secrets. Then his cell phone rang and saved me. Or damned me—I'd never know. But the interruption must have been meant to be and I kept everything hidden inside while he pulled away and answered the phone.

"Lucius," he barked before waiting for a minute for the other person to speak.

"Of course, we'll be delighted to see Uncle Sergio and Aunt Ava tonight. Yes, I know, Mother. And she's looking forward to meeting you too. Yes, I'll tell her." His voice had changed, even his body language becoming softer.

I grinned at the exchange. A son who obviously respected his mother was high on my list.

Lucius hung up. "I hope you're prepared for this. I think my mother has invited the entire Luceres clan to our dinner tonight. It's now going to be held in the ballroom with a live orchestra—and the first dance is ours."

"Ballroom? Dancing?" The words lacked substance. I was so stuck in survival mode that such frivolous pursuits didn't compute in the haunted recesses of my brain.

"Yes, beautiful. You do remember how to dance, right? If my memory serves me correctly, we swept the competition out of the water in the Shetlands."

"Ahh—yeah. Why is the first dance ours?" We had been awesome together that night. But it was also what had landed us in our current predicament.

"Just traditional when introducing a new member of the family. Nothing to worry about. We've got to go shopping today. I want to buy you the most beautiful ballgown imaginable."

"Hold on. Isn't that a bit extreme? I mean, we've just met and all?" My head was spinning with confusion.

"Our relationship has been on steroids since the very beginning. Hell, you're already pregnant with my baby. Might as well let the family know how serious we are."

"Is everyone going to be okay with my being born a witch?" Guilt struck even as I said the words. Was I dissing my own kind just in asking?

Lucius growled. "They'd better be, or they'll answer to me."

His sense of honor and level of trust in us only made me feel worse. How was I going to navigate this minefield that was getting wider by the minute?

"Okay, let's finish up here and hit the stores. I want you finding the most beautiful of gowns before all my female relatives snap them up in a shopping frenzy no one should be subject to." He gave a faux shudder. "Unless you'd rather have a designer of your choice come by with samples?"

"No, going out would be good." A change of scenery might help, get my mind busy with other occupations other than the dismal truth. I needed to find that damn cup already and get the hell out of here. I'd have lots of time to heal a broken heart languishing in a well-protected and hidden safe zone. That was, if it could be healed. It didn't help that I'd read somewhere that elephants die of broken hearts on occasion, refusing to leave the side of a dead mate. I jumped up, needing to do something, *anything* to stop the damn thinking already. Even shopping, which was not normally my thing.

"Great. Can you be ready in fifteen minutes?"

"Duh. Just try me!" I ran from the room, delighted to hear Lucius hot on my trail. Breathless, I rushed into the bathroom and stripped off my clothes, leaving them in a heap in the middle of the floor. In seconds he had done the same and we entered the rainforest-like shower together. *A tropical paradise.*

"This is good," I said, the soft water anointing my limbs. Of course, it didn't hurt that he was helping me at every stage, using his talented hands to massage shampoo into my hair then assisting in the rinsing before dedicating himself to washing every part of me so thoroughly that I'd never been more squeaky clean.

"My turn." I went to work on his six-pack, enjoying the lustful thrill of running my soapy hands over his magnificent body. His cock stood out proud from his groin and rubbed against my thighs as I worked. "So soon, big guy," I teased. "Maybe we'd better review that timeline?"

"I could make love to you all day, beautiful. I think we have time for one more," he murmured as he got to his knees to plant a full-on kiss on my waiting lips. And I don't mean on my face, but much, much farther down.

"Oh yeah!" I screamed as my body, still sensitive from the happy go in the kitchen, immediately prepared itself to undergo the exquisite torture of yet another glorious orgasm. "Right there! Oh yes, keep it up. *Yes!*"

Fifteen minutes later than planned, we finally managed to get some clothes on, even if it spoiled the view. I could look at that man all day.

"What's your favorite color?" Lucius asked as we stood in front of an obviously insanely expensive store on the Strip, Entrancing Fashions Boutique.

"Purple," I said without hesitation. "Yours?"

"Ah, a member of royalty in our midst," he teased. "I could definitely see you perched high on a throne. Maybe for our vows we can get matching thrones."

"What do you mean for our vows?" My heart literally stopped beating for a few seconds. This had gone *way* too far.

He frowned. "You are aware that you're carrying my child? I would never let a child of mine be born without legal parentage. How you want to do it—that's a woman's domain. But we will be doing it—long before the baby makes an appearance or even pushes out that nice flat stomach I love to kiss."

I had no comeback. What could I say to that other than to delay the process as long as possible? And no way would it happen this week, anyway—occasions like Lucius was talking about took weeks, if not months to plan. I was safe, for now.

"What? Speechless now? That mouth of yours was so busy scolding me earlier this week I thought you'd have a lot to say on the subject of marriage." He leaned down and kissed me right there on the street. A wonderous kiss that made my toes curl in my shoes.

I found my voice finally and tried for a lighter approach. "Going to cost you a bundle—an event like that. Hope you're up for it?"

"Or we could just elope? Head on over to the justice of the peace and have done with it right now. I'm game if you are." The mischievous look on his face made me swallow hard. Oh Goddess, but he was going to be so hurt.

I shook my head back and forth a few times with my eyes closed, as much to dispel the image of Lucius as much as to say what needed to be said. "No, I want it done right with all the bells and whistles, not a shotgun wedding in Vegas."

"Then that's what it will be, milady. Now, let's shop. I can't wait to see you in some sexy formal gown with a split right up to your hip."

"Sure that's the way you want to go? Others might find that look enticing as well." I began to search through a promising rack of glittering gowns as I spoke.

A deep growl alerted me to the fact I'd gone too far. He pulled me into his arms and took me by the chin, forcing me to meet his eyes. "If anyone looks at you wrong or says anything at all, you come to me. I'll take care of it. You're under my protection now and soon as we announce ourselves the better, then any other wolf had better keep his eyes and hands where I can see them."

"Jealous much?" I teased, capturing my bottom lip between my teeth.

"No. But that's the way I operate. Might as well know it up front."

"Gotcha," I said. "Now can we get back to dress shopping? I want to get my hair done today as well."

"What? Your hair is perfect the way it is."

"Right, hanging all over the place and getting in the way. I want to make a good first impression with an elegant updo to match an elegant gown tonight."

He blew out a breath. "Women. Never realize that just looking plain is the best look of all."

"Plain! That's a terrible compliment," I exaggerated my comeback to full effect.

"I didn't mean that you're plain. Hell, you're the most beautiful woman I've ever met."

I swallowed hard again, enjoying his chagrin before letting him off the hook. "Aww, thanks. You are definitely the most attractive man I've ever met."

"Our baby is going to be so beautiful. I won't be letting her date until she's thirty at least." The hard look in his eyes suggested he was not entirely joking.

"Okay, proud papa. Maybe we'd better concentrate on the matter at hand?"

"I'm going to announce our intentions tonight. Let everyone make of it what they will. Any objections to that?"

"I guess not." Long as it wasn't an official ceremony. I didn't need that extra burden to bear—dishonoring my vows.

"Good. Then we have another place to hit before we head back to the hotel."

"Not to mention that hair salon."

"Fine. Just don't go too fancy. I want to be able to run my hands through those luscious long locks when we get home. Breathe in that natural fragrance of yours that drives me wild."

Oh crap. *Home.* The word hit me hard in the gut and I had to steel myself to look at gowns that my eyes couldn't seem to focus on, hard as I tried.

"How about this one?" Lucius pulled out a silky purple number cut to a deep v in the front and held it up for inspection. The flowing chiffon skirt was a nice touch. with a gold border of mosaic design stitched around the hem.

January Bain

I forced myself to check out the gown like it mattered. "Sure. I like it." It could have been burlap for all I cared. Well, I wasn't being totally truthful—I did care a little bit that his family not find me wanting, at least in those things I had control over.

A young woman rushed up and took the dress from Lucius. "I'll start a dressing room for you. So nice to see you again, Mr. Luceres." She bestowed a winning smile on Lucius.

"This one looks good too." He took out another purple dress, only strapless this time with a silvery overlay patterned into flowing vines that danced around the skirt.

The pretty girl took if from him, her eyes lingering on his face. "We haven't seen you in here for a while. I guess you've been pretty busy, huh?"

"Yes." He continued to make his way carefully through the rack, adding to the growing pile in the clerk's arms.

I, however, was keeping a close watch on the female eyeing my soon-to-be fiancé like he was good enough to eat for lunch. I might or might not have had a touch of malice in my eyes. It didn't help that, other than a cursory glance, I was being totally ignored by said female. She was following him like she was the world's cutest puppy. *Goddess, give me the strength.*

"I heard your twin brother got married? Must have been amazing. He's so tall, dark and handsome. Just like you. All the Luceres men are so awesome." The store worker sighed heavily, like she was having an orgasm right there.

"You know what would be more amazing? If you would set up that room you've been promising," I said, adding a death-ray glare for good measure. I wouldn't stoop to using my magical powers on such an adoring fan. *Couldn't rule it out either.*

"I'll be right back, Lucius. I want to be as much help as I can. Anything you need, I'm the girl for you." She then batted her fake eyelashes like she was a character in *Gone with the Wind* and gave me a baleful look.

A discreet hand gesture and low and behold, the roof right above the girl's head began to hurl torrents of streaming water down on her and it wasn't even raining outside. *Funny that.*

"She's a bit young and inexperienced for any of the Luceres," Lucius said over the squeals of the clerk who rushed out of the way but not before she was soaking wet. I'd give her points for holding the garments away from her body so they wouldn't get drenched. The waterfall was very location specific. *When I'm good, I'm good. But when I'm bad, look out.* But this was just a bit of harmless fun.

"Phttt. The way she was throwing herself at you, I have my doubts she's that innocent," I countered. I could hear the young girl talking angrily with someone on the phone as we continued shopping, probably complaining to the manager. At least she had lots of choices available right where she worked for a dry set of clothing.

"You are so beautiful when you're angry, you know that?"

"I'm not angry! I just want to buy a gown in peace without the clerk hitting on my man."

"Your man, is it? I like the sound of that."

What am I thinking! I was supposed to be grown-up about what this week was all about and not let a silly emotion like jealousy rear its head. I landed with a thud.

"Okay. Time to try these on," I said with a sigh, ending the discussion. I stomped into the dressing room and began the annoying process of removing clothing and redressing, something I'd never been fond of. If the first gown worked, I was out of here.

"I want to see each choice, Isadora," Lucius instructed from just beyond the closed door. I knew then he had taken a chair in the gallery where he could watch the fashion show.

"Fine," I said between gritted teeth. I shimmied out of my sundress and pulled on the first violet gown, enjoying the sensuous touch of the fabric against my skin in spite of my mood. Okay. The fact it was very flattering was confirmed by my reflection in the full length, three-sixty mirrors that lined the huge dressing room including the closed door.

I stepped back out into the store proper and gave a twirl. "This is it. I love this one."

"Very nice. But I need some comparisons. Next." He waved a hand at me and I about lost it.

"I don't have time for this!" I protested.

"And I always have time to see my woman dressed to perfection." He raised an eyebrow at me.

What in the hell could I say to that?

"Just two more," I said, setting my limit.

"Five," he said, a grin beginning to manifest itself.

"Three," I countered, beginning to enjoy the exchange.

"Okay, you win."

Huh, not really. I had to undress and redress three more times. I about-faced and re-entered the dressing room.

Thirty minutes later we had a winner bought from a subdued clerk with wet hair and dry clothing. Well, she would get a nice commission for selling the expensive item, right? We'd chosen the very first dress Lucius had pulled out and the first one I'd tried on. It made me feel like a queen with its plunging neckline and gold Aztec design around the hem that caught the light as I walked. The gown bestowed enough confidence that I should be able to manage the meet and greet tonight with flair.

"We have time to hit the jewelry store before your hair and makeup appointment," Lucius said.

"Right." I plastered a happy smile on my face. Meanwhile I was dying slowly on the inside. The Goddess might forgive me for my transgressions against this man, but I never would.

Chapter Twenty-Three

Lucius

There was something that she wasn't sharing, something so important that it was eating away at her. We were too close now for me not to read her body language. I longed to read her thoughts, though that normally only happened after final vows, holding nothing back from the other. But what was my beautiful witch hiding? I had done everything to reassure Isadora, short of taking her to the preacher man today and have done with it.

But I understood her need for a fancy wedding. She'd only be doing it once and I wanted to provide her with wonderful memories for all the years of our lives. But she was hiding something. It ate at something deep inside me as well. I could only hope her worry would fade with time, that I would be able to give her enough faith in us to let it happen.

"I don't want anything too ostentatious, okay? Just because you're as rich as sin doesn't mean I want to flaunt it." Isadora set an impossible rule as I escorted her into the most expensive jewelry store in Vegas.

"You know, maybe I should go back and apologize to that girl? I did rather overreact."

I gave a snort. "You think? But no, if you do, she'll know you're a witch. Probably best to keep that secret. It was just a little water. No real harm done."

"I want to be a better role model for my daughter from now on. Wow, never thought that having a baby could change things so much. It's like the blinders have come off my eyes."

"True. I know what you mean." I reached for her hand and gave it a gentle squeeze. "I feel the same way."

She frowned and I took it to mean she was feeling badly about her actions with the clerk.

"Don't worry about it. Learning from our mistakes is what life is all about."

She turned away and began to studiously study the velvet-lined case with all the glittering engagement rings.

"These are all so fancy. I want something quieter, less all up in your face."

"Whatever you want. Just so long as it declares you mine."

"I'm not a possession, Lucius! In fact, I want to buy you an engagement gift too. How about a ring through the nose?"

Her angry tirade pushed me off balance. Was it the pregnancy hormones? One minute she was fine and now she was in some strange place. I scrubbed a hand over my face, considering what to say.

"I don't think you're a possession, Isadora. I want you to be my partner in life."

"Right! No man is that generous. They always have a hidden agenda in my experience." She crossed her arms over her chest, shutting me out.

"What are you talking about? Haven't I been there for you? Well, since we connected on the island anyway. I cleaned up my act for you, let you into my life—"

"Let me in to your life! How very generous of you!"

Her skin had flushed and her eyes were glinting fire. Was I about to be dowsed in a torrent of water or something worse? The thought made me uncomfortable that when things went south in our relationship, she might resort to witchcraft. It wasn't something I wanted to ever see happen. Not with us. We were special. *Chosen.*

"Where is this coming from? What's the matter?" I pulled her to a quieter corner of the store. "Are you not feeling well? Is it the baby?"

"I'm fine. The baby's fine. I just—I don't know, okay?"

"Just breathe. No need to rush this. We can come back another time. Would you like something to eat or drink maybe?"

"No. Let's get this over with."

I frowned. This did not sound right. Didn't women normally enjoy ring shopping?

"How about we go to the coffee shop across the street and I surprise you with the perfect ring tonight? Would that make you happy?"

What was wrong with this picture? I hardly recognized myself. My alpha-ness was slipping. I needed to get to the bottom of things before it got any worse. But having no manual on how to deal with a pregnant female was about the worst thing that had happened to me. Give me a fight to the death in the pit any day over this situation.

Then I grinned. Ah, but it would be all worth it. Soon we'd be a family. If I survived the interim. Who was I kidding? I was an enforcer for the pack. Getting through this should be a breeze, once I'd consulted with my mother. Surely, she would have some ideas on how to handle the situation?

"Fine. Let's go."

Five minutes later I had Isadora safely housed in a booth with lots of caffeine and sugary treats. I'd worry about the health benefits later. Right now, I just wanted her to feel better.

She gave me a look before beginning to fold and unfold her napkin. "I want to apologize for my uncalled-for behavior. You've been nothing but kind to me." She took a deep breath. "I'm sorry, Lucius."

I waved her words away, though they did touch me. "No problem. I know you've been through a lot."

She snorted. "You have no idea." She took a sip of her coffee and grabbed a chocolate donut, biting in to it with a look of ecstasy on her pretty face. "I love the chocolate ones."

I let her finish the donut in peace. "What's going on with you? Is Lucifer giving you more grief?"

She nabbed another donut, probably to keep from having to answer.

"Is Lucifer and his demands the problem?" I asked again, my own coffee sitting untouched.

She gave me an inscrutable glance. "Ever wonder what your life would have been like if you'd been born into a different family? Because I did, all the years I was growing up. I kept thinking my real parents were out there some place, heartbroken that I was missing from their lives."

"I think all kids that have it tough think that. But no, I was always happy to be a Luceres. Even happier now that we're about to become a family. I want to spend the rest of my life making yours the best it can be. But I can't, if you don't tell me all that's bothering you."

She grimaced and daintily wiped the crumbs from her plush lips with a paper napkin. "Not that I would change having a sister and brother. Elena and Ian are both great. And my mother meant well. It was just such heavy obligations so young, you know. But you've been the enforcer of your pack for years. Obligations must be practically your middle name."

I shrugged. "It's different. I always knew my role growing up and was happy to do what I could to keep my pack safe. You had obligations thrust on you. I think it's time we negotiated with the guy. We have more than enough money to buy anyone off."

"It's not money he wants. He trades in souls."

"Well, he can't have yours. So quit doing his bidding. I'll back you all the way. I'll tear him limb from limb before I'll let him harm you. We need to set up a parlay, so I can have access to him. See where things stand." I leaned forward in the booth and grasped eagerly her hands. Now we were getting somewhere.

"If only it was that easy." She looked undecided. I was certain she was about to break her silence. Good, it was time. Now I could help and be her knight in shining armor. Something I'd never dreamed I'd want to be so badly.

Chapter Twenty-Four

Isadora

Time's almost up, witch. You want to keep your family safe, come to me before sunrise tomorrow with the girl in tow.

Breathe. I pulled my hands away from Lucius, Lucifer's words ringing like a death knell in my mind. The bastard loved his announcements, using words like a medieval executioner's lash. "I need to use the ladies' room. Be right back."

Why had he shortened the deadline all of a sudden? *Right.* He must have gotten wind I was weakening.

I quickly used the facilities, then splashed cold water on my hot skin. My stomach roiled with nerves as I patted my skin dry. The mirror reflected my devastation. I had to get my act together, steal the damn chalice already and head back to Egypt on the next available plane. I pulled out my phone and began furiously setting up arrangements for travel. I would need all the good luck charms ever invented to pull this off.

When I had calmed down enough to face my wolf again, I made my way back to the booth.

"Everything okay?" he asked. He still had that look of expectation on his handsome face and it tugged hard at me.

"Sure, all good. I think I should hit that hair salon now."

I didn't look him in the eyes as I spoke, not wanting him to see the truth of it. I was definitely *not* fine and would most likely never be again. I had to get off this insane merry-go-round. It was tearing me apart and was not good for my unborn daughter.

It was my responsibility to keep everyone safe now. Even the House of Luceres had no idea who they were really dealing with when it came to Lucifer. He could attack anywhere. Any time. I wanted Lucius far away from my problems, more than ever. Even if his whole family would despise me for my actions.

He sighed. "Okay. Let's go."

The rest of the day passed in a whirlwind. Never had I wanted to slow down time more. Before I knew it, it was time for the party. I checked my appearance in the mirror with only minutes to go before I was expected to appear, uncaring that I looked better than I ever had. The hair, makeup and dress were perfection. Under any other circumstances, I would be ecstatic. But now I just felt dead inside, focused solely on stealing the chalice and getting away. I sat on the edge of the bed, using all my energy to slip into a deep meditational state. I sent out an inquiry into the universe, visualizing what I wanted. The precious cup made from the blood and bone of the first wolf. *Where are you? Show yourself.*

I had waited to do this until now, knowing I would be on Lucifer's radar for using my remote viewing power. Once he knew what I was after it, he would know something unusual was afoot. I could only pray he would wait, thinking I was offering it to him as homage to make amends, not force me down to the underworld until I had the chance to escape.

An image came to mind, indistinct at first, then clearing to show a rather simple-looking drinking vessel encased by four gray-colored cement walls. It was hard to believe the awesome magical powers the simple cup contained. The vision moved backward slowly to show a larger frame of reference. It was in the penthouse, Cristaldo's and Everly's floor, hidden in a wall safe behind an image.

Ah. The painting was by Peter Lik. *Phantom*. I loved the image he'd created. *So otherworldly and awe-inspiring, the perfect place to hide the Lupus Sanguis Chalice.* The mechanism that opened the safe was complicated, two locks and two fingerprints needed. The House of Luceres wasn't taking the protection of the cup lightly. As impossible as it seemed, I had a plan.

A sudden noise made my heart skitter. Lucius stood in the doorway. We stared at one another for a few seconds. Did he suspect something?

I got up and made myself relax, stood before him. "You look very handsome." Indeed, he did in his impeccable black tux and smoothly brushed hair.

"Your beauty takes my breath away. I wish I were a poet and could capture it in words. Instead, I'm going to have a thousand photos taken of you and the best one chosen for your portrait."

"A thousand?" I tried for a lighter tone but even I could hear the stress in my voice. I cleared my throat. "Only if you're in them too, Lucius."

He reached for my fingers and took them in his far larger, far warmer ones. "No, I want one of you from floor to ceiling, even if no artist on this planet can possibly capture your beauty. One with silver-tipped angel wings, I think. But I will always carry your image in here." He tapped his chest with one hand as if he were making his vow right then and there.

"As I always will too, for all my days," I said, feeling the true connection of us in the moment before turning away and fussing with the skirt of my gown to avoid his gaze.

The words hung between us, both spoken in truth, words capable of tearing the other to pieces when promises were broken. But the truth would always be there. We were meant to be Forever Mates, but life was getting in the way, setting us up for failure.

Why? Why had it come to this? Was it a test? A cruel situation thought up by demons? Was Lucifer somehow behind this? He was a mastermind, capable of controlling the universe. Well, it was no matter. I would do what I had to, keep everyone safe physically, even if it meant breaking their heart. But the worst part was a daughter who might never know her father.

"Time to go, beautiful. I want you to enjoy tonight. My family will welcome you, so I don't want you to worry about that. And once they hear about our daughter, they will be celebrating for weeks." He wrapped his arms around my waist and pulled me against him.

"But you won't tell them that tonight, right?" I panicked, imagining it. "It would raise all sorts of questions. Like how we could know so soon?"

"Fine. But I want you to know how proud I am of us—of you. Hold your head high, Isadora, you have nothing to apologize for." He bent down and kissed my lips, making the world fall away.

I clung to him, not wanting to let go. This might be the last time we were ever alone together. I shivered and pressed even closer.

"Are you cold, little one?"

He'd never called me that before and it brought a rush of tears to my eyes that I blinked away.

"No, I'm fine. We should go." *While I still can.*

"They'll wait for the guest of honor." But he did let me go and offered his arm. "Shall we, milady?"

"Oh, what about the ring?" I asked as we stepped out of the room. He'd said he was going to give it to me tonight and I wanted to wear it, thinking maybe it would bring me good luck for the terrible adventure that awaited me. *A small connection to the past when everything was perfect.*

"Later. I have something planned."

"I don't want a fuss," I warned. *Please let it happen before I have to steal the damn cup and escape.*

"I thought every woman wanted a fuss?" He smiled at me, his good humor intact.

"Not this woman. I like things to go as peacefully and smoothly as possible."

He laughed aloud at that pronouncement, his eyes alight with merriment. "You could have fooled me earlier this week."

"Well, I've changed," I said a bit huffily, striding beside him down the hallway.

"Yes, and for the better. I promise not to make too much of a fuss, all right. But can you blame me? Finding a woman like you? I want to shout it from the rooftops."

"Look. I'm not that special, okay? I have my faults." My protests fell on deaf ears.

"Say what you will, you're perfect for me." He pressed the button for the ballroom on the control panel inside the elevator.

I'm so far from perfect I should be allowed a do-over. "My whole life's been a lurch from one crisis to another, much as I've hated that. So please, don't expect miracles from me." *In fact, best to not expect anything at all.*

"I just want you to be yourself. No expectations beyond living in the moment, enjoying getting to know each other better." He hugged me again, rubbing my back in soothing strokes.

"Lucius, there's something else you should know about me."

The doors of the elevator opened just then, revealing a crowd of milling faces, all dressed to the nines in glittering gowns and tuxedoes.

"Hold that thought. We have the rest of our lives to get to know one another. Mother, Father, I want you to meet, Isadora Molay Champagne."

"But it's really important. You need to know —"

An older, very handsome and expensively dressed couple came forward to greet us, stopping my words.

"Isadora Molay Champagne, may I present my parents, Cesare and Sophia of the House of Luceres."

My face heated as I worked to control myself, to hide my discomfort at betraying their son. Cesare and Sophia both had such penetrating dark eyes, like they could see right into a person's soul. I prayed they couldn't see into mine. Was it tainted with all the interactions with the devil himself? Their son deserved so much better than me. I took a deep breath and held out my hand to shake. Instead, his mother stepped forward and embraced me.

"Welcome to the family, Isadora. I'm very pleased to meet you." She pulled back and patted my hand. "Finally, someone has decided to take on my Lucius. Not an easy task, I warn you. He's always been the quiet one, the sensitive one, hiding his true feelings behind his necessary work as an enforcer. Be good to my boy, that's all I can ask. Promise me that and we will be the best of friends."

The look she gave me then pierced the depths of my being. I swallowed, unable to answer her, floundering for a proper response.

"Mother, Isadora doesn't need to promise to do anything. She's a good woman and my choice. That should be enough." Lucius coming to my rescue hurt all the more.

"Of course." She reached over and pushed a lock of hair that had fallen forward off her son's forehead. A tender gesture that tore me asunder. "I just want a woman to love you for you, Lucius. To know you like I do. To promise to protect that tender heart." She pressed her elegant hand against his chest.

"Isadora has no intentions of doing anything untoward. Just because she's a witch, no need to think anything other than she's a good woman who's been through more than enough in her life already. She wants peace and quiet just like I do. Well, not too much peace and quiet. We do have our moments." His remarks were punctuated with a boyish grin.

"Welcome to the family, Isadora. Am I to understand that you are related to the Templar Knight's last Grand Master, Jacques de Molay?" His father stepped forward and I was thankful for the interruption. He kissed me on both cheeks in the traditional greeting.

"Thank you, and yes, I am a descendent of Jacques de Molay," I said, kissing him back. His aftershave tickled my nose and I had to suppress a sneeze, ending up making a weird, snuffling sound.

"I told you not to use that new cologne, Cesare," Sophia said. Her admonishing her husband, even though we were separate from the other guests at the moment, surprised me. This group of werewolves had a lot better structure than others I had met. A yearning pang that I was never going to be a part of it going forward made me rub my forehead in a self-soothing gesture.

"Do you have a headache?" Lucius asked, instantly concerned.

"No, I'm fine. Just a bit tired is all." I was not fine. In a way I was glad that Lucifer had shortened the deadline. This was murder. Wanting to stay, but having to go.

"We won't stay longer than necessary. Can I get you anything? Water or a soft drink?" he asked.

"Maybe some wine or champagne would settle your stomach?" Sophia asked.

"No alcohol, thanks."

"Aww, that is lovely news. Congratulations, my dear! I thought you were glowing. My instincts were correct," Sophia said, her expression proud as punch.

She hugged and kissed me again, whispering in my ear. "Don't you dare hurt my son or I will have you for breakfast, witch. Nod if you understand?"

I nodded, my throat tightening. Her warning had at least taken the too-bright glow off the introductions. But I understood. If anyone messed with my child, I would fight tooth and nail against the perpetrator. *Goddess, I'm so damned.* Had any woman in the history of the world known what to do when faced with a similar choice? *If they have, please send them to me, show me how to make this right. Stop. Thinking.*

Okay, I hear you. My plan was solid. One foot in front of the other—just do what must be done.

"Are you sure you're up for this?" Lucius asked.

"Of course." I gave him my brightest, fakest smile.

"Come. I want you to meet all my children," Sophia said.

A whirlwind followed. So many faces, so little time to absorb it all. When dinner was announced, I had a headache for real.

"You're a bit pale, beautiful. Come, sit down beside me," Lucius said.

Just then Cristaldo interrupted us, leaning in and whispering in his brother's ear.

"Right now? Couldn't it wait? Isadora is famished and I want to see her fed."

"Do you mind, Isadora? I just need my brother for a few minutes. I promise to return him safe and sound."

"Of course. Go right ahead. I'll just have an appetizer while you're busy."

"If you're sure?" Lucius got to his feet, kissed me for the last time on the cheek, and strode off with Cristaldo from the ballroom. Soon as they were out of sight, I got to my feet.

"If you'll excuse me, I need to visit the ladies' room," I said. Lucius' mother had taken the chair next to me. Cesare sat at the head of the table, the obvious center of attention by all the looks being bestowed by the crowd.

"Of course, dear," Sophia said.

I felt eyes penetrating my back as I hurried from the room. I didn't have much time. Just enough to grab the cup and hightail it to the airport. The plane was leaving within ninety minutes and catching it was my only hope to save everyone from Lucifer's wrath.

I stood outside the penthouse office, listening. "When are you two tying the knot?"

"I haven't officially asked her to marry me yet, bro. Give a guy a chance."

The sounds of the safe being opened. *Now.* It had to be now.

"Dragon breath and Merlin sight, I command Avalon to blend the mist, hide my presence from sight, my scent obscured by night." I repeated the mantra two more times while power gathered and welled up from deep inside me.

A vortex of light and shadow danced and swirled in the air, layers of camouflage patterning itself against my body, making me blend into the surroundings. The ghost of my grandmother blinked then vanished in an instant on the edge of my vision and I had her blessing. No doubt she would do the same to see me safe.

I pushed the stopwatch app on my smartphone and slowly moved into the office where Cristaldo was holding the famous chalice, studying it with intense interest. "It looks so plain, yet it has such great power to save lives."

"Right. Let's get it to the House of Anche. I have an important announcement and I don't want any more delays."

I swallowed, knowing exactly what Lucius was talking about. If only I could stay, live the fairy tale. But it wasn't for the likes of me. Advancing ever closer, my mind turned to more practical concerns, I began praying no one would catch my scent, something notoriously difficult to hide from a werewolf. Though that would not be enough to stop me, it would forever change how Lucius saw me. As it was, I had left a note for him in his bedroom, trying to explain things as best I could. Not that he would ever understand. But I did owe him an explanation.

Lucius froze, his eyes moving about the room, his expression mystified. "Did someone just walk in here?"

I wanted to whisper in his ear. *I will always love you.* But I couldn't take the chance.

"You seeing ghosts now, bro?" Cristaldo teased, setting the cup down on the office desk, then turning and dealing with the safe.

I immediately picked up the chalice, knowing as soon as I touched it that the cup would vanish from view enabled by the magic swirling around me. Now I had to move like the wind because it only lasted ten precious minutes and Lucifer would know within seconds I had called upon it. That was, if I was on his radar at the moment — the guy had lots of others to track as well. But he'd either be wanting me to bring the precious artifact to him or demand to know why I wanted it.

My only hope was to keep moving and ignore him until I was safe in Egypt, hidden by Cleopatra. I raced from the room and ran down the hallway.

I couldn't chance the elevator, so I hit the stairs, running full bore, the cup cradled against my chest. Two flights down and I cranked a left and took the elevator to the lobby. It was a long way to run from the penthouse and I didn't want to exhaust myself.

My phone dinged. Only five minutes until the spell wore off. I had programmed it earlier, counting down the minutes until all would be revealed.

Outside the Glitter Palace, I raced down the sidewalk, heading for a place to hide while I called for a taxi to take me to the airport.

Chapter Twenty-Five

Lucius

I will always love you.

One second, I swore I could hear Isadora whisper her love for me, then the cup vanished in front of my eyes. A terrible sense of betrayal froze the marrow in my bones, slithered down my spine like an alien creature consuming my life. The cup had well and truly disappeared. Only one person who had the power to pull off a vanishing spell of that magnitude.

Isadora. She'd played us. She'd wanted the cup all along. My god *why*, when I would have given her anything? The whole world, if she'd asked for it.

"What the hell just happened?" Cristaldo asked, his face swamped by astonishment and disbelief.

Did I admit it or hide it? Give her a chance to explain before calling her out to the family? *No coming back from that.* She'd be branded a traitorous witch for all time. That I couldn't endure. Not the mother of my child. I rubbed the back of my neck, the muscles held tight by tension. *Why, Isadora? Why have you done this to us?*

"I don't know. I'm as in the dark as much as you are. But I'm going to get to the bottom of this, that I swear."

"Shit. What am I going to tell the House of Anche? That we lost the cup right before our very eyes? We'll look like idiots! And who's going to believe it anyway?"

I had to head this off. If I didn't, everyone in the ballroom would know what had happened. I wanted to get to her first, find out why she'd betrayed me if nothing else. *Make her say it to my face.*

"I think I know what happened. You wait here. I'm going after it."

"What do you mean? Tell me what you know. And what the hell do I tell the Anche?" Cristaldo looked worried, his frown creased with concern.

"Make up a story. Tell them someone else borrowed it or the safe got damaged and we're drilling it to get it out. I don't care. I'll be back as soon as I can. Just hold the fort until I get back."

"Call me. Keep me updated. I don't know how long I can keep the truth hidden, Lucius." Cristaldo suspected what had happened but was going to give me the chance to fix it. I heard it in his voice and saw it in his eyes. A sense of gratitude for his loyalty helped the horrid sense of betrayal I was undergoing.

"Of course." I embraced my brother, then made a quick exit, heading for the airport. I realized now what I hadn't wanted to when I was in Egypt. Isadora had made some kind of deal with the Egyptian vampires of Alexandria. Who else on the planet wanted to raise the dead more than Cleopatra?

The airport was crowded, making looking for her difficult. I pushed to the front of the line, uncaring of the angry stares I was receiving in return. This was an emergency. Any one of them would do the same.

"I need to book a flight leaving for Alexandria, Egypt."

The middle-aged clerk looked uncomfortable, pointedly looking behind me at the line I had just circumvented.

"Ah, sir—"

"Lucius of the House of Luceres. We own the Glitter Palace, among other things. Perhaps you've heard of us?"

Her expression cleared. "Yes. Of course." Her fingers flew over the keyboard as she checked out my request.

"I'm sorry, sir, the flight is totally booked. If you want to go on standby—"

"I'll pay whatever it takes. I must get on that flight. It's a family emergency." As I said the words, my blood pressure rose, my skin began to itch and the urge to transform nearly overcame me.

She gave him a look of sympathy. "Maybe I can get you the jump seat? Usually it's reserved for airline personnel, but if you're willing to pay, I can check on that? I know the person scheduled to fly with us today and maybe I can persuade her to give it to you?"

"Yes. Tell her I'll pay a king's ransom."

"O—kay. Do we have a specific amount in mind?" She leaned in to whisper the words. I realized others were eyeing us with more interest now.

I drilled my fingers on the countertop.

"Does she have a child?" Thoughts of my own baby clouded my mind and I pushed them away. Now was not the time. I had to stay strong.

"Yes. Why?" The woman frowned, uncertain where I was going with the inquiry.

"Tell her I'll pay for four years of college, one of her choosing. Specific enough?"

The flight attendant's eyes grew rounder. "I wish I had a seat to sell you. I've got a daughter with her sights set on medical school."

"No problem. You're in on the deal as well." I relished the happy glow that immediately emulated from the woman, even in my torment. And paying for schooling? That was one of my favorite endowments that our family had always been into.

She gestured frantically to another clerk that was standing off to the side and told her to look after the line because she had something *very* important to take care of.

"Come with me, sir. I'll get you settled in right away." She took my arm in a commanding manner like she was afraid her big fish might yet escape and we were off down the ramp that led toward the plane.

Even though I had been keeping a careful watch out through the airport, I had not caught any signs of my errant witch. But she would have to show herself soon, if she wanted to get to Egypt. All I had to do now was wait her out. She'd never expect me to do this, to be on the same plane as her. I refused to believe I had chosen her destination incorrectly. My gut said she was headed to Alexandria and that was what I was going to rely on.

"My daughter is going to be over the moon! She's so smart and I was so worried that the debt she was collecting was going to drown her come graduation."

"The Luceres family is happy to be of help." Being magnanimous with the woman was easy. Waiting for Isadora to make her appearance, not so much.

"Is there anything you need?" she asked, fussing and pulling down the seat to secure if for me. The jump seat was located near the cockpit of the plane and situated so that I was not visible to passengers arriving. It wasn't the most comfortable of seats, but it would have to do for now. Generally, one or two passengers didn't make any given flight, so I'd asked to be upgraded soon as possible.

"Of course," she agreed.

"And here's what you need to do." I took out two business cards from my suit jacket and wrote a few lines on the back of each. "These are the code words that will allow you to access the money. Take this to the Glitter Palace and ask for Cristaldo when you flash this card. He'll see to it that the money is transferred to your accounts."

"Thank you."

"What's he doing in my seat, Mary?" Another flight attendant had arrived, her expression suggesting she was not at all pleased to find me occupying what would have been her seat.

"Oh, Helena! The most wonderful thing has just happened. Mr. Luceres here has offered to pay for four years of schooling for your Julie and to pay for Sarah's medical school if we get him to his destination today on this plane." She thrust one of the business cards at the perplexed woman. "This is our ticket to collect."

"Is this for real?"

"Yes, you have my word."

"I don't know, Mary. I wanted to get to Egypt today and meet up with that guy I met last trip. And how do we know this is for real?" Helena was peering at the card with skepticism.

"This is Lucius of the House of Luceres. They own the Glitter Palace."

"Helena, is it?" I asked.

The woman nodded.

"I'm going to put a call through to my brother Cristaldo and he will explain it to you. Will that work?" I slipped my cell phone from my suit pocket.

She gave me a quick assessment, taking in the expensive clothing and handmade Italian shoes.

"No, that won't be necessary. Thank you, Mr. Luceres. I recognize you now. My daughter will be very pleased."

"Great. Then it's settled. And if a seat in first class becomes available, I'll move you right away," Mary reminded me before ushering her friend off the plane.

Within minutes, the plane began to fill up with the sounds of passengers busy settling in and stowing their belongings. The noise was muffled by the small partition that separated my seat from the travelers in first class, the perfect place to hide in plain sight. In this small an enclosure, I'd most likely locate her scent before anything else. A spell as powerful as the vanishing could not last for long.

Chapter Twenty-Six

Isadora

Head down, I walked onto the plane, the chalice stowed in a carryall bag I'd purchased from the gift shop. Each second that passed allowed me to breathe a little easier. No way could Lucius know where I was headed. Not that he would care now after the way I betrayed him. Nausea overcame me. Holding back tears, I stumbled along after the other passengers down the impossibly long isle way. Soon this part of my life would be finished. I'd be living among the cold ones for who knew how long. The idea chilled my soul as if a deadly spirit walked on my grave.

Finally settled in my seat, I clutched the carryall to my chest. The cost had been too dear to let it out of my sight.

"Miss, you'll need to store that."

"Excuse me?"

"Your bag. It needs to go under the seat." The steward pointed to the offending item, his patience looking a little frayed around the edges. How long had he been standing there, trying to get my attention?

"Sorry. Bad day." I leaned down and stowed the canvas bag carefully within reach of my feet.

"Thank you."

The man moved on to admonish other passengers crafting similar infractions. One guy was even demanding a drink and we hadn't even left the runway yet. I stared out at the tarmac. I'd been fortunate enough to get a window seat, though I'd had to pay for first class. Well, it would be my last trip for some time. *Might as well go to hell first class.*

By the time the plane was scheduled for takeoff, a headache was pounding mercilessly inside a skull that felt too small. Waves of nausea were impossible to ignore and I unbuckled, lurching to my feet. At least no one was sitting beside me, making it even more difficult to get out into the isle.

"Miss! You need to sit down. Right now!"

"I'm sorry. I'm going to throw up! I have to go to the bathroom."

The steward handed me a folded barf bag, his expression tight. "Here. Use this."

I slumped down, trying to breathe. Gasping for air, I was in too much torment to care that I had become the center of attention. I opened the bag with shaking hands and held it to my mouth. The roiling in my stomach increased and in seconds my stomach emptied its entire contents into the plastic-lined container.

"Can I get you some water? Mouthwash?"

"Water, please." My throat was parched and tender, my voice scratchy.

The steward hurried away. With trembling fingers, I secured the offending bag and placed it on the floor. I felt marginally better. Pushing back my hair, I leaned back against a seat that smelled of disinfectant and took a few deep breaths, rubbing my stomach in soothing circles. "Sorry, baby. I'll eat something soon."

"Here you go." The man handed me a bottle of water. "Give me the bag and I'll dispose of it."

I handed it to him, avoiding meeting his eyes. It was horrible to have made such a spectacle of myself. Very unlike me. I normally keep to myself. Though that incident with Lucius in the elevator might say otherwise, it had been a one off. Never, *never* to be repeated.

It was only a couple of minutes later that the engines began to rumble, gaining power and racing across the runway, headed for the open skies. I braced myself, the lurch to my stomach as the plane left the ground not helping my equilibrium. I swallowed against the bile that rose in my throat. Surely my stomach was empty now? When we reached cruising speed, the seatbelt sign flashed off. I left mine on, not wanting to take chances.

"Fancy meeting you here." A familiar voice echoed inside my brain, bringing a rush of emotion, instantly followed by the hollowness of deep regret. Tears threatened to fall.

"Lucius! What on earth are you doing here?" Stunned, I could only stare at him helplessly. He sat down and made himself comfortable, his presence a comfort and a curse.

"I believe you have something that belongs to the House of Luceres." It was not a question but stated as a fact. No denying it now.

"I know you won't believe me, but I need it more than anyone. I had to take it—I had no choice."

"Really? That's what you want to talk about after you betrayed me and my whole pack?" His eyes were hard to read. Had all the affection and love he had for me had gone away? Could that be? I knew I deserved it, but the pain his disinterest was afflicting on me hurt worse than anything that had ever happened to me.

"I didn't mean to b-betray you," I said, stumbling over the horrid word. How was I going to escape him now? I was all out of ideas, the clock ticking down so rapidly I swore I could hear the distant sounds of an alarm ringing somewhere in the universe.

"Then why did you?" His expression hardened and his words lashed, fueled by anger or pain.

How has it come to this? "You shouldn't have followed me." I had nothing, nothing left to say or give. He would never forgive me, I could see that now. He was shutting us out of his life. I rubbed my stomach, trying to reassure my unborn daughter.

"I was supposed to let you steal a priceless artifact? One that has the power to change the world and requires safeguards? Do you know how foolish that sounds? What did you intend to do with it? Sell it to the highest bidder?"

"It wasn't like that."

"Then tell me what it was like. Explain yourself. We've got nothing but time now."

Could I really do that? Throw myself on his mercy and share my worst fears? Nothing good would come of it—he'd never forgive my not telling him and stealing the chalice, but maybe he'd understand I had to protect others.

"I couldn't tell you. I was sworn to secrecy."

"Your loyalty lies elsewhere. I can see that now." His mouth firmed into a straight line. The lush lips I loved to kiss had vanished. The love and affection he had felt for me had gone away. I had lost him. Nothing really mattered now except protecting my child. Could my sad tragic tale at least do that?

"Okay. I will tell you the full story. All I ask is you wait until I'm done before you pronounce judgment."

He nodded, his expression bleak.

And so, I told him, left him in no doubt that if I didn't choose this path, others would be hurt. Emily. My siblings. His family. The legacy that would be visited on our unborn child.

"I needed to buy safe passage while Lucifer scoured the earth for me. I could think of no one else but Cleopatra that could offer that. And she wanted the Lupus Sanguis Chalice, so I made a trade."

"And you didn't trust that I could see to your safety and our unborn child's? I would have figured a way to keep her out of Lucifer's clutches." His expression shifted and raw pain was visible for an instant, making my heart squeeze with a pain so sharp it drew blood.

"No one can guarantee our safety. Surely you can see that," I shot back. "That debt is a black mark on our souls."

"And the queen of the damned can?"

"She's in the best position to hide us. Even Lucifer fears her. And I couldn't give him Emily."

"Emily started all this. I had no idea that her prank was this serious." His voice changed again with the realization. "But you should have come to me first. Told me this, not stolen from the pack. If they found this out, they'd tear you apart, Isadora. The cup is dangerous. Why would Lucifer need it anyway?"

I shook my head. "I don't know. He has his own agenda. Maybe he wants to create an army of werewolves?"

"Lucifer always wants more power. He's been sucking off yours for years, keeping you tied to him. And now you're expecting a half witch, half werewolf baby. And a debt that can never be paid looms in the balance. How the hell did it come to this?"

The silence between us grew as we both withdrew into our own worlds. He would have to let me go now. Maybe even let me keep the cup, for I knew he would do nothing that would harm our baby. That I could count on, if nothing else.

Chapter Twenty-Seven

Isadora

At some point I fell asleep, then woke up to an aching stomach. Starvation loomed if I didn't get something into my system.

I rubbed my eyes and straightened up in my seat. I had been leaning against Lucius, his warm body soothing, his fragrance a balm. I had no right to his comfort, though that didn't change the fact I desperately needed it.

"How are you?" he asked. He appeared calmer now, though his eyes were still wary. Or was that weary? I got that. I just wanted this whole thing to be over and done with. What he thought of me, well, I'd earned, but I hoped I'd have his blessing on hiding out now that he knew the full story.

"Fine. I'm famished though."

"I thought you might be. I've kept a meal for you." He reached over and pulled down the serving tray latched against the seat ahead of me, then placed a plastic-wrapped dish in front of me.

"Thank you." I tore off the covering and set to work. The first bites went down fine, giving me the confidence to continue eating. I made my way through the entire meal in record time and sat back, rubbing my full stomach. "We needed that." I wasn't above pushing his sympathy when and were ever possible. I wanted my baby safe. Now he would have to let us go. No other way about it.

I ignored the pain that knowledge pressed down onto me, as if a physical presence was crushing my mortal soul. There was nothing else for it.

"You should be home safe and sound. Not traveling across the world in your condition."

His words stung. "You're not my mother. I'm fine. I wouldn't put my baby at risk."

"Then stop running. Soon as we set down, I'm taking you home. No ifs, ands or buts. I'll deal with Lucifer. That's my job."

"*No!* That's exactly the wrong thing to do!" How had I not gotten through to him? "If you do that, you're setting all sorts of danger into the world. No, I forbid it. I'll hide out until this chaos dies down and the baby is born. Then, and only then, will I consider what to do next." I may have to stay hidden for the rest of my days. So be it. Anything to keep my child safe.

"The baby will never be safe as long as *he* has a hold over you. You know that, right? At some point he will find you. No, we deal with him now."

"That's crazy talk. I won't hear of it." *Crap*, what could I say to persuade him of the wrongness of this idea? "Besides, what can we offer him? He doesn't want money, he wants power. Souls."

"Let me handle that. I'll make him an offer he can't refuse."

"What does that even mean?" Confused, I looked at him. His closed-down expression gave nothing away.

The captain's voice came on over the intercom just then, announcing we were about to land. I had to try one more time.

"Please, Lucius, let me handle it. I know him better than you do. I can buy time with Cleopatra's aid, surely you can see that?"

He didn't answer me. Just shook his head slowly. Defeated, I felt the weight of the world descend on my shoulders. Time was running away. Now I would have to do the unthinkable to stop this.

When the fasten seat belt sign pinged off, we filed out with the rest of the passengers. With no luggage to collect, only the carryall that Lucius now carried over his shoulder, we headed over to the ticket counter.

"When is the next available flight headed back to Vegas?" he asked the startled clerk.

"I'm not sure. Let me check."

"I need to use the ladies' room," I said, anxious to get away. I hopped from foot to foot to punctuate my point.

"Give me a minute. Then I'll escort you."

"I have to go now!"

He sighed. "I'll be right back," he said to the agent.

"Okay, let's go." He took my arm and directed me down the airport to the entrance to the bathroom. "Don't try any funny stuff. I'll be waiting right here." He took me by the shoulders. "Promise me you will come right back. I can't have you hurt, Isadora, you know that, right?"

He had to be kidding. I had to try 'funny stuff' or he'd be leaping into the middle of the deepest ocean without a life jacket. The part about hurting him made me bleed, but what choice did I have? This was so far from being over.

I hurried into the bathroom, praying I could pull it off. By now Lucifer had to know of my recent actions. Any moment he could call me back, using my blood oath as the catalyst. I had to get to Cleopatra first. Let her know the cup was in Egypt. That I would have it for her soon.

I quickly used the facilities as I really had to go, then began to enact a spell that would allow the pair of us to communicate. One I normally hated to do, because forever after she could call upon me, the spell forging a strong link between us that was impossible to eliminate.

"Tomb of death, enact the light, let me join with – "

"Don't do it, Isadora! Stop!"

Lucius stood in behind me, visible in the mirror I faced. "Please, Lucius, I have to do this," I begged.

Come to me or he will die. The horrible voice I had prayed never to hear again filled my mind. *Time's up.*

He saw the look of fear in my eyes. "It's too late! Lucifer is calling me."

"I'm going with you. We end this now."

"No. I love you. I want you safe." The realization hit hard, that I would do anything to keep my mate safe. And I saw the same look reflected back in his eyes.

"I still love you, Isadora, body and soul. Let me come with you."

I surrendered at that moment, for what choice did I really have? I couldn't live without Lucius. And I couldn't protect him. But maybe together we could protect our child? "Okay, we go together. But for the record, I would not have you harmed in any way. Lucifer will likely use that, so be warned."

"Lucifer be damned. Bring it on. I protect my own." The steel in his voice further convinced me. It was true. We were the best of Forever Mates, willing to do what had to be done.

"Hold on and brace yourself," I said, then began to enact the spell to take us down to the underworld. He came forward, his arms holding me tight as I spoke the words.

"*Underworld portal reveal and open, send us across the invisible divide. Keep us safe from harm and allow us back when we return.*"

A small round disc tore into the fabric of space and time, forcing open a swirling tidal entrance directly before us. Then we fell through it, headed for the most damned place on earth. But for the first time I kept my footing with Lucius' help when we landed.

"We have to move fast. Terrifying creatures lurk in that mist," I urged.

"Stay close." He reached for me and we walked hand-in-hand to our destiny.

"This is interesting." Lucifer's raspy voice rang out before he came into view. "You bringing me fresh meat, Isadora?"

A growl from my mate sent a shiver down my spine. "Ignore him. He's just trying to rile you."

Volcanoes began emitting more fire and ash all around us, obviously caused by his proclivities.

"I've come to buy you off," Lucius said, his voice hardened by steel. "What do you want?"

"That chalice you have on your shoulder would be a start. Then that niece of yours that hasn't paid her due would be a nice gesture. What was her name? Right, Emily. She sure landed you in the pits, Isadora." He grinned at his pun, showing a full set of teeth that would do justice to a shark.

"Emily's not up for negotiations," I said.

"Then what do you propose, witch?"

"You collect souls, right?" Lucius.

The monster that possessed surprising beauty nodded once. But then some serial killers are also attractive, allowing them to charm their victims to their lair.

"Take mine and end this contract with Isadora, right now. My soul is ancient, far more powerful than most any other on earth. I've lived dozens of lifetimes. It would be a real coup for you, having an ancient werewolf soul from the time of the Romans, right?'

"No, Lucius, I can't let you do that!" I could hardly believe what I was hearing. He had to know that this ultimate price would cost him for eternity? He'd never see his daughter. Lucifer would see to that.

He turned to me, his deep brown eyes filled with love and regret. "I have to do this. There's no other way. A huge sacrifice is needed to save you and our child. Let me do this. It's my cross to bear. My guarantee of a future for you and our daughter. All I ask is don't let her forget me."

"Before you make a decision there's no coming back from, let me take you on a little tour. Show you what your foolish sacrifice will earn you." Lucifer spread his black wings widely, satisfaction obvious in his confident pose.

"No. None of that matters. I stand by my word."

Lucius had turned pale, but his stance was strong, his feet planted like Atlas holding up the world on his broad god-like shoulders. How could I have betrayed such a man? He was magnificent, so much better than me. I felt humbled just being in his presence.

"No, I can't let you do that! I love him!" I fell to the ground, preparing to beg for his life. "Take me, but please, all I ask is let me have our child first. Then I will willingly come back and do your bidding. Live here with you. Be your slave. Just leave Lucius and our baby out of it." The words were ashes in my throat, making it scratch the tender lining. I swallowed hard, unable to believe what was happening. Unable to believe what I was offering.

Lucius reached down and pulled me to my feet. "No, we don't beg. And I will be the one to do this. Not you." He hugged me for a second, whispered in my ear. "I love you and I always will. That will be enough to sustain me here. You must go back. Raise our child. My family will help."

He turned back to address the black-winged angel. "I, Lucius of the House of Luceres, do hereby barter my soul for the soul of Isadora Molay Champagne and her unborn child. I will take her place in hell. May God forgive me."

A bright flash of lightning followed by a loud crack of thunder rent the night skies.

What was that about? Terrified, I could only wait, sensing the worst was about to happen.

Lucifer grew larger in statue, his wings rising high above him, his expression horrible to behold. He was no longer beautiful, but a creature of great monstrosity. My heart twisted inside my chest, ripping the breath from my lungs.

"You dare challenge me? The most powerful fallen angel, who survived the greatest battle of all in Heaven, forced to live his days an outcast?"

Instantly, Lucius sprang forward, going from man to wolf in a split-second. His jaws clamped around the throat of the evil one. The pair staggered backward, a frenzy of motion as they fought tooth and nail. Unable to see what was happening, unable to help, I was only able to stand and watch, horrified. The blood lust, the sounds of battle, everything hung over me as I stood frozen, unable to move.

"You know the rule. The pact is ended." The commanding voice came from way above us, an all-knowing voice that electrified me. *Who had spoken?* Confused, I was grateful for one thing—the fight ceased and the pair separated, like magic.

Lucifer didn't say anything for a moment, just shook his head. Then he twisted up his face with distaste. "Never saw this coming." He turned his face upward, like he was talking to someone we couldn't see. *God?* "So, you win this time."

We stood, both of us stunned. I trembled with emotion, my pulse echoing in my ears like I had just completed a marathon.

"What are you talking about, devil?" Lucius finally asked for both of us.

"You don't even know what you just did. You just voided her contract, damn it, with your self-sacrifice and do-gooder shit. Now get the hell out of here, both of you, before I figure out some kind of clause or fine print that allows me to keep you here."

"But you're Morning Star, King of the Underworld." I was beyond mystified.

"I am aware." The black eyes narrowed, making chills sweep up my spine.

"Come. We need to get out of here," Lucius said, his voice prompting me to turn and race away with him.

I enacted the reverse spell and we were both instantly transported back to the banal bathroom, our arms locked. A woman was just leaving and she turned to give us an incredulous look before shaking her head and scurrying away.

"Are you okay?" Lucius asked.

I stared up at him, feeling unworthy. "You were willing to do that for us, for our baby, throw away your soul?" It wasn't a question, but a fact.

"Talk is cheap. Only actions prove a person's worth."

"Oh, Lucius, I'm so sorry." I began to weep at what I had almost let happen. How had I not realized how deep our love was? What an amazing man I was in love with? To think I had been willing to betray him. Defeated, I cried all the harder.

"Dry those tears, beautiful. I understand why you did it. Not that the betrayal didn't hurt, because it did. Stung like hell, in fact. But you did it to protect our daughter. I can understand that."

My tears diminished with his amazing support. He shifted the carryall on his shoulder, reminding me of another obligation.

"I promised the Vampire Queen that I would let her have the cup to see if it would bring her lover back. She's tried everything else." A part of me actually felt sorry for her. Cleopatra had been without her Antony far too long. And yet she had never given up hope.

Lucius stood still, thinking about it from his intense expression. "Then that's what we will do. I won't stand in the way of true love, now that I know how overwhelming that passion to be with another is."

We kissed then. A kiss filled with the deepest love and the wildest passion. We were celebrating being free. *Being together.* It was only the loud put-on cough of another woman making herself known that pushed us from the room and into the airport.

Chapter Twenty-Eight

Isadora

"Even the sky looks prettier," I said as we strode out of the front electronic doors hand-in-hand. Today truly was our new beginning.

"Nothing or nobody could look prettier than you do right now, my love."

"I'll bet you say that to all the women." To have gone from hell's embrace to topside, free as a bird? Hell, I had a right to be giddy.

"No, just you." Lucius gestured for a taxi, a half-smile lighting his handsome mug.

A cab promptly appeared and we were off, speeding toward our destination in the encroaching darkness. Cleopatra would soon be awake.

Near the tomb, Lucius paid the cabbie with a generous tip to wait for us before advancing toward the Vampire Queen's stronghold.

"I should maybe go in alone? You know, werewolves and vampires don't exactly mix well."

"No. We do this together. If she wants the use of the chalice, she'll set aside our differences. I know I'd do anything for us."

"Don't I know it!" I hugged Lucius again. I swear my feet hadn't touched the ground since we left hell together.

"Okay, we're here." We stopped in front of the rockface that loomed foreboding in the moonlight.

I placed both hands out, palms up and head bowed in the formal greeting, asking for entrance for us. When a surge of energy emulated from the rockface, the ward enacted to obscure the entrance vanished. We stepped through the stone portal turned to a thin membrane then into the chamber beyond.

The stillness hit a person first. The air too quiet, too suffocating. I glanced at Lucius, noticing his nose twitching in discomfort. No doubt the odor of vampire was nauseating to his faculties.

"Why did you bring him here?" The steely voice of the vampire Cleopatra bounced off the rockface, her expression even deadlier when she revealed herself.

"We've brought the chalice to you. You can try to raise Antony."

"Is it a gift?" she asked, her voice calculating.

"A gift for your use tonight, from the House of Luceres to you. Then we take it home with us to keep it safe for future generations," Lucius said, his tone strong and commanding.

"Who do you think you are, wolf?" she asked, advancing closer, a sharp-clawed hand reaching toward us in the darkness. She was only visible due to our advantage of otherworldly sight.

"A man who knows the value of love in this harsh world. Tonight, I would have given my eternal soul for Isadora's, if that's what it would have taken to free her from the devil's clutches."

I rushed in. "And that's what he did. Earlier tonight. Broke the pact with Lucifer. Even made the devil admit to God that he'd won this time."

"Is this true?" Her dark eyes glittered with keen interest. "Do you love her that much?"

He nodded. "Yes. I would do anything for Isadora. Even give up all that I am to save her and our child."

"I understand you. We both have a soul that yearns for completion. I will try your chalice. Perhaps your love bond can help me," she said in a musing tone of voice.

"What do you mean?" I asked.

"The Lupus Sanguis Chalice operates on blood, correct?"

"Yes. My sister-in-law Trinity's life was saved by my brothers Maximus and Alexandro after she was bitten by a Nomad wolf. Both of them gave their blood for her," Lucius said.

"I have no blood from my Antony." A deep sadness appeared in her eyes, so sad it even encroached on my shinning new path.

"Bone marrow may work. The chalice is made of blood and bone," I suggested. Hard not to feel sorry for her loss now that I understood what eternal love truly means.

"I think it needs more. An active blood pairing. The two of you have the most powerful bond I've ever seen in the modern world. I think it's your blood added to ours that will seal the deal."

"No. I forbid it," Lucius said, spitting out the words. "I don't want a bond with vampires."

Cleopatra's anger at being thwarted was immediately apparent. Her eyes turned blood-red and her teeth grew long and deadly. "I could take what I need."

"Stop. This is not the way," I said. I had not survived the underworld to be lost now. "We came with good intentions. To help you. We know your pain. But threatening us is not going to solve the problem. Why not try it with just your blood and Antony's bone first? Then see if something more is needed."

"The victim of the bite is supposed to drink the blood. How's this going to work?" Lucius asked, doubt apparent in his expression. "Who's the victim here?"

"Antony is. Maybe we need the blood of Cleopatra in the cup, then placed on his mummy? His wrapped body is still here, right?"

"His heart," Cleopatra said with a sharp nod of agreement. "That's where the blood should be placed. But I want the blood from all three of us. That's the true test. My Antony had wolf blood, did you know that? Made him a warrior. I will give you anything you want if you'll do this for me. Anything." Her swift move from threatening to begging tugged at me. She was desperate, that was more than obvious.

"Lucius, it's just a little blood. Surely we can spare it?"

"But what if it ties us together, all four of us. What then?"

"I can live with it if you can? You know what it feels like to lose your Forever Mate. I know the pain for me was indescribable."

"All too well. For you, Isadora, I would do anything. But don't ask this, it's too risky."

"Then do this thing. Maybe it will work. Bring back a pair of famous lovers. It can't hurt to have their blessing in this world."

He frowned, obviously thinking. Then his expression cleared. "Just a little blood. You're pregnant. I won't have you taxing yourself or harming the baby."

I nodded. "Thank you. I promise you, we'll be fine."

"Okay, let's do this thing and get out of here."

"Come." Cleopatra beckoned us and we strode after her. Deeper and deeper below the tomb we descended, past a labyrinth of chambers beneath the tomb all carved from the rockface. Who lived down here? Furtive sounds of scurrying filled me with a sense of dread. It became harder to breath and long before we reached our destination I was wanting to run. It took much courage to continue. It was only with Lucius by my side that I managed the feat. Finally, we reached our destination and Cleopatra stopped in front of Antony's shrine. The gold-engraved sarcophagus shone in the darkness, an oil lamp flickered and burned nearby.

"Show me the Lupus Sanguis Chalice," Cleopatra demanded.

Lucius removed it from the carryall and held it out to her.

"Rather plain," she said, her expression doubtful.

"It has great power," he said. "Use it wisely."

A vampire is strong—it was a known fact—but when Cleopatra easily removed the lid of the sarcophagus that weighed hundreds of pounds with no visible effort, it made me shudder.

Please, Goddess, made this work. I prayed, not wanting to see what would happen if it didn't. Vampires are also known to have anger issues. Not that she could best a wolf and a witch. Together Lucius and I were unstoppable, right? Unfortunately, there's always a seed of doubt until proven true. But more than likely, we'd have to temper that knowledge, not let absolute power corrupt us. No, that would never happen, I reassured myself. Our pair bonding was based on love and understanding.

The Vampire Queen used a sharp jewel-encrusted dagger she removed from her belt to cut through the dusty linens the mummy was wrapped in. Exposing the sunken chest, she continued to cut carefully into the top thin layers of skin and bone until she reached his heart.

"I refused to keep his organs separate in a vase. I wanted his body intact, praying this day would come," she said by way of explanation for why he'd been buried in such a unique way.

Turning to us, she nodded. "The blood of eternal lovers."

"Give me the dagger," Lucius said.

Quickly he did the deed, making a small cut on my offered palm, then his own. Our blood mingled in the bottom of the bone cup, its deep red color mesmerizing. It emanated life, its fragrance rich with the metallic odor of copper.

Handing it back to Cleopatra, he said, "Now yours."

"If this works, you must leave immediately," she warned. "He will wake hungry."

She sliced her own palm and the blood dripped down inside the cup. Swirls of spiraling white mist rose above the edge of the chalice.

Time seemed to freeze as something filled the chamber with an infusion of invisible energy, electrifying and terrifying at the same time. I had no idea what would happen when she dripped the blood on the mummy's heart, but I held my breath and waited.

"We must hold hands."

The edict made me uncomfortable. I wanted to flee, get the hell out of there just in case this time she was successful in raising the revenant. No vampire on earth could be hungrier than one starved for over two thousand years, right?

But we did as she asked. *Just hold on. It's almost over, baby.*

The three of us joined hands over the open sarcophagus, only breaking the physical bond for a few seconds when Cleopatra poured more blood over Antony's exposed heart.

"Blood and bone and the power of the original wolf, I ask your blessing in bringing back my own true love, Marcus Antonius. Heal his heart and body, save his immortal soul. Bring him back to me, this I command in the name of Osiris, god of the afterlife and keeper of the immortal."

The queen bowed her head, her urgent grip on my hand painful and oh so cold.

"It might take a while. Trinity didn't come back for a number of hours," Lucius said.

"Then we wait," Cleopatra said.

"No. I can't wait that long down here," I protested. I yanked my hand away, not willing to go that far.

The offering of blood began sizzling, tendrils of mist rising above the coffin, drawing my attention again. I watched in rapt fascination. Was this it? Would it actually work this time? I had been pretty certain that it would not, just willing to do it because it was the right thing to do. I had made a freely given pact with the Vampire Queen and I would never go back on my word. Honor was at stake.

I would not have believed what I witnessed next, if I had not seen it with my own eyes. The heart began to fill out, the color changing from dead ash to purple-red, then came something that looked like a twitch. Very slowly the organ undulated, almost imperceptible to the eye.

"Blood. He needs more blood!" Cleopatra's expression had changed, almost maniacal, her eyes unfocused. Horrified, I stepped back from the sarcophagus.

She cut her wrist deeply, making me shudder again. Blood flowed from the wound onto the telltale heart.

"Time to leave," Lucius commanded. He grabbed the priceless chalice that the Vampire Queen had abandoned on the edge of Antony's gold coffin, thrusting it back inside the carryall.

I didn't need a second invitation. We fled, hand-in-hand, back through the endless labyrinth, a sense of something coalescing in the darkness behind us pushing me forward. I didn't want to know what it was, afraid of the unknown harming our unborn child. Not until we reached the surface was I able to take a full breath.

Stepping out into the moonlight beyond the tomb, I felt released from whatever powers that had sucked me in, leaving me calmer. Exhausted to the core, I stood and stared at Lucius. I could tell by his dynamic expression he had felt it too, the powerful entity or entities that inhabited the tombs. Probably something we'd not bring words to going forward.

"Let's go home," Lucius said. I nodded, grateful for our escape. I'd not be visiting Cleopatra and Antony soon, if indeed he was in the process of being resurrected. I could only pray our bond wouldn't be too much of a problem going forward. But I'd worry about that later. Now, it was our time. Me and Lucius, my very own forever love.

The taxi had waited nearby and we climbed inside.

"To the airport," Lucius directed the driver.

We sped off into the night. I laid my head on his broad shoulder and drifted off before the taxi even took off, his arms cradling me. A while later, Lucius gently shook me awake.

"Time to board, sweetheart. Then you can sleep again."

I stretched and exited the taxi with his help. "You ordered a private jet?" I said, looking over at the aircraft parked on the tarmac with the familiar House of Luceres family crest stenciled on the white metal in red and gold.

"Nothing but the best for my Forever Mate," he said, love lighting up his creamy brown eyes.

I could live right there, I decided, with that much love to bathe in. So much it flowed through me, warming everything I possessed.

"I love the sound of that," I teased, my good humor restored now that we were free.

"I love the sound of your voice, Isadora. The touch of your hand, and the purity of your soul."

His simple tribute spoke to me and humbled me. "As I do you. You and I—you were right, we were chosen. I'm so sorry I ever doubted it. Please, forgive me, I should have told you everything that was going on."

"I do forgive you, Isadora. You did what you thought best. We'll keep this little incident between us going forward. The pack may not be quite as understanding."

"Thank you. I'm so grateful for this—for us. It's a dream come true."

Mama. The sound emanated from my belly. Lucius splayed his hand over my stomach. "I heard that. Our daughter's spirit is speaking to us. She must be an ancient one."

"You know she will be a handful, right?"

"Good. Then I will be doubly blessed."

He was right, we were blessed having found each other. Bright days forged ahead in my mind, days free of darkness and filled with love. Never had I expected this amazing outcome which made it all the sweeter. My own family to love and cherish. It didn't get better than that. Werewolf, vampire, human or witch, all creatures need love, and that alone would make this world a better place.

Epilogue

Isadora

Lucius stared into the eyes of our daughter, Bella, for the first time, his expression filled with wonderment and love for the miracle. Nearly nine months had passed since those first fateful days. Things were different now, and yet so much had stayed the same. I still had access to my witch powers, my ability to help was treasured by my new family and my siblings were protected.

What had changed? My deep love for Lucius had grown stronger, my place in the universe felt assured. And what of Cleopatra and Antony? Yes, it had worked. The pair had been reunited, though it had taken weeks and the blood of many ancient beings before the deed was competed. The event had softened the animosity between werewolf and vampire, something that ensured more peace going forward.

"She has your eyes," Lucius said, still gazing at Bella with fascination.

"And your hair. Black as a raven's wing."

Our daughter looked at me now, her expression so wise, her eyes so filled with ancient knowledge, it took my breath clear away. Yes, the new generation would make the world a better place.

All a mother can ask.

Want to see more from this author? Here's a taster for you to enjoy!

Sin City Wolf: Hellfire
January Bain

Coming Summer 2022

Excerpt

Amara

I ripped off my headphones, throwing them down beside my computer. The terrible words from the medical thesis that I had just started to edit for a grad student made me want to run screaming into the streets.

Calm down. Breathe.

The name of the disease that had taken my mother too early mocked me. I too carried the RPS25 gene, the hallmark of ALS or Lou Gehrig's disease. I didn't need reminding of the inevitable while I worked, though I did require the steady money from the various departments at the university that sent an ongoing stream of journals, papers and dissertations my way. I had acquired the contacts during my time working in the administration department and I was grateful for them, needing to be self-employed at home to help my mom during those final months.

Crap. This moment had to happen sooner or later. I lived with the lurking symptoms every day of my uncharmed life. I thought I'd be better prepared for the inevitable. Apparently not.

"And I need a break from this," I said aloud, jumping up from my office chair.

"*I love you, Amara!*" My parrot Rainbow began to prance back and forth on his perch, his dance moves timed in perfect sync to his words. Talented guy.

His colorful plumage of a deep blue head, orange-yellow chest and green cape, a hallmark of the little Lorikeet, gave my sweet baby a surreal appearance against the dying of the sunlight behind him. Of course, I'd taught him to say, *I love you, Amara*, since in my lonely existence, exacerbated by COVID-19, I probably would never hear the words said by an actual human being. For me, this was as good as it got. But at least the pandemic restrictions had been easing of late, meaning I could join my fellow humans once more if enticed.

My cellphone rang. I checked the number. Aw, Shay, the best person in the world to take a person's mind off their troubles…mostly because she had so much stuff going on in her own insanely busy life.

"Hey, girlfriend, what say we get all gussied up and hit the town running? I got the entire weekend free to be me! My sister's arrived this time as locally advertised. She's promising to look after dad until the sun rises over Vegas Monday morning."

I hesitated, though I longed for some forget-the-crappy-world time. How did a person who just turned twenty-five in August manage to find her way to such a boring existence? If it wasn't for Rainbow, I'd go mad locked in my small apartment with just my computer for company.

That, and the endless line of work that needed editing with the ever-diminishing hope I might actually get to write my own stories one day. A minor in literature looked to go to waste at this juncture. "I don't know… I got this thesis due next week. I promised the guy and I can't afford a penalty for being late."

"*Phttt*. You always finish in time, Amara. One night off isn't going to hurt. Please, I need this like the earth needs the rain, like the sun needs the stars, like the—"

"Okay, if you lay off the literary devices, I'll bite. Where do you want to meet?" I handfed Rainbow pieces of cut-up apple while we talked, enjoying the bright alertness of his rich blue-and-red-rimmed eyes. We shared the same eye color, though mine were not normally red-tinged, unless I'd indulged in too many apple martinis.

"I've been dying to try out the Glitter Palace Casino. I'm hearing their karaoke bar is insane. And free drinks for the ladies," Shay said, her voice lilting with her trademark enthusiasm. "Of course, I can't guarantee I'll be acting like a lady after a few drinks, if you get my drift."

I got her drift. Shay might not be going home alone like yours truly after a plethora of Singapore Slings, her drink of choice. "If you promise me I just get to listen and not sing."

"No! Just one duet, *please*, you can't deny your best friend one measly song. Please, please with candy cane elves sprinkled on top."

I laughed. Shay knew how to work me—hand feed me a new image to fire my imagination. *Candy cane elves indeed. Last time it was miniature chocolate marshmallow bears.* "Fine. But only one. Now I gotta go if I'm going to have time for a shower and a bit of primping."

"Sure. Meet me at the entrance at nine. I'll be the one grinning ear-to-ear and doing a highland fling with an entire weekend off."

"That would be fun to see." I imagined my tall, thin friend high-stepping over crossed swords, her curly fair hair, the polar opposite of my extra-long ebony-blue locks, flying in the wind.

"And wear something red and showstopping."

"Maybe, if I can be bothered to shave my legs. Later."

I hit End on my iPhone and turned to Rainbow. "Can you do a night alone or should I call a babysitter?"

"Yes, *I love you, Amara!*"

"Your wish is my command. How about we see if Jeannie from upstairs is available on short notice?"

I glanced back at my computer and sighed. I love novels that feature supernatural creatures that don't exist. My decadent escape from my boring existence. I'd pay that debt forward one day, if I could find the time, writing a slew of genre romances featuring uber-bad boys tamed by the heroine.

"Too bad vampires aren't a real thing. Not having to worry about getting sick would be sweet. Can you say fangbanger, Rainbow?"

"*Can you say fangbanger, Rainbow?*"

His words lifted my spirits. "Guess you can, sweetie." Maybe I should be more careful of what I said around my exuberant tweetie friend. Saying the wrong thing at the wrong time might end up biting me in the ass. Well, not like anyone ever visited me other than take-out service. I had them on speed dial. *And the local liquor store.*

"Time to call Jeannie." I scrolled down to her cell number and clicked on it.

"Hmm, no answer." Now what? I hated to leave Rainbow alone, thought in reality it was a common practice and it would only be for a few hours. Maybe I should cancel? But Shay seldom got a night off from looking after her dad. She deserved one. I couldn't let her down after getting her hopes up. She wasn't the type to head out on her own, no matter the brave front she always plastered on.

"How about I leave some music on? Do you want light jazz, showtunes, Christmas songs or classic rock?"

"*Christmas, Christmas, Christmas.*" Rainbow bopped up and down, seed flying everywhere. One thing about birds, they were messy little creatures. Endearing, but messy.

"Perfect. We have exactly the same taste, kiddo." I was a big fan of Christmas movies all year long. I quickly turned my iPod on and found the perfect albums, setting them to play in a loop. *Okay, time to get a move on.*

I ended up taking the time to shave my legs, wash and condition my hair and put on makeup. Drying my long hair, I debated on curling it or not, deciding in the end smooth and sleek was easier, before pulling the red number Shay had requested from my closet. Did I dare? It was over the top for me. Cut low and short, riding my thighs.

If not now, when. *I'm only going to be young once, right?*

"Okay." I approached the cage, my wrap and purse in hand, ready to head for the elevator that would take me downstairs. I'd already called for an Uber to the casino. "You be a good boy and I'll give you some peaches tomorrow."

"*Peaches now. Peaches now.*"

"No way, bud, I don't want my dress covered in fruit. Not a good look." Rainbow was a notorious eater, spilling and spitting food all over the place. But then what did I have to do other than look after him? *A good friend is hard to find.* And what was the other part? *Oh yes, a hard friend is good to find too.* I sighed again. I couldn't remember the last time I got laid.

In the lobby, I enjoyed the moment of looking good when Gary, our doorman, gave a low whistle. Everyone liked the guy. He always had a kind word to say and was full of good cheer.

"Special night, Amara?" he asked, coming out from behind his desk.

"Meeting a friend at the casino."

"You be careful. Full moon's rising. Means troubles on the way."

I shivered. It wasn't like our amiable doorman to be so maudlin. "You okay, Gary?" I glanced at him. His round face with the enviable dimples looked a bit paler than usual.

"Yeah. Not sure why I said that. Must be that song I was listening to earlier. I forget what it's called." He scratched the back of his neck. "You have a good time tonight, you hear. You meeting up with Shay by any chance?"

"Good guess. Oh, there's my Uber now."

Gary opened the door for me, adding a small bow. "Say hello to Shay for me."

"Will do." I hurried toward the compact car, praying I wouldn't twist an ankle in my unaccustomed high heels. But sometimes, a gal has to look good and flats don't do my petite frame much justice. *Being short can suck. Just sayin'.*

"Where to?" the driver asked, twisting around in his seat to give me a look.

"Glitter Palace, please."

It was a short ride and I was soon standing on the street waiting for my best friend to put in an appearance. Shay was notorious for running late. But I totally understood. Her dad always managed to need one last thing from her, even if her sister was there to help. I glanced around. Other people were meeting up and joining with friends before heading in. It warmed my heart. Social isolation sucked even worse than being height-challenged.

I pulled a mask from my purse in preparation for going inside. I was about to slip it on when a man sauntered up, his eyes glittering strangely in the light from the marque. His glance locked with mine with the kind of supreme overconfidence I could only dream of. But something about him sent my hackles into overdrive. Every instinct said he was the kind of man I would move heaven and earth to stay right the hell away from.

My heart slamming in my chest, I pretended to ignore the off-putting effect he had on me, but I took it seriously. *Always pay attention to your gut instinct. It can save your life.* Gary's warning in the lobby came back to me in that instant. I busied myself with putting on my mask, not wanting to give the stranger any encouragement. *Go away.*

He leaned his head toward me just as he passed by, whispering in my ear. "I'll be keeping an eye out for you, inside, sweetheart. You're just my type."

I reacted like he'd spilled fire down my dress. "Get lost. You're not definitely *not* my type." I held the ground, staring him down. He seemed confused by my reaction. Good. I hate being singled out by a man I instinctively didn't trust. *Women. We get to chose who we go with. It's not up to the male of the species.*

My missile worked. The guy walked off, not bothering to respond.

I took a few deep breaths to calm myself, feeling satisfied I had handled myself well.

"Hey, Amara, you're looking good, girl!" Shay said with a beaming smile as she came striding up.

"So are you," I complimented her right back. And she did look great, her curls a cascade of loveliness down her back, her midnight-blue lace dress a marvel of creation the way it hugged every curve.

"Sorry I'm late. Dad wasn't too happy tonight with me leaving." She pulled a mask out of her purse and put it on.

"No worries."

We took our time going inside, trying to catch up before we hit the casino. But we never would. That was the best part of being with Shay. Our depth of understanding of each other meant there was never an end to the conversation.

We found a choice table in the karaoke room, ordered our drinks from the friendly waitress then sat back to check out the room. Singing was one of the few pleasures we both shared. Shay was much better than I was, but I could harmonize and keep us from looking too shabby.

"You guys here for the karaoke?" the waitress asked in a cheery tone as she placed our drinks in front of us.

"Yup. What's the money tonight?"

"A thousand dollars for first place."

"Wow, what's the occasion?" I asked. That was a lot of money for singing a song, if a person wasn't a professional. Of course, that meant the competition would be stiff tonight. We'd never win. But the entertainment value just went through the roof.

"Semi-finals and the owners wanting to get more people in here, you know, since COVID reared its ugly head."

"Yeah, I hear you."

"You don't have to wear the mask when you sing, if you have proof of vaccination on you?"

I nodded and pulled out my phone. "Here you go."

Shay did likewise and we were all set.

An icicle of dread silvered down my spine. There was that guy again, staring at me from an alcove nearby. The look in his eyes made me pause. It was so ancient and cruel. If I didn't know vampires weren't real, I would think this guy could be one.

I had instantly disliked him outside and the feeling was growing stronger by the second. *Stay the fuck away from me.*

I shot the idea as best I could across the room at him, narrowing my eyes with dislike. He raised his drink at me as if offering a toast. Or asking if I wanted a drink? I shook my head—a firm no—and turned away. The sense of dread that seeing him again had brought on annoyed me. I worked to keep all my focus on my friend. I was safe here, right, surrounded by a growing crowd of people?

Full moon be damned. I wasn't letting that asshole ruin my evening. An image seared my brain at that second. One of hellfire, of pain and ruin beyond belief. Then it was gone, leaving a trail of discomfort in its wake.

What the hell is up with the universe tonight?

About the Author

January Bain has wished on every falling star, every blown-out birthday candle and every coin thrown in a fountain to be a storyteller. To share the tales of high adventure, mysteries, and full-blown thrillers she has dreamed of all her life. The story you now have in your hands is the compilation of a lot of things manifesting itself for this special series. Hundreds of hours spent researching the unusual and the mundane have come together to create a series that features strong women who don't take life too seriously, wild adventures full of twists and unforeseen turns, and hot complicated men who aren't afraid to take risks. She can only hope the stories of her beloved Brass Ringers will capture your imagination as much as they did hers when she wrote them.

If you are looking for January Bain, you can find her hard at work every morning without fail in her office with two furry babies trying to prove who does a better job of guarding the doorway. And, of course, she's married to the most romantic man! Who once famously replied to her inquiry about buying fresh flowers for their home every week, "Give me one good reason why not?" Leaving her speechless and knocking her head against the proverbial wall for being so darn foolish. She loves flowers.

January loves to hear from readers. You can find her contact information, website details and author profile page at https://www.totallybound.com

Home of Erotic Romance

Sign up for our newsletter and find out about all our romance book releases, eBook sales and promotions, sneak peeks and FREE romance books!

www.ingramcontent.com/pod-product-compliance
Lightning Source LLC
Chambersburg PA
CBHW021519240626
47154CB00002B/699